Thomas Delf, Charles Martel

Diary of an Ex-Detective

Thomas Delf, Charles Martel

Diary of an Ex-Detective

ISBN/EAN: 9783337122171

Printed in Europe, USA, Canada, Australia, Japan

Cover: Foto ©Raphael Reischuk / pixelio.de

More available books at **www.hansebooks.com**

DIARY

OF AN

EX-DETECTIVE.

EDITED BY

CHARLES MARTEL.

"Crime may be cunning, but Justice is more sagacious; the one may have
long legs, but the other a more unerring stride."

LONDON

WARD AND LOCK,

158, FLEET STREET.

MDCCCLX.

WINCHESTER:
PRINTED BY HUGH BARCLAY,
HIGH STREET.

TO

JOHN AND DANIEL FORRESTER,

OF THE

MANSION HOUSE, LONDON,

IN RECOGNITION OF THE VERY GREAT SERVICES,
PUBLIC AND PRIVATE,

THEY HAVE RENDERED IN FURTHERANCE OF
THE ENDS OF JUSTICE,

This Volume is Dedicated,

WITH SENTIMENTS OF PROFOUND ESTEEM,

BY THEIR

OBEDIENT SERVANT,

CHARLES MARTEL.

CONTENTS.

APPENDIX.

LEAVES

FROM THE

DIARY OF AN EX-DETECTIVE.

MONSIEUR PELIGON.

I HAD just reached home—if home it might be called, as I was seldom in it, and never knew when I quitted it when I should return again. I had just reached home, as I was saying, a little after seven o'clock in the evening, and was pulling off my wet and muddy boots— London mud—thinking my day's work was over. I had had no dinner—could seldom find time for that—so I had sent my old housekeeper for a steak, and its savoury odour was stealing up the kitchen stairs, when a loud knock came at the street door—something between a postman's knock and a small tradesman's. I knew it too well; it boded no good for my peace.

"There's that plaguy fellow Josh, I'll be bound, come to drag me out again this horrible night. What's in the wind now? Why couldn't they have sent for someone else? There's Rayner and Collard, they have

B

a pretty easy time of it; but as for me—they seem to think they can never find too much for me to do."

I felt I had a right to grumble at that particular moment, for I had been hanging about the banks in Lombard Street and its vicinity since nine o'clock in the morning, in as nasty, cold, drizzling, foggy a November day as London ever saw; and I had missed my man, a bank-clerk defaulter, whose company was particularly requested as a favour by the Lord Mayor. Why, any man would have escaped on such a day as that, when you could not see an inch before your nose. No wonder I was a little out of humour.

But that knock at the door. Well, my old house-keeper reluctantly quitted the gridiron, upon which my steak was discoursing most eloquent music, vowing all the way upstairs "it would be spoiled;" and as soon as she opened the street door my worst forebodings were confirmed.

"Well, Master Josh, what brings you here to-night?"

"Well, old gal, guv'nor in?"

"Yes; just going to have a bit o' dinner, so don't bother him."

"That's all very well, 'don't bother him,' but bis'ness is bis'ness, and must be attended to. So just tell the guv'nor I wants to see him—something special and urgent."

"Come in, Josh," said I, putting my head out into the passage. "What is it?"

"Here's the perticklars," said Josh, handing me a

large sealed envelope. "Captain says, 'Josh,' says he, 'look sharp and find Mr. F—— in less than no time, for he must go to-night.'"

I broke the seal and read as follows :—

"Gustave Peligon, merchant, dealer in oils, &c., is declared bankrupt, and has absconded from his creditors. He has not been seen for two days, but it is not known whether he has left England or not; if he has not, it is certainly his intention to do so. You will take him and lodge him in Newgate. Warrant inclosed. G. P. is a spare man, age forty-five, about five feet nine in height, stoops a little, sallow complexion, black hair and eyes, large beard, grizzled, no moustache, large mouth, thin lips, thin Roman nose, dresses in black, wears a good deal of jewellery, supposed to have a large sum of money in his possession."

While reading this my steak was brought in, flanked by a pot of coffee and a plate of toast. Then commenced a struggle between appetite and duty. I was cold, chilled through, and very hungry; and I reasoned in this wise: "Nature must be supported, and if I do not eat I shall be incapable of doing my duty."

"Josh, fetch down my carpet bag, and hand me that pair of dry boots; put them to the fire, and get me down my thick coat and comforter, for I must be off to France by the mail-train to-night. Call a cab."

While Josh was occupied with my equipment I managed to snatch a few mouthfuls, and in ten minutes I was ready to step into the cab.

My first business was to go to the French Consular Office, and ascertain if my *protégé* had taken out a passport, or had been *viséd.* For myself I always carried my passport in my pocket, ready for sudden emergencies. I knew the office would be closed for the day, but that made no difference, as I possessed the *open sesame,* and in a few minutes I was examining the passport-book to see if any one answering to the description of Monsieur Peligon had taken out his ticket-of-leave to revisit his native shores. Making careful search, I could find none exactly tallying with my description, so I concluded monsieur had taken his chance to do without one, to make use either of his old one, or of an accommodating friend's. So, taking my leave of the Consular official, I next turned my steps to the Dover railway-station. There was no time to lose ; the train started at half-past eight, and it had struck the hour while I was in the consul's office. What with the fog and the slippery state of the roads, cabby made but slow progress ; so when we arrived at the foot of London Bridge, I made up my mind to run for it on my legs. Snatching up my carpet bag, I made a start ; but before I could say " here goes," I found myself sprawling on the muddy pavement. Every stone seemed as if it had been greased, and it was with the utmost difficulty I could set one foot before the other. The slipping backward was more easily achieved than the moving forward.

"Confound all roguish bankrupts!" said I, in the deepest vexation. "What a deal of trouble it would save if people could only make up their minds to be honest."

After a hard struggle with the mud I just managed to reach the door of the station as the porter, with one hand on the portion already closed, was with his other about to pull-to the remaining half.

"Hold hard, my man," said I; "I'm for Paris."

"Too late," said he.

"That be ——. I'm F——, the police officer. I must go, if the train has to wait for me."

"Step in, sir, quick!"

And in I went—no time for ticket. I rushed to a first-class carriage, whispered to the guard a few words which seemed to make an impression on his feelings, and calling a porter, gave him a couple of sovereigns to get me a ticket for Paris.

"Through? All right, sir."

I walked up and down in front of the carriages to see who among the travellers would best suit me for company, and I picked upon one in which there were three vacant seats. I immediately took possession of one by ensconcing my carpet bag in it.

"Ready, sir?" said the guard.

"Waiting for my ticket. Ah! here it is. Thank you, my man. All right, go ahead."

A groan—a grunt—a cough—a whistle—a scream—
and off! My last half-hour's exertions had rather
ruffled my composure, but I had now plenty of time to
smooth down, and therefore proceeded to make myself
comfortable, then to take a survey of my travelling
companions. Opposite to me sat a bloated animal who
looked as if he were fattening for a cattle-show. I
reckoned upon a coroner's inquest—verdict, apoplexy
—as being his speedy fate. He glared his glassy grey
eyes upon me like an ogre, and I fancied he was
speculating upon the chances of my proving juicy and
tender after two hours' basting before his kitchen fire.

Being a not very agreeable object to contemplate, I
turned my attention to his neighbour. I put him down
for a commercial traveller : he pulled out a Welsh wig,
and quickly composed himself to sleep.

There was yet another traveller. He was buried in
the folds of a capacious cloak, his travelling cap was
pulled tightly over his head, and I could see nothing of
his face but a pair of keen black eyes, which, whenever I
looked at him, I found were intently fixed upon myself.
I do not mind being looked at, but this man's silent,
steadfast gaze made me, I don't know why, exceedingly
uncomfortable; so I took a newspaper out of my
pocket and commenced to read.

We were not a very talkative party. Now I like
talking ; one can always learn something if the talkers
are in earnest. So I resolved to make an effort. After
perusing my paper for some quarter of an hour, I

changed my seat to one opposite my fellow-traveller in the cloak.

"Money market seems flat," said I.

No reply : try again.

"That bankruptcy of Peligon's has caused some excitement in Mincing Lane."

The black eyes opened a little wider, but still no response.

"They say he has absconded—sailed for America it is supposed."

Still silent : I thought it was time to give in. Either this man is deaf, or he won't hear, I thought to myself.

Then I began to ruminate. This may be Monsieur Peligon himself; but there is no finding out while he is bundled up in that corner, so I 'll just keep my eye upon him.

At Reigate station we stopped a few minutes, and I got out to take a look at the passengers in the other carriages, to ascertain if they contained a more likely customer than the one I was riding in. But I could not see one that would for a moment admit of a comparison with the description I had received of Monsieur Peligon. A few passengers got out ' to stretch their legs,' but they were unmistakable members of the Bull family, and made no sort of claim to my attention.

In due time we arrived at Dover. Before stopping I again addressed my neighbour in the cloak.

"Going to cross the channel to-night? We shall have a hard time of it."

The same imperturbable silence. I was not at all anxious for a sea voyage on that dark, cold November night, and would have given up all chance of reward for my services could I have escaped it. My suspicions had gradually grown stronger as to the identity of Monsieur Peligon with my silent fellow-traveller, but suspicion was not enough for my purpose: I must have something like proof. "I'll look at his luggage," thought I, "when the train stops; perhaps that will help me."

So when the train stopped I got out first, and quickly retired into the shade, where I could see without being seen. Monsieur should have turned to the left to go to the luggage van, but he turned to the right.

"Oh, oh!" thought I, "my gentleman has got no luggage. Had no time to pack up, I suppose. Monsieur Peligon, I am your faithful servant."

And in that capacity I stuck to his heels closely. He might choose to sleep in Dover, but it was more probable that he would cross the channel. And in truth he made his way down to the pier, where the mail-boat was noisily blowing-off steam.

My gentleman no sooner got on board than he dived down into the cabin, and quickly took possession of a settee, upon which he stretched himself to sleep. Bad as the night was, I preferred the deck to the concatenation of foul odours that assailed my nostrils in the cabin. I was sure of my man until we reached Calais, at any rate; so I set myself to thinking what course I should pursue when I arrived there.

"Monsieur will be obliged to go to the Custom House to show his passport, and so shall I. Here's to our better acquaintance." Then I took a thimbleful of brandy out of my pocket flask, and a pair of pocket pistols out of my carpet bag, with the "bracelets," which I placed ready in my outside coat-pocket. As monsieur was accused of felony, my warrant had been endorsed by the French consul, and I could, in virtue thereof, lodge my gentleman in prison at Calais, if I could satisfactorily make out his identity.

When we were about half-way across the Channel I thought I would step below to see what state of health monsieur was enjoying. The sea was very rough, and what few passengers there were on board were terribly sea-sick.

I dived below and looked on the settee where I had left monsieur, but, thunder and ——, he was not there!

Seeking the steward, I inquired if he knew where the man in the cloak was who had lately occupied *that* settee.

"Don't know, indeed, sir. Oh, Mr. F——, glad to see you, sir. Rough night, sir. I expect he's gone on deck, sir. He had a glass of brandy just now, sir. Been very sick, sir."

I returned to the deck, but it was too dark there to see one's own hand. Several moving objects passed me; but it was impossible to make out the identity of any one of them. There was nothing for it but to restrain my impatience until we reached Calais. A faint suspicion crossed my mind that monsieur might have thrown himself overboard; but I did not allow it to gain any ascendency over my hopes. At length, after four hours' buffeting with the waves, the boat made the lights at Calais pier.

"All ashore!"

I was the first at the gangway; and up they came, one by one, the score of voyagers that had tempted the perils of the deep on that stormy November night; but I could not recognise my neighbour in the cloak among them. I flew to the steward, and inquired of him if all the passengers had come up from below.

"All up, sir," said he.

"The devil!" said I. "Here, take care of my carpet bag till morning. I'll see you first thing."

"All right, sir!"

I hurried across the gangway, and soon came up with the file of passengers proceeding to the Custom House, and by dint of squeezing got to the head of the procession, and into the passport office. The passports were taken from the passengers as they entered the door, to be given up in another room when duly examined.

After a short pause the names were called out in rotation by a gendarme, to which the owners duly responded. I had made myself and business known to the sergeant, who had placed a couple of his men at hand to assist me in the arrest, should it prove necessary, and I was allowed the privilege of standing just within the door of the room to which the travellers had to come to receive their passports.

I listened with both my ears to every name that was called. One after another, Smeeth, Jonnes, Broon, duly responded, and it was, I think, about the eighteenth summons that the welcome name of Gustave Peligon met my ears.

The owner of that precious name hurried forward. He was greatly metamorphosed in his outward appearance since he had taken up his position on the settee. Then he was in a black or dark blue military cloak and foraging cap, now he wore a grey cloak and a hat; but I could see at a glance he was the man I wanted. So as soon as he had received his passport I stepped up to him, and, slapping him on the shoulder, said quietly in his ear,—

" Monsieur Peligon, you are my prisoner."

" *Sacrè !* No, no."

" Yes, yes ; no nonsense ; come along quietly." And taking him by the hand, I quickly slipped a handcuff over it, the other being attached to my left wrist.

Nodding to the sergeant, he made a signal to his men. I lit a cigar, and we took up the march.

In the daytime I can find my way about Calais pretty well; but in a dark November night I found it quite another thing. Sometimes I stumbled, at others my companion—he so often that I thought he did it on purpose. One gendarme led the way, the other brought up the rear. It was now past four in the morning; the town was silent as a churchyard. Every one but ourselves seemed locked in the arms of Morpheus. After some twenty minutes of groping and stumbling we arrived at the prison gate, and by a stout pull at the bell endeavoured to rouse the guardians.

Neither one summons nor two sufficed for that purpose. At last a little window over the gate was opened, and a parley ensued, the result of which appeared to be satisfactory, for a few minutes afterwards a wicket in the gate at which we were waiting was opened.

" *Entrez, messieurs.*"

" He might as well have brought a light, I think," I said to myself. "We cannot manage to do much business in the dark."

But there was no such thing as a lucifer-match in the prison of Calais. Fortunately my cigar was not burnt out, so taking a newspaper from my pocket, I applied it to the vital spark, and by dint of much fanning and coaxing I managed to produce a blaze, by the light of which I showed the jailer my warrant.

Releasing my prisoner from the link that united us together, I wished him and the rest of the party good night, and hastened to retrace my steps to the pier, in the hope of being able to return to London by the morning mail-boat.

I had not proceeded far before I heard steps behind

me, and voices shouting, " *Allons. allons, monsieur !*" I
halted for a moment, and was soon joined by the two
gendarmes, who were returning to the Custom House,
and kindly undertook to escort me on the way. For
this little attention I was very grateful, as the road was
not easy in such a night.

I should have been glad of the opportunity of
bringing Monsieur Peligon back with me to England ;
but as some legal formalities had to be gone through,
which would have detained me two or three days in
Calais, and having a special affair to attend to in
London, I was compelled to return alone, very well
satisfied, however, with the result of my expedition.

I reached Dover in time for an early morning train.
In the carriage in which I was seated an elderly French
gentleman sat opposite to me. We entered into conversation, in the course of which he informed me that
he was going to London respecting the affairs of a
creditor who had become bankrupt, and, it was supposed, had absconded with a large sum of money, the
property of his creditors.

"I do not care so much for the money I shall lose,"
said he ; "but this man has been ungrateful. I
established him in business, and he has used my name
without authority to get large credit, and now he robs
everybody. I would give a thousand francs to find
him."

"May I ask his name ?"

" Gustave Peligon."

"Gustave Peligon! Good; I can tell you where you can find him at this moment. I left him but a few hours ago."

"You, *mon ami!* Tell me where I shall find him, and the thousand francs are yours," taking out his pocket-book.

"I am a police officer. I arrested him this morning at Calais, and safely lodged him in the prison there."

Starting to his feet, he threw his arms around my neck and fairly hugged me. When he had resumed his composure he drew a note for a thousand francs from his pocket-book, and handed it to me. I declined it, but he gently insisted, so I made a virtue of a necessity.

As for Monsieur Peligon: a short time after this trip to Calais I was in attendance at the Old Bailey during the sessions, when, to my great surprise, I saw monsieur arraigned at the bar for forgery.

He was found guilty, and sentenced to fourteen years' transportation. "*Bon voyage*, monsieur," I whispered as he passed out. He glared upon me like a hyæna.

THE CONFIDENTIAL CLERK.

"No. —, WOOD STREET, CHEAPSIDE,
"*March 15th, 184—.*

"MESSRS. BARTON, BROTHERS, would be glad to see Inspector F—— at his earliest convenience, respecting a matter in which they require the aid of his services."

The above note was put into my hands while I was hanging about the Mansion House one morning, waiting the arrival of some of my shadows, who were out on a little affair that made a considerable noise at that time.

I lost no time in proceeding to Wood Street, where I had an interview with the principals, at which the confidential clerk was also present.

"Good morning, Mr. F——. You are very prompt. Greatly indebted to you. We have been very much annoyed lately from missing a large quantity of valuable goods — silks, satins, laces, furs, and other articles— amounting to several hundred pounds; and, although we have for some time kept a strict watch upon those we employ, we have been unable to attach suspicion to any one upon a good foundation. All our young men have been in our employ for some years, and are very steady and respectable. I said *all*, but I should except two, who have been with us but a couple of months or so."

"Is there any peculiarity in the goods you have lost, gentlemen?" I asked. "Could you identify them if you were shown them again?"

"We could only identify them by our own private marks upon them. If these were removed they would be just the same in appearance as other parcels manufactured by the same houses. There is one piece· of Lyons satin, however, of a new pattern, which we could identify, as it is the only pattern yet taken from the loom. It is sent to us on approval, and we have ordered several hundred pieces of it; but this sample piece is missing since the day before yesterday, and has given us a great deal of annoyance, because we have taken a large order from a West End house, and they have shown the pattern to the Duchess of W——, and she wants a dress made up of it to appear in at the next drawing-room."

"Can you show me a pattern of this particular piece of goods, gentlemen?"

"Here is a small piece: you see it is quite novel and very elegant."

"That will do, gentlemen. I should be able to recognise it among a thousand. Now, gentlemen, am

I to understand that you consider that some one in your establishment is the thief?"

"It must be, for the goods are taken from places to which our customers have no access; and whoever has stolen them has taken into calculation the difficulty there will be in fixing suspicion, among so many, upon any particular one."

"Who is the last to leave at night? who locks up the premises?"

"Mr. Perkins; this gentleman here," pointing to the confidential clerk, "is always the last to leave. He stays to see all safe, and when the porter has padlocked the outer door he tries it; the porter then gives him the key, and calls for it at his house next morning."

"Well, Mr. Perkins, have you any suspicions as to which of the clerks may have committed these robberies?"

"No, Mr. F——, I cannot say that I have. Most of our young men are exceedingly well conducted—I may say all, in fact; for we have had the two who were last engaged watched at night upon leaving the warehouse, but nothing improper was seen in their conduct. One goes home to his mother's, a respectable widow lady, the other generally goes to the Literary Institution in Aldersgate Street, stays there till it closes, and then goes straight home to his lodging."

"Well, gentlemen, we must take it for granted that the thief is in the house, and must be discovered. You wish me to find out who it is, of course. I will undertake to do so, although it may prove a very long and troublesome job, for I shall have to investigate the habits and doings of your whole staff. How many do you employ ?"

" Forty-two, all told, including the porters."

" Forty-two ! Why, if I put all my hounds on the scent it may take three months, if the rogue should happen to be the last taken in hand. If I undertake the business I must stipulate to have the whole matter left in my hands, without any interference on your part."

" Oh, certainly, Mr. F——. We cannot go on with the present state of matters; we would rather give up business. We do not mind the expense of your labours; we only hope you may be successful."

" Well, gentlemen, I shall begin at once; I should like to go through your warehouse, and take a look at your assistants. I am something of a physiognomist, and can tell a thief almost as soon as I look at him. I suppose I can pass for a customer."

One of the partners escorted me through the warehouses, and the way we turned over things and " took stock " would have amused you. I took the likenesses of all the young men employed.

" You have no idea, Mr. F——," said the senior partner, on escorting me to the door, " how distressingly painful it is to me to have to suspect any one we employ. We feel an interest in them all, and would promote their welfare by any means in our power. Whenever a young man shows industry and zeal, and after a few years' service desires to set up in business for himself, we do not hesitate to help him as far as we can consistently with prudence."

"I can understand your feelings, Mr. B——, very well, and I hope it will not be long before I am able to relieve your mind. Good day."

Upon returning to my crib I found several of my boys waiting to see me.

"Now, lads," said I, "as soon as you have got through with R——'s affair I have another job for you, which will amuse you on evenings. Bartons, of Wood Street, suspect some of their clerks of robbing them, so you must watch them at night when they quit the warehouse, and see how they amuse themselves."

At dusk I had rigged myself up in the "fast style," with plenty of flash jewellery, &c., and took my stand at the corner of Wood Street and Cheapside. I had marked nearly every man in the establishment, and I felt sure that at least one or two would come up the street past where I was standing, and I was not mistaken. Soon a couple came along together, and they held a consultation at the corner where I was standing as to whether they should go to billiards or coffee. Coffee gained the day.

I followed them to a coffee-shop in St. Martin's-le-Grand, and waited till they had refreshed themselves. Upon coming out they turned into St. Paul's Church-yard, and proceeded up Fleet Street to the Strand.

Arriving at a certain "billiard-room," they proceeded upstairs. I waited outside for a quarter of an hour or so, and then followed up.

I found my gentlemen busied in knocking the balls about. I kept dark: they did not bet, and played for a shilling a game. About eleven o'clock they made signs for departure. I got quietly down into the street first. They walked together till they reached the corner of Arundel Street, where they parted, one proceeding up the Strand, the other down Arundel Street, where I concluded he lodged.

Next evening the same young gentlemen were favoured with my special attentions. This time they went to the Olympic theatre, where also I took a seat in the pit. Upon quitting the house they proceeded to a public-house, and after partaking of some ale they parted, and proceeded on their respective ways as before. I took a fancy to see where the one who went up the Strand lodged. He led me a long dance down to Pimlico. Arrived at a door in Charlwood Street, he applied a latch-key, and let himself in.

"So then," I argued with myself, "there is not much to be made of these young fellows; they are like thousands of others who, after getting through their day's work, consider themselves entitled to what they call 'pleasure,' and find it in billiards and farces." I followed up some of the other young gentlemen in their turn, and derived considerable amusement from the way in which they spent their leisure hours.

Two of the clerks were members of the Whittington Club, where they generally spent their evenings—harmless enough, if not profitable. Another went every night to some theatre; but as he generally resorted to the gallery, I did not consider his habits so expensive as those who smoked and frequented casinos. One seemed to have a passion for old books, and generally pulled up at some book-stall in Holywell Street, where he would spend an hour or two, and then stroll leisurely home. Another had a taste for engravings, and seemed to be a collector. Most of the others were of the moral school : one was a member of the Young Men's Christian Association; another a member of a Bible class and a Sunday-school teacher. After leaving his class at Exeter Hall one evening he proceeded along the Strand, and stopped to speak to a young woman at the corner of Wellington Street. In a few minutes they both proceeded together to a house of ill-fame in —— Street.

Thus matters went on for some three weeks, and finding nothing tangible in the suspicions I might have formed of different individuals, I then made my report to Messrs. Barton, and we had a long discussion over the various comings and goings of the young gentlemen in their employ. I cannot say that my communications were calculated to make those gentlemen more comfortable. It was naturally concluded that a member of a club might have use for more money than a salary of £120 a year afforded. A patron of the fine arts could spend his year's income upon a few engravings or a picture; a billiard-player might venture to play for high stakes occasionally; and an admirer of the drama might meet, in his visits to the Temple of Thespis, a goddess before whom he might be tempted to fall down and exclaim, " I am thy slave for ever."

Upon each of these travellers on the road of life not a little time had been fruitlessly spent, but nothing was elicited to justify a suspicion that any one among them was false to his employers. There were two or three of the clerks who were allowed to leave half an hour earlier than the others, on the plea of being members of certain religious associations which met at seven o'clock. These were the nice young men of the house, the saints of the community, and I had been forbidden to watch them, as they were beyond suspicion. As soon as I learned these facts I determined to take them in hand, and a week or two served to put me in possession of some very interesting facts respecting two of them.

One, who wore the most sanctified face you ever saw, and who was constantly lecturing his companions for their want of piety, was found to be addicted to low sensual vice. On the score of economy, I suppose, he kept a toy to play with, and kept her in very elegant style: still I could not venture to say that he robbed his employers, although I was puzzled to find out where the money came from. I have known ambitious young men who, upon coming into a salary of seventy-five pounds a year, thinking, probably, that it was not easy to get through so large a sum, have at once taken to smoking and to women, and soon found it necessary to make up the unexpected deficiency by embezzlement.

I must say I began to despair of success, and thought seriously of giving up the matter as a bad job, when one evening I was riding in an omnibus along Piccadilly. Opposite the end of Bond Street, the omnibus was hailed, and presently a lady dressed in the most expensive and fashionable style got in. The richness of her toilette, and the abundance of jewellery on her person, would have attracted my attention under any circumstances. I thought them singularly out of place in an omnibus. But I was fascinated by her satin dress. It was the identical pattern of the rare piece Messrs. Barton had lost!

"Now then," I thought to myself, "if this is not the Duchess of W——, the time has come at last; I am to be rewarded for all my care and anxiety on behalf of Barton and Co." There were no other passengers in the omnibus beside the lady and myself, consequently I felt quite justified in bestowing all my attention upon her. She seemed grateful, and evidently gratified at my silent admiration of her splendid *tournure,* as the French would say; "make up" as *we* should say. The lady, I thought, was of a rather nervous disposition; every five minutes she drew out a splendid gold watch set with brilliants, noted the time, and forgot it as soon as noted.

"Madam," I said to myself, "we must be better

acquainted. I cannot ask you for your card, so I will
be your page or footman, and escort you safely home.
The night is dark, and wolves are abroad : I 'll be your
watch-dog."

I was in a Brompton 'bus. When we came opposite
to Brompton Square the lady begged me to stop the
vehicle. I did so, and took the opportunity of getting
out first. My lady soon followed, and proceeded to
No. —. Upon her arrival there she assailed the
knocker with a vigour of arm equalled only by that
of the Marchioness of Cheshire's powdered flunky.

Of course I made a memorandum of the number of
her house, and waited long enough to satisfy myself
that she resided in it ; for in a few minutes a light
appeared in the second-floor front room, and I fancied
I could see my lady arranging her hair at the mirror
between the windows.

It was too late that evening to make inquiries, so I
hastened up to the neighbourhood early next morning,
with a dummy parcel made up for Mrs. Vernon,
No. —, Brompton Square, the lady's number. I rang
at the bell ; the servant who answered it assured me
that no Mrs. Vernon lived there, only a Mrs. Glossop.

That was all I wanted. I made inquiries among the
shopkeepers in the neighbourhood : all the information
they could give me was that she had not lived there
long—they believed she was newly married.

Of course a watch was set upon the house that
evening. I was quietly ensconced in the parlour of a

public-house close by, waiting for anything suspicious that might turn up. I had not sat there long before one of my boys hurried in, and tipped me the signal. I quickly finished my grog, and proceeded to the square. In about an hour a gentleman came out, whom I at once recognised as one of the staff of Messrs. Barton, Brothers.

Next night the watch was set again. At about eight o'clock the clerk made his appearance in the square, knocked at No. —, entered, and remained there all night.

I had now some curiosity to see the inside of the house, but it was necessary to resort to some *ruse* to obtain that privilege. Next morning I presented myself at the door dressed as a mechanic, with flannel jacket, corduroys, and a basket of tools over my back. "I was sent by the landlord to look to the gas-fittings." Admitted of course, and obtained access to every room in the house, accompanied by a chatty little housemaid, upon whom I was very sweet; praised her little foot, promised her a handsome husband, and she, out of pure gratitude, told me lots of news—told me how extravagant "missus" was, and how master and she were always having words—showed me "missus's" wardrobe —remarkable truly for its richness and variety. The house was elegantly furnished—everything of the best description—carpets, curtains, mirrors, paintings, rosewood furniture—bed-curtains satin. The bedroom was like a jeweller's shop. O my! I was perfectly dazzled.

I had in my pocket a sixpence with a hole in it; this I gave to the little housemaid, as a charm, for luck, and I am sure that night she dreamed of "that nice man, the gas-fitter."

"Where did the money come from for all this luxury? Who pays?" These were important questions in the business, and must be solved by me before I could satisfy my clients. The house was hired in the name of one of Messrs. Barton, Brothers', clerks. Could he keep such an establishment on his salary, liberal though it was? And the lady—what was she? Well conducted, or only a Delilah, ready to betray her *friend* the moment it became her interest to do so?

Next day a watch was again set upon the house, and towards evening I strolled up to see if anything had transpired. While standing at a corner, talking to my man, I saw one of Messrs. Barton's porters pass by with a good-sized bundle. We followed him up. He stopped at the door of No. —, and was about to ring the bell, when we laid hold of him, and told him he was wanted.

He seemed too much alarmed to offer any resistance or to ask for any explanation, so he followed us quietly to the station. The bundle was found to contain a roll of rich satin and other valuable articles; and the man, without any reserve, told us that they were given to him to deliver by Mr. ——, clerk of Messrs. Barton, Brothers, and that he was constantly in the habit of bringing parcels to No. —, Brompton Square.

We locked the man up for the night, and next

morning took him with the bundle to Wood Street, leaving him outside in charge of an officer, while I went in and communicated to the firm what I had seen, and what had taken place.

Messrs. Barton appeared thunderstruck. They could not believe it. Thought there must be some mistake. What! the man of all others in whom they had reposed the greatest confidence — the one of all others the least to be suspected! They were incredulous.

"Better send for Mr. Perkins, gentlemen, and hear what he has to say."

The confidential clerk was then summoned. When he entered the room, as soon as his eyes fell upon me, I observed a convulsive twitching at the corners of his mouth, and he cast his eyes down upon the floor.

"So we have discovered the thief, Mr. Perkins," said I quietly.

"Ah!" said he, "discovered—how?" and his voice trembled with emotion; "and who is he?"

Catching his eye for a moment, I looked steadily at him, and slowly repeated his name :—

"Mr. George Perkins!"

"'Tis false," said he. "Who dare accuse me?"

"I'll find one who will do that very soon," I replied. And the next moment the porter and his bundle were confronted with him.

Finding himself caught, he dropped his bluster, and put on an air of injured innocence. Finally, when he found the damning evidence too strong against him he made a full confession. He had plundered his employers to the extent of some thousands.

That same day we paid a visit to a certain lady at No. —, Brompton Square, with a polite request that she would surrender her ill-gotten plunder. How she fretted and fumed! She was just going out for a drive in the park, dressed like a duchess going to a state ball. The brougham was waiting at the door.

"But must I give everything up? Can I not keep anything? Where is that wretch Perkins? Why is he not here to protect me?"

"Mr. Perkins will not come here again, and has quite enough to do to protect himself. Everything here seems to be obtained from plundering his employers. If you do not wish to be arrested as a receiver of stolen goods you will make no more trouble, but surrender the house and its contents quietly. Here is a note from Mr. Perkins, which will show you that we do not act without his knowledge and sanction."

"My God! what shall I do? Where shall I go?"

"If you will take my advice, ma'am, you will immediately pack up a small trunk of articles necessary for a lady's wear, and go and take a quiet lodging for a week or two, until you can turn yourself round."

"Stolen! All these things stolen! Perkins a paltry thief! I am astonished! He told me he was a partner in the house of Barclay, Perkins, and Co., and I believed him. What a fool I have been!"

"Not the only one, madam; but make the best of it."

The lady took my advice. She ordered a servant to bring a small trunk into the room. It was brought by the chatty little housemaid, who, recognising me in my new costume, started upon seeing me, and dropped the trunk on to the floor.

"I am going into the country for a few days, Ann. Bring me a change of things, and put them into that trunk. You may send the brougham away and call a cab."

I had a hard struggle with the lady when we came to the jewellery, which she was extremely unwilling to part with, especially her watch set with brilliants. She seemed to have a perfect passion for these baubles.

"Must I give up my rings?"

"Everything, madam."

Then the water-works were set going. She threw herself into an easy chair and sobbed violently. The fingers of each hand were covered with rings. She drew them off one by one, till only a wedding-ring and keeper remained. When I saw that I said,—

"There, that will do; you had better keep those."

There was a pair of diamond earrings that it took a long time to get out of the lady's ears. I fancied they must be riveted in.

"Cab's at the door, ma'am."

Sobbing more violent than ever. Ann looked on in blank amazement. I dare say she wondered what all this had to do with gas-fitting.

At last my lady summoned resolution enough to bid

"a sad farewell to all her greatness," and she ordered
the cab to drive to Waterloo Station, and drove off.

A few days afterwards there was a sale of furniture
and other effects at a certain house in Brompton Square,
and the articles fetched very good prices.   Little Ann,
the housemaid, helped me to make out the inventory.

As for Mr. Perkins, his employers dealt leniently with
him, on account of his wife and young family.   He was
not prosecuted.   The proceeds of the sale of the furniture, &c., at Brompton, reduced the losses of the firm
to a few hundred pounds ; and, on condition that the
late confidential clerk would emigrate to America or
Australia, Messrs. Barton, Brothers, paid for the passage of himself and family out.

I met one of the firm a few months ago.   He told
me that Perkins had gone to Australia, had been very
successful as an accountant and shipbroker there, and
had just remitted them a bill for five hundred pounds,
to indemnify them for any loss they might have sus-
tained through him.

They made me a present of that gold watch you see
hanging over the mantel-piece, as an acknowledgment
of my services, besides paying all expenses.

There are a good many such fools as Perkins, who
will risk everything for a Delilah.

THE PAWNED JEWELS.

CHAPTER I.

I DARE say you have heard of the robbery of Lady Thistledown's jewels. Pretty stiff haul that! Why, the diamonds alone were worth fifteen thousand pounds, and there were many articles that had been in the family I may say for centuries.

How did it happen? Why, I'll tell you. Her ladyship was proceeding from her residence to the railway station. A box containing her dresses, dressing-case, jewels, &c., was placed *outside a cab*, which, in the care of a servant, followed behind the carriage; but when they arrived at the station, lo and behold, the box was missing!

Wasn't there a pretty how d'ye do! I was sent for to my lady. She was like a crazy woman. I really thought she was mad, she went on so; and it was only by repeated assurances that we should be certain to recover the property that I could in the least pacify her.

Did we ever recover it? Wait a bit, we haven't come to that part of the story. I am not going into that at all just now, but to tell you a bit of romance that grew out of it.

It was shortly after the robbery that one day I received a message from Mr. Simpson, the pawnbroker, who, I dare say, you know very well, saying he wished to see me as soon as possible. I at once concluded that it was about something in connection with the lost jewels, so I put on my best coat and hat, and walked up to the Strand.

'Although a pawnbroker, a title almost as significant as a " flinty heart," Mr. Simpson was a man of refined feelings, with as good and kind a heart as ever beat in a human breast. When I arrived at his office he was engaged, so I took a seat at a desk, and made myself quite at home, which I could very easily do, as Mr. Simpson and myself had had a great many confidential affairs together.

While seated at the desk, scanning my note-book, the door of a box nearly opposite where I was seated opened, and a female closely veiled entered it, remaining, however, as much in the shade as the limited space which inclosed her permitted. Just at this moment Mr. Simpson became disengaged, and he advanced to the box to attend to this new visitor. She threw up her veil, and revealed one of the most lovely faces I ever beheld. Her age was apparently four or five-and-twenty; tall, elegantly attired, well proportioned, a fine oval face, deep blue eyes, auburn hair, with that air *distingué* which can never be put on or mistaken.

When she spoke she displayed a mouth full of well-formed, pearly teeth, and her hand, from which she had removed the glove, was of the true aristocratic mould.

What passed between Mr. Simpson and his fair customer I could not hear. She spoke in an almost inaudible voice, and he responded in whispers. This appeared to me mysterious, and my curiosity was piqued; so I made a signal, well understood by Mr. Simpson, but not by any one else, which signified, "What have you got there?" In a few moments Mr. Simpson looked at me with a significant glance, which I interpreted to mean, "Here's a bit of romance."

When he had taken the article she had brought to pledge, Mr. Simpson came alongside of me to write out the ticket, and took advantage of the opportunity to whisper, "What do you think of that?"

"I'll tell you presently," I replied.

Trying to look as much like one of the assistants as possible, I made some excuse to get nearer where the interesting young lady was standing, so as to have a good look at her. Certainly the scrutiny was favourable. She was a most commanding, captivating creature; beautiful, but of that haughty style which, while it attracts, reminds you that there is an impassable gulf between yourself and the proud conscious beauty that condescends to be gazed upon by inferior mortals. There was evidently a nervous flush upon her cheeks, and an unnatural brilliancy in her eyes, that assured me that every motion, look, and gesture was prompted by

D

the feeling that she was undergoing a torture of the feelings. Certainly a pawnbroker's shop was not the proper sphere for so elegant and refined a person. Her air of high breeding interested me deeply. As she was in the act of leaving the box she turned round full upon me, and gave a withering glance, which seemed to say, "I am obliged to submit to your scrutiny now, but you don't belong to this establishment I know. I should like to know who *you* are."

Discretion has formed a very important element in my education, so of course I kept my position and held my tongue; but the face of that magnificent beauty illumined the box for some moments after she had quitted it.

"Do you have many such customers as that, Mr. Simpson?"

"I cannot say that I do. There, look at that, and tell me what you think of it."

He handed me the article the mysterious young lady had just pledged. It was a large and singularly-shaped breast-pin, the centre being composed of various precious stones, fantastically but artistically set, representing a coat of arms. It was surrounded with a wreath of smaller stones, which, from the peculiarity of their arrangement, had some significance—probably, as I thought, spelled the motto of the coat of arms.

"This looks like a family relic," I said, after a careful examination of the pin. "It is certainly an ancient——"

"You may well say that, Mr. F——. There must be something extraordinary in that young lady's history. I should like much to find it out, for I have become greatly interested in her. She has been a regular customer of mine for some time, and I have come to the conclusion, from what I have observed, that she is getting hard up."

"What do you mean, Mr. Simpson?"

"The only explanation I can give is to tell you what I have observed. About three years ago—my books will show—she first came here with some articles of silver plate marked with a family crest and initials; then she brought various jewels, among which I particularly remarked a tiara of great value, set with diamonds, which she was extremely anxious should not be sold or lost. I must confess that my interest in her became very strong, for she was evidently much above the class with whom I ordinarily deal; and I assured her that, so long as she continued to pay the interest, she need be under no fear of losing her property. The earnestness with which she thanked me convinced me that there was something more than mere want of money at the bottom of the affair, and this still further increased my interest. The pin she just pledged was for money to pay back-interest on previous loans, and I really hope something may turn up to save me the pain, and her the mortification, of a sale of her property."

"What name does she give?"

"Valerie De Vere."

"Do you suppose that is her real name?"

"I cannot answer that. Such is the name she gave me."

"Do you think she is English?"

"She speaks with a slight, the slightest possible accent. I have come to the conclusion she is born of French parents in England. The crest on her plate is not that of an English family."

"And her address?"

"No. —, Craven Hill."

"A good neighbourhood, at any rate," I replied, smiling.

"Yes; but I do not suppose that she lives *there.* I am half inclined to think that she belongs to some exiled family, which has gradually fallen into poverty, but whose pride encourages them to hope that something will turn up to enable her to redeem those relics of former greatness."

"Of course, Mr. Simpson, you won't sacrifice the things?"

"Certainly not. The world, I am afraid, has made up its mind that pawnbrokers have no hearts, and that our only object is to make the most out of the necessities of our fellow-creatures. I can't help what the world thinks, but I can say that I go to my bed nightly with a conscience as void of wilful wrong as that of any man in London. I don't mind telling you, Mr. F——, because you will understand me, that I have taken a deep interest in that lady, and there is nothing in reason or honour that I would not do to serve her."

"I believe you, Mr. Simpson, and am glad to hear

you say so. Her appearance is so prepossessing that I
am already prepared to say that my poor services are
entirely at your disposal, if they can in any way be
useful to you and to her."

I well knew Mr. Simpson to be a shrewd as well as
a kind-hearted man, and the very fact that his interest
was aroused in her behalf awakened a curiosity in me
to know more of her; so I at once made up my mind
to learn what I could, if it might be accomplished
without alarming her sensitiveness, or unnecessarily
wounding her feelings; and with this intention I
prepared to take leave of Mr. Simpson.

"But before I go, Mr. Simpson, I should like to
know what was the business you sent for me upon."

"Well, the fact is, this is the very matter. You know
my mind, and if anything comes in your way that will
throw any light on this lady's history or position, all
I can say is, I should be very glad to know of it."

You will not think it strange if I tell you that next
day I took a stroll out to Craven Hill. With some
misgivings, and with my mind not quite made up as to
what excuse I should invent, I rang the visitor's bell at
No. —, the address the fair stranger had given.

A man-servant responded to the summons: on the
spur of the moment I asked for Mrs. Armitage.

"There is no such person here," was the reply.

"Are you quite sure?" I asked, not having made
up my mind as to the course I would pursue.

"Sure! Yes, quite sure. No one lives here but
Mrs. De Vere and her family."

This was just what I wanted, and all I desired to
know. So pulling out a memorandum-book from my
pocket, and turning over the leaves, as if in search of
some name,—

"Is not this Craven Hill Gardens?"

"No, this is Craven Hill."

"Oh, is it? Then I have made a mistake. Sorry to
have troubled you;" and bowing, the door was
promptly shut in my face.

So, after all, she had given her real name and
address. But what on earth could have occurred to
compel one living in such style to resort to such shifts
for a living? As far as I could make out, from a brief
glance into the hall, the house was handsomely furnished, and there was every indication that comfort, if
not luxury, surrounded the inmates.

When quitted the door I was as much in a quan-
dary as when I went to it, and I was half ashamed of
myself to think I had been so easily foiled. However,
barring the passing interest which Miss De Vere's
appearance and manners had excited in me, I had no
special reason to care for or think about her. She
could not be connected with the robbery of the
countess's jewels, as I had at first thought; so, important matters engaging my attention, she gradually
passed from my thoughts, like so many others have
done, whose cases apparently claimed much more
sympathy and action than hers had excited.

CHAPTER II.

" You know Jack Tupling, and Joanna Wray, and Davy Rutt, and Emma Rolander, and Nat Larkins— eh ?"

" I cannot say that I have ever had the honour of their acquaintance," I modestly replied.

" Well, I have. I can tell you something about that gang, for they all played into one another's hands."

" What have they to do with Miss De Vere and her story ?"

" That remains to be seen. Some few years ago I was inspector at —— station : there was, I remember, a case of a Frenchman, whose name was——Well, I can't recollect it now, but it is in my pocket-book. He arrived in London from Birmingham, where he had been purchasing a large quantity of real and sham jewellery, to take with him as merchandise to Martinique, among which was a large number of watches. The lot had probably not cost him over five hundred pounds, but it was so elegantly got up ' for exportation,' that, if he had ever reached the island with it, he would have realised a fortune. He put up at a French *café* and hotel near Leicester Square, and was patiently awaiting the day of sailing of the ship in which he had taken passage for Martinique.

" Nat Larkins, to whom I introduced you a few moments ago, a Prussian by birth, and one of the most expert thieves that ever infested any community, who

passed himself off for a Frenchman by birth, was in the
habit of daily frequenting the *café* where the Frenchman with the jewellery had put up.   It did not take
him long to strike up an acquaintance with the unsuspecting Frenchman, who was delighted to meet with
a fellow-countryman, and it was not long before their
acquaintance ripened into intimacy; for Nat was a
perfect master of his profession, and knew exactly when
and how to make his game.   The Frenchman—whom,
for brevity's sake, I shall call Monsieur Boulange—had
confided to Nat all his business, and had gone so far in
his confidence as to show him one trunk filled with
watches and jewellery, destined for the gay, dashing,
sable beauties of Martinique.   Nat, although tolerably
wide awake, forgot on the present occasion that all that
glittered was not gold, and set about racking his brains
to get possession of the treasure.   His first move was
to secure a room adjoining that occupied by Monsieur
Boulange, with a door communicating; and having
established a perfect intimacy with his intended victim,
he proposed to show him something of life in London,
to which Monsieur Boulange, with true French polite-
ness, consented.   Nat had so laid his plans that Emma
Rolander should spread her net for the unfortunate
merchant, and this she did so successfully, that he
became deeply enamoured of her.   She was soon a
daily visitor upon Monsieur Boulange at the *café* : he
showed her his treasures ; and it was arranged that she
should accompany him to Martinique.

" One morning Monsieur Boulange reecived a tele-
graphic message, purporting to have come from Birmingham, stating that his order was completed, and awaited his
inspection. With many regrets at leaving his *charmante*
Emma, and after many tender adieux, Monsieur B——
started for Birmingham. This was another move in
the scheme planned by Nat Larkins to get possession
of the trunk of watches and jewellery, which the praetice
of the telegraph companies dating a message from any
place the sender may think fit, enabled Nat to do
with facility. He had only to walk into the office at
London Bridge, and indite his trap message dated
Birmingham, and the poor unsuspecting Frenchman
would be enticed away. Nat took care to secure the
services of Jack Tupling as his body servant, or
factotum, and of course communicated to him the
contents of Monsieur Boulange's trunk. Nat took care
to accompany monsieur to the station, and see him
fairly under weigh; he then returned to the *café* to
consummate his cunningly-devised scheme.

" On that same afternoon, Nat, with a face as long as
his arm, informed his landlord that he had just received
information that his ' modder' was taken suddenly and
seriously ill, and that he would be obliged to go
immediately to see her; not alone because filial duty
demanded it, but because, as her only son, he would
inherit a handsome fortune. Accordingly he ordered
Jack Tupling, who had been acting the part of valet,
to pack up his trunks immediately, and take them to

the Dover rail, where he would meet him ; and he was
very particular to impress on his landlord the necessity
for keeping an eye on his room during his absence, as
there was much valuable property in his trunks, which
he would leave until his return.   These arrangements
being completed, Nat Larkins, by means of a pair of
nippers, found an easy entrance into the room of
Monsieur Boulange through the connecting door, and
the contents of the unfortunate Frenchman's trunk
were speedily transferred to one of his own.   This
done, he relocked the door with the nippers, and Jack
Tupling, shouldering the trunk, marched out of the *café*
with it as boldly as if it had been his own, and
deposited it in a cab waiting at the door."

CHAPTER III.

I do not now remember exactly how long it was
after my first sight of Valerie De Vere at Mr. Simpson's
that I saw her again ; but one pleasant evening, while
I was propping up a lamp-post at the corner of St.
James's Street and Pall Mall, I saw a tall woman,
closely veiled, coming towards me at a rapid pace.
At the first glance I thought it was Emma Rolander;
but another look dissipated that idea, for she did not
transact her business in that way.   The woman, just
before she reached me, went up to a gentleman and
accosted him, but what she said I could not hear.   I
observed, however, that after a very brief conversation

the gentleman turned away with a coarse laugh, while the female dashed on. I can find no other word to describe her gait.

My curiosity was a little roused, for I felt sure she was on the " lay "—some new hand at the business, not well posted up in the mode of proceeding. As she passed me I turned to follow her, when, at the moment, who should pass me but Emma. Of course she knew me, and stopping, said,—

" I wonder who that woman can be. She has been going it up and down for a couple of hours; but," she added with a chuckle, " I don't think she has done much business."

" Go along, and let her alone. Mind your own business. How 's Nat and Jack ? You 'll have enough to do to keep yourself out of trouble, without putting your nose into other people's affairs."

I passed on rapidly in the hope of overtaking the stranger. She could not have gone very far, for in a few moments I saw her coming back at the same race-horse speed, accosting such gentlemen as she thought might serve her purpose. At length she reached me, and I threw myself purposely in her way, expecting she would accost me, and in this I was not disappointed; for, approaching me in her quick nervous manner, she laid her hand on my arm, and bending her face close to my ear, asked,—

" Have you got five pounds ?"

" I have, and something more," I replied; " but I

should like to spend it in my own way. Let me see
your face."

She slowly lifted her veil: the light from the gas-
lamp fell full upon her face, and disclosed the features
of VALERIE DE VERE!

CHAPTER IV.

I have been astonished a good many times in my
life, but never so much as on this occasion; for of all
the persons in this great Babylon, she was the very
last I should have expected to find in that sad voca-
tion.

"Come," she said, in nervous, tremulous tones,
"have you five pounds now?" and she looked eagerly
in my face.

For a moment or two I hardly knew what to say or
do; but recovering my self-possession, I said:—

"Come over into the park; it is not so public there;"
and I crossed over to the gate by Marlborough House.
Hastily drawing down her veil, she followed me across
the street; and when I had passed through the gate
I waited until she reached my side, when she hurriedly
repeated her singular demand for five pounds.

"Miss De Vere," I said; but I had no sooner
pronounced her name than she gave a start and a suppressed scream; and clutching my arm, she exclaimed
hysterically:—

"My God—my God! what have I come to? Who
are you that knows Valerie De Vere?"

"Do not agitate yourself—you have nothing to fear from me. I dare say you have heard my name. I know everybody. I am Inspector F——."

Had she not leaned heavily on my arm for support she must have fallen to the ground. I perceived that she trembled violently, and I could hear her choking sobs, which she vainly endeavoured to stifle by pressing her handkerchief to her mouth.

"Oh, sir, you'll not expose me, will you? I never thought of such a crime till to-night. Ah, if you knew all!"

And she shook her head sorrowfully, as if reluctant or unable to say more.

"What am I to understand? Fear nothing from me. My duty is to aid you if I can, not to injure you. Let me know all, that I may judge how I can best serve you. Will you come with me, and tell me what on earth has happened that I should meet you under these circumstances? I see you do not remember me."

"I never saw you before that I remember," she replied in a low, choking voice, but without raising her head.

"But I have seen you, and know you. Do you remember when you pledged that large breast-pin at Simpson's?"

"Ah! that's it, is it? You were there, then, and saw what took place? Then you can understand my position. Oh! for God's sake, if you can help me and will, do so now, and I will bless you as long as I live. I will go with you anywhere, and tell you everything. God help me that I have so much to tell ! "

"My dear lady, do not go on so ; it is of no use to fret and grieve ; no sort of good can come of it. Rely upon my doing anything, everything in my power to serve you."

During this discourse we had kept on walking, and were now by the Duke of York's steps. I turned towards the Horse Guards, intending to cross over to Great Scotland Yard, but upon reflection I thought it best not to do so for my companion's sake; so I turned into a coffee-house by Charing Cross, and took possession of a little quiet room, intimating that I did not wish to be disturbed. I asked my companion to take a seat in the chair I had placed for her on one side of the table, and she fairly sank into it ; and leaning her head on both hands, her tears and sobs increased so fearfully, I almost dreaded an hysterical fit.

I saw that in her present state of mind it would be useless to offer any condolence, so I concluded I would let her have her cry out ; and when she had in some measure checked her grief and stifled down her sobs she raised her head, and throwing back her veil, displayed her beautiful face, red and swollen with weeping, and wearing an expression of distress really pitiful to behold.

"Oh! Mr. F——, pity me, and do not condemn me; for when you know all—— God forgive me ! "

she interrupted, again burying her face in her hands; and giving way to tears and sobs, recalled the memory of the past, and the shame of the present hour.

I was convinced that there was no use in making any attempt to change the current of her feelings; so I patiently waited till they had run themselves out, till her own time arrived to disclose the circumstances which had led her to such a position.

Suddenly she aroused herself, and fairly dashing away the tears which blinded her eyes, she said nervously,—

"I believe—I know—yes, I am sure you are a gentleman. You do not, I am certain, believe I voluntarily chose to do what you prevented me from accomplishing to-night—the ruin of my body and soul."

"No—on my word, no; and I tell you frankly my interest was aroused by a few words from Mr. Simpson, which he spoke to me after you had left his office. Why, Miss De Vere, I have even been to your house."

When I said this she fairly glared upon me with astonishment.

"Yes," I continued, "I was so much interested then in you, that I thought I would learn more, if possible, and, if possible, serve you."

"You did not enter the house?" she inquired eagerly.

"O no! I merely went to the door, under pretence of inquiring for another name, but really——"

"Really what?—what?" she asked nervously, forgetting her grief in her new excitement.

"To know if you had given your real name and address to Mr. Simpson."

She looked at me earnestly for a moment, with an indefinable expression; then, suddenly extending her hand, while a sad smile lighted up her face, she said,—

"Forgive me, Mr. F——. I did not mean to say anything offensive."

"You have not, Miss De Vere; and now, if you can, tell me all your griefs. Whatever you say will be religiously kept secret; and believe me when I say I sincerely desire to serve you."

"I believe you from my heart, Mr. F——," she exclaimed suddenly, leaning back in her chair, and laying her clasped hands in her lap. "Do you remember the banking-house of Bacon, De Vere, and Scott?"

"Certainly I do," was my reply; for I recollected them well, as the predecessors of a firm which has since occupied a conspicuous place in the financial history of the country.

"My father was a member of that firm."

"In the name of all that is singular and mysterious, is that possible?"

"Not only possible, but true."

"One moment," I said; for I wished for a moment to think and reflect. "Do you mean to say that you are the daughter of Henry De Vere, who was——"

"I know what you were going to say, but do not say

it.   I am his unhappy daughter, and I have two
brothers less able to provide for themselves than I
am."

I half rose from my chair in sheer bewilderment.
She perceived the impression that her words had made
upon me, and renewing her sad smile, which fairly
captivated my heart, she continued,—

"Yes, Mr. F——, you have heard of my father;
but probably you never heard of his children—still
less of his daughter, perhaps.   You little dreamed, I
am sure, that you would ever meet with a daughter of
his as you have met me to-night."

I could only bow a reply; for there was something
so extraordinary in the information she had imparted,
that I could scarcely realise its truthfulness; yet I felt
it was all true.

"I promised to tell you all, and will have no
concealment from you, now that you know me.   At
the time of the French Revolution, my father, then a
young man, escaped with the wreck of a large fortune
to this country.   He became a partner in a banking-
house.   Soon after his arrival here he met my mother
who was of Irish parentage, and married her; and for
many years everything went on prosperously and happily
with them.   My father's position as member of so
eminent a banking firm necessarily brought him and
his family in social contact with the wealth and fashion
of this metropolis.   He lived in a style becoming his
wealth and standing, keeping open house to all comers.

E

Every advantage in the way of education and accomplishment which money could procure was bestowed upon me; and when I reached a proper age I was introduced into the society which, up to this present hour—yes, Mr. F——," noticing my look of surprise, " which, to this present hour, I have maintained; but oh, at what a sacrifice!" and she leaned her head upon her hand, and for a moment was lost in thought.

"When I was — no matter how old," she continued; " but only a few years ago my father became entangled with a set of aristocratic swindlers, honourable and fashionable sharpers, the result of which was that they introduced him at Crockford's, and he was there, at the gaming table, stripped, or say cheated, of everything he possessed in the world. I need not tell you the rest—you must know what ensued as well as I do myself.

" An examination into his affairs showed that everything he had owned was so deeply mortgaged, and his debts so numerous and heavy, there was nothing left for his family except the house in which he resided, which gave us a shelter, and nothing more. His partners, naturally incensed at his conduct, refused to have anything to do with us; but one friend, who did not condemn us for his faults or vices, clung to us. My mother possessed jewels and plate—family relics of much value; but beyond these, and the furniture in the house, purchased by her father at her marriage, there was absolutely nothing we could call our own.

It was not long before the terrible and sudden shock began to show its effects on my mother, and I could perceive that at times her mind would wander, until at length she sank into a state of hopeless idiotcy. The entire charge of everything—even my young and helpless brothers—thus fell upon me; and, worse than all, on me devolved the duty (for such I considered it) of keeping up the appearances of our former position. And then commenced that terrible struggle between *pride* and *poverty* of which you, with all your experience, can form no idea. Many a night, Mr. F——, have I passed at parties, leaving my mother in charge of a servant, when my heart was nearly bursting with anguish, and many a smile that has wreathed. my face only served to hide the terrible struggle going on within. The little ready money we possessed at the time of my father's death, though carefully hoarded by my mother, was soon exhausted, and then I had recourse to Mr. Simpson. First I took some of our family plate, then jewels, and our treasures faded away one by one, in the foolish hope that something might turn up among our wealthy relations in France which would enable me with truth to keep up the appearances which had cost me such terrible trials and sufferings. You say you saw me at Mr. Simpson's when I pledged that breast-pin ?"

"Which was true, Miss De Vere; it was the first and only time I have seen you until to-night."

"Do not speak of that," she said with a shudder,

while a blush of shame crossed her cheek. "Forget it;
for I shall pray that even the recollection may for ever
be blotted out of my mind. Mr. F——, will you
believe me, knowing what I have told you, when I say
that for days past we have suffered from absolute
hunger?"

I looked up in surprise. She continued:—

"Hear me out. It was not for that you saw me as
you did. O no! I would have starved first; for I
feel that to live with virtue lost, only to be first the
toy, then the football of purse-proud libertines, would
indeed be to experience the woes of hell upon earth.
It was a purer and nobler impulse that impelled me to
the sacrifice. My poor *dear mother*, now that she
approaches her last hours, has resumed her reason, and
her incessant cry is for *that breast-pin*. It was my
father's first love-gift to her, and she prized it beyond
anything she ever possessed. Her distress drove me
almost mad—*it must* have been madness—for now her
voice is ringing in my ears, entreating but to be permitted once more to behold that precious relic of the
plighted faith of my father, who was dearer to her than
all the world beside. Could you have seen them
together before the fatal hour when those cursed fiends
beset his path, and followed him day and night till they
had worked his ruin, and witnessed his singleness of
devotion to my mother, and the tenderness with which
he treated her, and how kindly he anticipated her every
want, and even her desires, you would not wonder that

his terrible fate should have made a wreck of the heart
that was so passionately wedded to him. O how the
remembrance of those scenes of unalloyed happiness
racks my poor brain, when I compare them with the
terrible death of my dear father, and the sadder condition of my helpless mother!

"I could not bear to hear her ask for that pin,
knowing, as I did, that it was beyond my reach. At
last I darted from the house, and fairly ran into the
street, scarcely realising what I was doing or where I
was going, and yet fearfully conscious that I was about
to thrust myself into the very pit of vice to relieve the
heart of my dying mother. This was my condition when
you found me, and providentially, I trust, your presence
saved me from ruin, and partially restored me to my
senses. I tell you, Mr. F——, we are all suffering
from want. My brothers are, I hope, in bed and
asleep, but they went there hungry. I have eaten no
mouthful this day, and my poor mother, accustomed all
her life to luxuries, is in want of the most common
necessaries of life; and yet I am sure that she and my
brothers would rather have gone to their graves than
know what you have learned to-night."

Thus far Miss De Vere had preserved comparative
composure while speaking; but as her narrative drew to
a close her voice was gradually raised, her words came
quickly, nervously, and the closing sentence was
delivered almost with a scream, so terribly was she
excited.

When she had concluded she leaned her face upon her
hands, and again gave vent to her tears and sobs. For
a few moments I remained seated in silence, reflecting
upon this strange revelation; but it was now time for
action, not for thought; so I rang the bell and ordered
some refreshment, which she had obstinately refused to
take when we were first seated. I had to use much
persuasion to induce her to take food.

"Think," she said; "my poor mother and brothers
have none. Why should I have more than they?"

"But consider, Miss De Vere," I said, "they are
looking to you, and how much worse it would be for
them if you were unable to exert yourself. Eat something to keep up your strength."

I prevailed at last. After swallowing a few mouthfuls
and a cup of tea she declared she felt so much better
that I took up my hat, and rose to go.

"Now, Miss De Vere, I must go home with you. It
is high time you were at home for your mother's sake.
As for that pin, she shall see it in the morning."

"Do you mean so?" she asked eagerly, as she arose
and wiped the tears from her eyes.

"As sure as your name is De Vere."

"Oh, thank you—bless you! Mother can die in
peace. As for me——" and she shook her head sorrowfully.

"Don't think of that now. Come, may I accompany
you home? It is growing late, and it will not be safe
or prudent for you to go alone."

Drawing down her veil, she followed me silently out of the coffee-house into the street. I hailed a cab, and we proceeded at once to her residence. No conversation passed between us, for she was too deeply engrossed in her own sad thoughts, and I was completely bewildered at what I had heard.

At length the cab stopped.

"Here we are, Mr. F——."

Alighting, we ascended the steps of the house. She opened the door with a latch-key.

A lamp was burning in the hall, lighting it sufficiently to enable me to perceive that it was appropriately furnished. A richly-ornamented hat-stand was on one side of the door, and near it was an old-fashioned carved oak chair. The stairs were carpeted, and the whole aspect of things was indicative of anything but the poverty she had described.

I turned with an air of surprise; but she met my glance with the old sad smile, and motioned me to ascend the stairs, which I did, closely followed by her. As we reached the first landing I noticed a tallow candle placed in a common tin candlestick, standing on a deal chair without a back. She lit the candle and xtinguished the lamp. Looking around, I could just discern by the feeble light that, except the chair and candlestick, there was no particle of furniture. The floor was bare, the walls were bare, and there was an aspect of cheerlessness and desolation which quite chilled my heart.

As I stood in mute surprise, she laid her hand on
my arm, and whispered,—

"Beyond what you have seen, there is not an article
of furniture in the house. My mother is sleeping on
the floor; she has but an apology for a bed: my
brothers have not even that. Do you understand me,
Mr. F—— ?"

"Perfectly," I said; for I could now perceive what
great sacrifices had been made to pride and appearances, the furniture in the hall being retained to
deceive or delude those who might call into the
belief that, if not rich, they were at least comfortable.

"Will you see my mother?" she whispered.

"No; I had better not to-night. The appearance
of a stranger might excite and alarm her injuriously.
I have promised to serve you, but will do so in my own
way. I believe now all you have said, even to the
desperate want which oppresses you. Take this,
procure what is needful for your mother, but do not
forget yourself; for remember her strength lies in you
now. I will see you to-morrow at ten, when you shall
have the pin; after that we will speak of the future."

"I cannot thank you now as I ought, Mr. F——; I
will try and do so hereafter; but my prayers will
follow you for this night's kindness."

Before I could prevent it, she seized my hand,
pressed it to her bosom, then to her lips, imprinting a
fervent kiss upon it. I left that desolate house
reluctantly; for I felt how much more remained to be

done for its unhappy inmates. When I found myself in the street again it seemed as if I had just awoke from an unpleasant dream ; for I could scarcely realise the truth of what I had heard and seen.

Next morning, before the hour I had appointed to call upon Miss De Vere, I had seen Mr. Simpson ; and on my becoming responsible that it should be returned in a few days, he readily intrusted the much-coveted breast-pin to my keeping, though, as he did so, he looked as if he wished very much to know my reason for asking for it. He did not, however, ask me directly, and I forebore making any mention of the occurrences of the previous evening.

Punctually at the hour appointed I called upon Miss De Vere; and when I showed her the much-prized jewel her eyes fairly glistened with joy.

"There," said I, "I have kept my promise to you ; and my word is given that it shall be returned within a week."

"And so it shall be," she replied, taking it and pressing it to her lips. "Oh, how can I thank you ? What can I do to show my gratitude ? "

"By conquering your pride, Miss De Vere ; by letting your *real* friends know your true position ; and by bending to the circumstances, unfortunate and unhappy though they be, which now surround you, and which you cannot at present overcome. You have no right to deny to your mother, your brothers, or yourself, the commonest necessaries of life, for the sake of upholding a false, foolish pride. Duty, humanity, honour, every sentiment which should animate a proud, high-minded girl, as you appear to be, demand this sacrifice from you, and you *must* make it. Promise me that you will."

For a moment she remained silent. Her colour came and went as I spoke. At length, raising her head, and looking me in the face with her large truthful eyes, she said,—

" I cannot refuse you. I promise you I will."

"And I am sure you will if you promise. Remember that breast-pin must be returned to me, and when you return it I shall expect to hear how faithfully you have kept your word."

She was anxious to take her prize to her mother, so I did not detain her longer. After many expressions of deep thankfulness and gratitude I took my departure.

CHAPTER V.

About ten days afterwards a lady in deep mourning was ushered one morning into my private office. I at once concluded that her mother was dead. After the ordinary salutations she said,—

"There, Mr. F——, I need not say how deeply grateful I am for your considerate kindness. There's the breast-pin again."

"And your promise, Miss De Vere?"

"Has been religiously kept, and again I owe you thanks. I made known our situation to Mrs. E——, so well known for her benevolence, and she proved herself not only the true lady, but a kind, considerate friend. Through her generosity and influence we have been bountifully cared for. My poor mother died surrounded at least with comforts, and provision has already been made for my brothers."

"So I was right, after all?"

"And I was wrong from the beginning. But for my foolish pride, such sufferings as we have undergone would not have been entailed upon us."

"And what about yourself, Miss De Vere?"

"I am invited to pass a few weeks at Brighton with an old schoolfellow of my father's, whose wife was a friend of my mother's."

"You will at least be contented there, and, I hope, happy. Try and forget the past, and do not let your pride again overcome your reason."

"Never, Mr. F——! The lesson I have received," and she crimsoned to the temples as she spoke, "is one I can never forget, any more than I could forget your delicate and considerate kindness."

"Do not speak of that, Miss De Vere, for I only discharged my duty in common humanity. I am heartily glad to hear of the change in your circumstances, and hope you will continue to prosper."

"If ever I do prosper, my first duty and pleasure will be to testify my deep gratitude to you. We may not meet again soon, but, believe me, your kindness is deeply engraven on my heart."

We parted. The next time I saw Miss De Vere she was walking down Regent Street. in company with a notorious prostitute and thief.

CHAPTER VI.

It is easier to imagine than to describe my astonishment when, one sunny afternoon, I was walking up Regent Street. It was in the height of the season, and you know how gay and lively it is about four in the afternoon at such a time. I was fairly staggered "struck all of a heap"—at seeing Miss De Vere, elegantly dressed, coming along full sail, in company with the notorious Joanna Wray and her "pal," Captain Shark, as they call him—Nat Larkins being his true name, with a dozen aliases. They were evidently on terms of close intimacy, and apparently engrossed in earnest conversation. Miss De Vere's head being turned towards Nat, she did not perceive me; but Nat and Joanna did, and the fellow gave me a wink—curse his impudence!

I would have turned and watched them, had I not been engaged in looking for other game; but I looked back upon the trio with undisguised astonishment.

What could it mean? Was it possible that I had been deceived by Miss De Vere? I could not be deceived as to her companions. Was she a companion in crime with that infamous Joanna Wray? I mused and pondered, but could not solve my perplexity. There is some mystery here, I thought; for I could not

find it in my heart to condemn Miss De Vere, although
appearances were so much against her. Fortunately I
was enabled to clear the matter up quite unexpectedly.

I must confess that sometimes thoughts unfavourable
to Miss De Vere would cast their shadows over my
mind; and I had some curiosity to know how these
opposite characters, as I supposed them to be, had come
together. I fancied that Miss De Vere might be one of
those women whose love of ease and display must be
gratified at any sacrifice, and had recklessly thrown
herself away.

One afternoon I was sitting in the private room at
the station, when a note was brought in to me by a boy
whose face I remembered to have seen at Mr. Simpson's,
the pawnbroker. It was from Mr. Simpson, asking me
to call upon him as soon as I could make it convenient.
I immediately proceeded to his shop, and seating ourselves in his private office, he commenced by saying,—

"What on earth does all this mean, F—— ?"

"Upon my word, I can't say," I replied, smiling, for
he spoke as if he took it for granted I knew what he
was alluding to.

"True; that was hardly a fair question, considering
you do not know what I had in my mind. Well, it was
this: Nat Larkins was here just now, with one of the
pledge-tickets belonging to that De Vere girl."

"I am not surprised at that, Simpson," I replied,

quite unconcernedly; for I well remembered my last
sight of her, though of course he as yet knew nothing
of the circumstances under which I had seen her.

"The deuce you're not! But I am; and I should
like to know what it means, and what you mean."

"I suppose he came by it in the regular course of
business," I replied, with the same composure.

"I really cannot comprehend you. A few weeks ago
you were completely carried away by her, and now you
seem to take it as something quite natural that this
rascal——But how the deuce do you suppose he came
by that ticket?"

"Well now, Mr. Simpson, I am obliged to confess
that I have come to the conclusion that we were both
taken in by that woman; and therefore I can take
this matter coolly, as you see."

Mr. Simpson opened his eyes very wide, and looked
marvellously chapfallen.

"You don't think they were stolen, I hope?"
alluding to the jewels pledged by Miss De Vere. Such
a discovery would have entailed a very serious loss
upon him, in case of reclamation by the owners.

"You haven't forgot the robbery of the Countess of
Thistledown's jewels, I suppose?"

"No, indeed, I have not. But these are none of
them, surely?"

"Not at all. I have no doubt that the jewels
pledged by Miss De Vere belonged legitimately to her;
but, from what I saw a week or two ago, I am satisfied

that whatever she might have been, she is no longer deserving of your interest or sympathy."

"Suppose you tell me what you did see," said Mr. Simpson, rather nervously; for he well knew that I should not speak in such a manner, or use such harsh language, without very good reasons.

I then proceeded to relate to the worthy pawnbroker the incidents connected with my first interview with Miss De Vere, and my visit to her house.

"You found everything there as she represented?"

"Exactly; and my interest in her was so deeply and painfully excited, that I assumed the responsibility of that breast-pin for her."

"But she returned that honourably."

"Very true; but possibly that might have been only a blind to prepare for some greater and more profitable operations."

"What possible reason can you have for such a suspicion?"

"Simply because I know she has fallen into bad hands—has very bad associates; and my suspicions are confirmed by finding one of her duplicates in Nat Larkins's possession."

Mr. Simpson looked something more than astonished at this communication, but made no remark. I continued,—

"A short time ago I saw her parading down Regent Street, with Nat on one side and Joanna on the other."

"I'll sell everything to-morrow," hurriedly exclaimed

Mr. Simpson, whose anger was only equalled by his astonishment at hearing this account. "But no; there may be some devilry at the bottom of this, of which she is ignorant. It can't be possible that one like her, giving such unmistakable evidences of birth and high-breeding, could voluntarily associate with such characters."

"As for that, they could deceive Satan himself. Nat is a plausible, accomplished scoundrel, with excellent address; while Joanna can play the lady when she tries hard. What did you do with Nat, and what was his ticket for?"

"The ticket was for a valuable diamond ring, upon which I advanced her twenty pounds—all she asked. I told Nat that it was in the strong room, and that I should not go into it again that night, and he had better come again in the morning. He was terribly disappointed, but afraid to appear too anxious; so he put the best face he could upon it, for I was determined not to give the ring up till I had seen you about it. He will be here again in the morning soon after ten. Now, what's to be done about it?"

"I really don't think it worth while to stir in the matter. She has evidently given that ticket to Nat, or else she has intrusted it to him to redeem and sell. You say it's very valuable?"

"Very. But, Mr. F——, I am not going to give up that girl so easily, if you do. I am satisfied there is some villany at the bottom, and it ought to be sifted out."

" But how ? " I asked, smiling at Mr. Simpson's earnestness.

" You know where to find her."

" I have the address she gave me."

" Well, then, try and see her, there's a good fellow, and we shall soon find if she be a willing associate of Nat and Joanna."

" Well, Mr. Simpson, you have been so kind to her that you ought to be satisfied in this instance. I will send her a note, requesting her to call upon me by nine o'clock to-morrow morning. If she belong to that gang it is not likely she will put in an appearance."

Accordingly I wrote and dispatched a note, requesting her to call upon me at nine o'clock on the following morning on business of the greatest importance. I thought I should but have my labour for my pains; but as Mr. Simpson was so nervously anxious, I acted more with the view of gratifying him than in the hope of obtaining any satisfactory information.

To my great surprise, my messenger to Miss De Vere returned with a note from her, in which she thanked me for the interest I continued to take in her, and promising to be punctual at the hour named.

CHAPTER VII.

The clock had not struck nine five minutes on the next morning when Miss De Vere was announced, and promptly ushered into my little private office.

She was dressed in deep mourning, and advanced towards me with extended hands, while a blush and a smile lighted up her beautiful face. "Is it possible," I thought, "that this noble-looking creature can be a willing associate of Nat Larkins and Joanna Wray?"

"You see I am punctual, Mr. F——," she said, as she took the chair I handed her. "I am under too many obligations to you for past kindness and consideration to neglect any request you make. Pray what is this important business?"

"I wish to know if you have parted with any of the tickets for the articles pledged at Mr. Simpson's," I asked abruptly, for I wished to take her off her guard.

"Why, certainly not," she replied, with an expression of the most profound astonishment. "What can be the reason for your asking such a question? I hope Mr. Simpson has no intention of disposing of the things?"

"O no! I am confident he has no such intention."

"I am glad to hear you say so, for of late I have had such a strong presentiment that brighter hours are in store for me."

"Have you those tickets with you?"

"Certainly; I always carry them with me. Do you wish to see them?"

"If you please. How many had you in all?"

"Seven." And she took a bead purse from her bosom, opened it, and drew out a little roll of paper, and laid it on the table. "There they are, sir; you can look for yourself."

"When did you examine them last?"

"I don't think I have unrolled them for several weeks."

"You said you had seven?" I said, unrolling the paper they were wrapped in, and counting the contents. *There were but six tickets!*

"Yes; Mr. Simpson's books will show the same. I have never been able to redeem any of the articles."

"Please to count them now, Miss De Vere; you will find one missing."

Her countenance turned very pale as I said this, and her hands trembled so, as she held the tickets, that she could scarcely count them.

"True, Mr. F——," she said, as the tears gathered in her eyes. "And was it for this you have been so kind as to send for me? How can I ever thank you?"

"I do not desire any thanks; if any are due it is to Mr. Simpson, for it is at his request that I have sent for you on this business."

"I do not know what to make of this. How did you know I had lost one of my tickets, when I did not know of it myself till now?"

"You must excuse me. I ask, but answer no questions. Now answer me two or three. I saw you walking down Regent Street the other day in company with——"

"O yes, I remember; Mr. Larkins and his sister-in-law," she interrupted, with a frank ingenuousness which

convinced me of her sincerity and truth, and which
made me really happy to think I had acted upon Mr.
Simpson's suggestions. "Why did you not stop and
speak to me? I would have introduced them to you.
They have been very kind to me;" and she looked in
my face so innocently, every word carrying conviction
of truth with it, that I almost dreaded the necessity
thus forced upon me of making known the real character
of her associates, whose acquaintance, I now felt sure,
had been forced upon her.

"They would not have thanked you overmuch for an
introduction to me," I said, rather dryly, though I
could hardly suppress a smile at the idea of an introduction to Nat and Joanna. They knew me too well
already. She looked at me inquiringly.

"Have you ever been to their residence?" I inquired.

"Oh, frequently! Our acquaintance was made quite
singularly—romantically I may say;" and her face was
lighted up with smiles as the recollection crossed her
mind.

"Well, I have no time to ask any more questions
now, nor to answer any of those you are so anxious to
ask me. We will go to Mr. Simpson's, and perhaps
we may recover your lost ticket."

As we walked along the Strand I asked her how
long she had known these kind friends, and, to my great
surprise, I learned that they had so ingratiated themselves with her as to establish an acquaintance that had

ripened into intimacy, carried even so far that she had passed several nights at their house.

On arriving at Mr. Simpson's we proceeded to his private office. Mr. Simpson, on entering it, looked surprised at the greeting with which Miss De Vere saluted him. Advancing towards him with extended hand, and a face beaming with ingenuousness, she said,—

"Mr. Simpson, Mr. F—— tells me that I owe you all thanks for the discovery he has made. Receive them now, and believe they come from a truly grateful heart."

Mr. Simpson could not find a word to say for himself; but, by a glance at my smiling face, he read the intelligence that his suspicions of devilry had been well founded. He therefore merely bowed and drew back, leaving me to do the talking.

"Mr. Simpson, you were right, and I was wrong in my suspicions. There has been a deep game played upon Miss De Vere, which, but for your intervention, might have been carried out to her cost. I have no time to enter into explanations, but I may say that the ticket Nat has got was obtained by fraud or roguery, or both. Now, is there any place where Miss De Vere can be concealed until I want her?"

"To be sure there is," said he, opening a door into a kind of lobby. The door was glazed, and a white curtain hung suspended over the glass.

"Now, Miss De Vere, if you are satisfied that we are your friends, you will do just as we wish you."

" I shall cheerfully obey whatever you command. I place myself entirely in your hands. I suppose the mystery will be soon cleared up. What am I to do?"

" Only retire into that lobby, and wait there till I want you. You will be able to overhear all that passes, and will judge from my language when I wish you to show yourself."

" I suppose it is all for my good, although I cannot understand what you are doing for me."

CHAPTER VIII.

By the time we had reached Mr. Simpson's it was just upon ten o'clock, and our arrangements were barely completed when Mr. Simpson was called into the shop ; and a sign from him, as he entered, assured me that the fly was in the trap.

It was Nat Larkins sure enough, who had taken time by the forelock.

" Perhaps you will not care to stay here while I fetch your pledge? Walk into the private office," said Mr. Simpson, in a voice loud enough to reach my ears.

I took the hint, and opened the door into the lobby, into which Miss De Vere withdrew. I walked to the window, and stood with my back to the door as Nat was ushered into the room. As soon as I heard the door closed I turned round and faced Nat. He looked as if he had been shot. I thought he would have sunk to the floor. He propped himself against the table, and said nothing.

"At it again, Nat?" I said boldly; for I knew my man, and read his guilt in his countenance, even if Miss De Vere's words had not assured me of it. "Hand that ticket to me," said I, holding out my hand.

"I don't know what you mean," said the consummate scoundrel, regaining his composure, which it took a good deal to disturb.

"I mean the ticket for the diamond ring you have come for."

"I'd like to know what you want with that? I bought it and paid for it, fair and square, and it's mine."

"I should like to know who you bought it of, and the price you paid for it."

"Now, Mr. F——, this isn't the fair thing," said the rogue whiningly. "When a fellow comes fairly by a thing I don't see why he cannot keep it."

"You scoundrel! you never came fairly by anything in your life except your infernal rascality. Don't think to fool me this time. Where did you get that ticket?"

"Bought it for ten sovs," said the unblushing liar, who little dreamed how much I knew, but who acted as if he were assured I was only trying it on, on suspicion.

"Is that true?" I asked in a loud voice, throwing my gloves against the window of the lobby door as a signal for Miss De Vere.

"As I live, it's false!" exclaimed Miss De Vere, as

she emerged from her place of concealment, and stood
before us the picture of shame and anger.

At the sight of her Nat's assurance and impudence
forsook him, and he understood at once that his only
refuge was in confession and restitution.

"There," said he, handing me the ticket; "if I had
known there was going to be such a blasted fuss about
it, I would have had nothing to do with it.   It was all
Joanna's doings."

"Like as not," I replied quietly, for I saw my advantage, and I placed the ticket in my waistcoat pocket.
"Ruthven is outside, and will show you the way to
Marlborough Street;" and I opened the door for him,
which he approached sullenly, and, turning to me with
a scowl, he said,—

"Perhaps I'll be even with *her* yet," pointing to
Miss De Vere.   Then he walked out, swearing awfully.

"So far, so good," I said, turning to Miss De Vere,
who stood in great perplexity; for what she had witnessed only assured her of that which I had before but
darkly hinted at by the questions I had asked her.

"Mr. F——," she gasped—"oh! you won't tell
any——" But, before she could finish what she was
going to say, she fainted.

The application of proper restoratives by Mr.
Simpson's servant soon brought back consciousness.
She found relief in violent hysterical sobbing, which it
seemed impossible for her to repress.

We let her grief exhaust itself, and when she·had

somewhat recovered her composure, she said, turning alternately to Mr. Simpson and myself,—

"Oh! what shame have you saved me from? What have I been about? I cannot believe my senses. Pray tell me what it all means."

"You must first answer me a few more questions. Tell me how you became acquainted with this man and his associate. How did it happen that I saw you walking with them? and how did he get possession of this duplicate?"

"How the duplicate went out of my possession I cannot imagine, for I had never missed it. How I became acquainted with them I will tell you candidly."

"You see I had no need of an introduction, Miss De Vere."

Resting her elbow on the table, and supporting her head with her hand, Miss De Vere remained silent, her countenance expressing both wonder and perplexity at the discovery she had partially made of the character of Nat and Joanna. After allowing her sufficient time, as I thought, to collect her ideas, during which I engaged in conversation with Mr. Simpson, I said,—

"Come, Miss De Vere, cheer up; there is no occasion to trouble your mind about the past. Consider yourself fortunate that matters are not much worse. You have had a miraculous escape from a possibility which I know you could never have dreamt of. Tell us how it happened that you became so intimately acquainted with this man and his associate."

Wiping the tears from her eyes, she said appealingly, —

"I hope you will think none the worse of me for this affair? I can explain everything."

"Assuredly," I replied, "neither of us was willing to forfeit the good opinion we entertained of you, however compromising appearances might be. Now tell us unreservedly all you know about this party."

"It is a very simple story. One day, about six weeks ago, I went out shopping, to buy myself some shoes and other things. It came on to rain very heavily when I was near Leicester Square, and I stepped into a shop at the corner of —— Street to take shelter. I trod upon a piece of orange-peel opposite the door, sprained my ankle, fell down in the mud, and was in such pain that I could not raise myself up. Two well-dressed men came from the shop to assist me, and they lifted me in. One of them—he who was here just now—appeared to sympathise with me very much, and urged me to accept the hospitality of his sister-in-law, who occupied the upper part of the house in the shop of which I had taken shelter. As the storm was very violent, and the pain and swelling of my ankle so great, I was easily persuaded, the more so as I was anxious for the assistance of a surgeon. Carrying me carefully upstairs, I was introduced to the sister-in-law, the lady in whose company you saw me walking down Regent Street."

I could scarcely refrain from laughing. Miss De Vere, seeing me smile, shook her head sorrowfully.

"I wish I could laugh, Mr. F——; but, from what I have already heard, I fear this is anything but a laughing matter."

"Go on, Miss De Vere," I said, composing my features. "I will tell you all that it is necessary for you to know when you have concluded your story."

"Mrs. Larkins (for that was the name by which she was introduced to me) received me very kindly, and I was treated by both with the greatest respect. The surgeon was sent for. He bathed my ankle with iced water, and gave me a draught which soon sent me to sleep. I reclined upon a couch in the sitting-room. When I awoke it was nearly eleven o'clock; and I concluded, upon their pressing entreaties, to remain where I was for the night. I knew my friends would not be anxious about me, because I had told them that I should probably call upon an old friend with whom I frequently stayed a day or two at a time. Well, I stayed all night, and I could not have received more care, kindness, and attention if they had been old friends. We had an elegant supper, with wines which Mrs. Larkins said were brought over by her husband, who was a sea-captain, trading in the Mediterranean. The evening passed away very pleasantly, and when the hour for retiring arrived, I was shown into an elegantly-furnished bedroom by Mrs. Larkins, who assisted me in undressing."

"Yes; and that was the time when the duplicate was stolen."

" They were so polite, attentive, and kind, that I was charmed by them, and have been a regular visitor there ever since, and always received with kindness. I know nothing more of them than what I have told you. Mr. F——, will you tell me what *you* know ? "

" I am sorry to be obliged to tell you what you must know. The fact is, you have fallen into the hands of one of the most notorious swell-mobsmen in London —a ' ticket-of-leave ' man ; and his sister-in-law, as he calls her, is the infamous Joanna Wray. You may well imagine my surprise when I saw you in their company.'

Miss De Vere looked quite bewildered, and was utterly incapable of uttering a word. After a silence, in the highest degree painful to Mr. Simpson and myself, she arose, and with the quiet dignity of a well-bred lady said,—

" I must go home now, Mr. F——. Excuse me from remaining any longer now. I feel much upset."

I bowed assent. Drawing her shawl around her, she took her departure, and I was alone with Mr. Simpson.

" Well, I was half right, Mr. F——, after all."

" All right. But really this is one of the most singular cases I ever had to do with."

" Ah ! I don't think we have seen the end of it yet What are you going to do about it ?"

" Break up that infernal nest of thieves, and send every one of them to the hulks. I will go now and look after Joanna, and hear her story as to how she got acquainted with Miss De Vere. Thus far all has gone well, but I think, with you, that we have not come to the end of the chapter yet; so good day, Mr. Simpson. I shall let you know if anything turns up."

CHAPTER IX.

I proceeded at once to the place occupied by Joanna. The door was opened by Emma, another of the gang. The moment she caught sight of me she let go of the door, and rushed upstairs like a deer. I lost no time in following her, but of course could not keep pace with such a nimble wench. She gained time enough to warn Joanna of my coming, and so put her on her guard, although that was hardly necessary, for she was a woman of remarkable self-possession, and with fertility of invention enough to meet any emergency. I entered her elegantly-furnished apartment, and she received me with that suavity and courtesy which made her so dangerously attractive; for she was not, in fact, a handsome, but only a very showy woman. I had, at the time, a serious charge against her; but the time for her arrest had not arrived, as matters were not ripe. It was possible that she might have known I was on her track, but she was too shrewd to evince any suspicion. She had already been arrested on the charge, but got off because the prosecutor failed to appear.

"To what am I indebted for this honour, Mr.

F—— ?" she said, smiling, and pointing to a chair, which, however, I declined.

I had made up my mind as to the plan I would adopt with this lady to discover the truth ; so I said out at once that I wanted to know how she came by the duplicate of the diamond ring pledged at Simpson's. The question was so abrupt and unexpected—for, as she knew my visits to her were always official, she had naturally attributed the present to the case I have alluded to, by which she had made a hundred and fifty pounds at one haul—for a moment she was startled out of her self-possession ; and I could perceive, from her hesitating manner, that she knew all about it, though she had not expected it would come to my ears.

" Oh !" she said, with a toss of her head, " you must ask Nat about that—got it from some woman he picked up.   You know he has a weakness that way."

" You know as well as I do you are tipping me a confounded lie.   As for Nat, you won't see him again for one while, for I have locked him up on that matter ; and now I have a little business to transact with you."

" You don't mean to say you have got Nat foul ? " she asked, looking earnestly at me.

" Yes, I have, and Joanna too," I replied, seeing on the instant that her suspicions were aroused, for she exhibited every sign of confusion.   " Come, now, tell me the truth for once if you can.   How did Nat come by that duplicate ? "

"I told you before," she said, trying to brave the matter out, "that you must ask Nat himself. I don't know everything he does."

"Well, if you don't choose to tell the truth, I must try some other plan; so put on your things and come with me."

"You're not going to pull me for Nat's doings, surely, Mr. F——?" she asked, with an expression of alarm on her countenance, which, despite her skill and experience in her *profession*, she could not entirely conceal.

"Nonsense! you ought to know better than to try such a game upon me. Come, put on your things, and go with me to Bow Street; and, by the way," I added, turning full upon her, "you had better send for bail in that other case. I have fairly 'planted' you in that affair now. You got off too easily before."

"You don't mean it, Mr. F——, do you, now?" asked Joanna, evidently alarmed at the aspect of affairs.

"I say what I mean. I don't trifle, if you do. Now, just put on your things, will you? or come without if you prefer it."

"I don't think it's of any use trying to deceive you," she said musingly. "I got it from that woman you saw with us in Regent Street."

"But how?"

"Well, I took it as I generally do, if you must know."

"I knew that before. I want to know how you made the acquaintance of *that woman*, as you call her."

"It was some of Nat's nonsense. He's always getting himself and somebody else into scrapes. She sprained her ankle during a thunder-storm—took shelter in the shop below. Nat invited her upstairs, and I took care of her."

"Oh! I think I know the rest. Joanna, old girl, you think yourself devilish clever, but you have overshot the mark this time. Do you happen to know anything about this woman ?"

Joanna looked a little malicious as she replied,—

"From what I have seen I should think you knew as much about her as I do."

I was half inclined to get angry at the hussy's impudence ; but, as anger is a luxury I seldom indulge in, I kept my temper, and merely said,—

"You have not told me how you came by that duplicate. It won't hurt you now to tell the truth."

"Well, when she was undressing, a bead purse fell out of her bosom, and she was in too much pain to heed it. I picked it up, opened it at my leisure, and weeded it ; and now you know as much about it as I do."

"Come, this and the other case will go hard with you. Put on your things and come along. You can easily get bail. Old Lugner will stand your friend, I suppose. Have a cab ?"

"Oh! pray don't, Mr. F——. It isn't fair to show

me up for Nat's doings. I never got a penny out of her, nor——"

" No confessions now," I interrupted ; " you have got to answer two serious charges, and I am thinking they will bother you a bit."

One of my men was waiting outside the street door. I opened the window and gave a whistle, and he soon worked his way up.

" Bring Joanna along with you."

That was enough. She broke out into an agony of tears, which, however, were only called forth by the shame at being found out. They did not shake my resolution. She was taken to the station and given in charge.

CHAPTER X.

My next business was to see Miss De Vere, to procure her testimony as to the duplicate. I called upon her at the house of a friend with whom she was staying. She was greatly confused and agitated upon seeing me.

" You don't think badly of me, Mr. F——, do you?"

" I assure you I do not. But pray be calm, and try and listen to me. No one knows anything of this affair but ourselves."

" Thank God! Spare me the shame of having it known to the world."

" I wish to prove myself your friend, therefore trust me. I have come now to serve you."

" You are always serving me, Mr. F——. I can never be sufficiently grateful."

G

" Will you prefer a charge against these people for robbing you of that duplicate ? "

" What would be the consequence ? "

" They will be transported."

" But I should have to appear in public against them, should I not ? " she asked eagerly.

" Certainly."

" I could not do it. Here, Mr. F——;" and she nervously drew from her bosom the bead purse containing the duplicates; " here, take them, burn them, do anything on earth with them, but spare me further shame and disgrace."

" If you are positively unable to say when and where, or by whom the duplicate was stolen, you may be spared."

" Oh! how can I say when, or where, or how it was stolen, when I first learned of its loss from you? I could not—I would die before I would—under any earthly circumstances."

This was said with such an air of determined resolution that I was sure it would be idle to argue against it. In fact, I had expected as much when I called upon her; and, under the circumstances, knew she was right, for she could not well swear that the duplicate had been abstracted at all. This enabled her to avoid the ordeal of public exposure, which she so much dreaded. The consequence was that the charge against Nat and Joanna could not be proceeded with, but they were kept in custody for another affair.

CHAPTER XI.

Months passed away without my having seen Miss De Vere, although I did not fail to think of her very frequently. Other cases as interesting as hers occupied my attention ; consequently her image was fading from my mind like a bad photograph, when one day a note was handed to me which ran as follows :—

"Mrs. Gardner's compliments to Mr. F——, and she will be glad to see him at Long's Hotel this afternoon at five o'clock."

Of course I concluded that the lady addressing me had been robbed of her jewellery, and desired my assistance to recover it. Being official business, I determined to wait upon the lady, although it was her place to call upon me.

At the hour appointed I reached the hotel, and was at once ushered into the sitting-room engaged by the lady at whose request I had called. It was unoccupied. After waiting a few minutes the door communicating with an adjoining room was opened, and a tall, elegantly-dressed gentleman entered, leading by the hand Miss De Vere!

I never act impulsively, but I suppose you will believe me when I say that the chair felt as if it had powerful springs in it which lifted me up mechanically ; for the first thing I knew was that I stood on my feet, shaking hands very heartily with the most beautiful woman I ever saw, whose face was radiant with the smiles of happiness.

"My dear, good, kind-hearted friend, how happy I
am to meet you again! Charles," she said, turning to
her companion, "this is Mr. F——, of whom you have
heard me speak so often, and to whom I am under so
many obligations."

"For my wife," said the gentleman thus familiarly
introduced, "I thank you, and am proud to make the
acquaintance of one who has rendered her such important service."

"Oh, I forgot!" said the lady, with a merry laugh.
"Mr. F——, this is my husband, Mr. Gardner."

"And Valerie's husband is happy to know so good
and kind a friend," said Mr. Gardner, advancing with
extended hand, which was, of course, cordially grasped.

I was so completely taken by surprise, for a few
moments I could scarcely find words to speak. Readily
divining the cause, Mrs. Gardner, as I must now call
her, said,—

"I see, Mr. F——, you are surprised, but not more
so, I am sure, than when you saw me with——"

"Hush!" said I; "not a word about that. I *am*
surprised, and I need not add, delighted, to see you in
your own proper position. You have passed through
many chances and changes ——"

"And now," she said, not allowing me to finish my
sentence, "there he stands;" and she pointed to her
handsome husband, who stood looking admiringly at her.

It is hardly necessary to relate by what means Miss
De Vere's position was so wonderfully changed. Rela-

tives to whom she had been too proud to apply for
assistance had sought her out, and Mr. Gardner had
been appointed to the task. Like a sensible man, he fell
in love with her at first sight, and, after due probation,
became intrusted with the care of her future happiness;
and I judge it is in very good keeping.

Mrs. Gardner's purpose in sending for me was to
thank me, and to ask her husband to thank me, for the
service I had rendered her. You can see her almost
any afternoon in Hyde Park : there is not a handsomer
woman to be seen there.

THE MURDERED JUDGE.

CHAPTER I.

It was my turn on the night-watch. About six in the morning of the 3rd of April, 18—, I was sitting in the station-house at ——, warming my toes by the expiring embers of what had been a pretty good fire; for it was a late spring, and the nights were damp and chilly. We had had a very quiet night of it—no charges of any consequence except a drunken tailor or so, and two or three quarrelling "unfortunates." I felt rather drowsy, and was not sorry that the hour for going home to my bed had arrived.

"Good morning, Mr. F——. Cold morning, sir. Have you heard the news, sir? Judge Black's been murdered."

I started to my feet, scarcely able to realise what I heard. For a moment I thought I had been dreaming. Repeating the words, I said,—

"Judge Black's been murdered! Who can have done that?"

"It'll be your job to find that out, I reckon, Mr. F——."

"When did it happen? Bless me! why have I not heard of it before?"

"Happened some time last night; found out this morning when the servants got up. Murderers got in through the housekeeper's room window. Old man found dead in his bed, with his skull beat in."

"House robbed too, I suppose?"

"No, think not; nothing missed at present."

However drowsy I might have been before, I was quite awake now, and thought no more of sleep. Familiar as twenty years' experience in the police had made me with strange things, this event completely staggered me. If plunder had not been the murderer's object, I could not conceive why any one should seek to murder the old man. He was too inoffensive, too upright, to have given any one excuse for taking his life; and the only thing I could think of to satisfy the inquiries of my mind was, that probably the relations of some one whom the Judge, in the discharge of his duty, had consigned to severe, perhaps capital punishment, had sought in this hideous manner to take a fiendish revenge. But even this notion I was, upon reflection, forced to abandon.

I proceeded at once to head-quarters. Several of the "heads" had already assembled, and were gravely discussing this astounding event. As soon as I entered the chief addressed me.

"Ah, Mr. F——, glad to see you. Here is a very bad case. Judge Black found murdered in his bed this morning.   We shall put the matter into your hands."

The scene of the tragedy was a small town in the vicinity of L——.   Of all places in the world, L——, I think, is the dullest.   The people appear to bury themselves within doors.   Pass through the place when you may, the chances are that throughout its entire length, which exceeds a mile, you will not see a dozen persons.   The town has an air of substantial comfort and order about it.   It always appears to be Sunday there.   You see no dirty children in the road, nor pigs scampering from under your horse's feet, nor stray cows, nor lost sheep, wandering in the highway; even the hens and chickens are kept within doors.   The first time I arrived there I was strongly reminded of Goldsmith's "Deserted Village."   There were the houses, and the churches, and the pump, but no living thing in view.

When, on the morning of this tragedy, I arrived at this place, it wore a very unusual aspect.   The whole town was astir.   At every door and corner groups of people in earnest conversation could be seen ; and it was not difficult to surmise the subject of their discourse.   I proceeded at once to the residence of the chief magistrate, and reported myself.   I found him in earnest conference with some of the leading gentlemen residing in the neighbourhood.   Perplexity, mingled with surprise and horror, was visible in every face.

"We have placed the house in charge of the head constable, Mr. F——; but you will do well to proceed there immediately, and examine the premises for yourself."

I accordingly did so. It was not difficult to find the way. People were all streaming in one direction, and that direction was the Judge's residence.

It is singular how danger or tragic events break the ice between men strangers to each other. At any other time I might have passed through this place a dozen times in the day, and not a man would have addressed me a "Good morning." But now, as I walked briskly up the main street, every one I overtook had a word for me.

"Bad business this, sir. Poor Judge! Ah! he was a good, kind man to the poor. Wouldn't have hurt a fly, sir."

"Have you any notion who did it?" I asked.

"Lord bless you no, sir—wish I had. It was nobody belonging to this place, I'm sure."

"All honest men, then, in this quarter, I suppose?"

"Not exactly that; but there was never a murder committed in it afore, that I ever heard on."

"Any bad characters in the town?"

"Well, as for that, there are, to be sure, a few idle, drunken fellows, who live nobody can tell how; but they wouldn't want to murder the Judge—he never harmed them."

"But mightn't they want some of his money? He had plenty I'm told."

"I don't suppose he was such a fool as to keep money

in the house. No, it wasn't money they were after, it was something else."

"What do you think it was, then, if not money?"

"Well, this is not the time to say what I think, and you're not the man to tell it to neither."

"Well, my friend, we are strangers to each other, it is true, and you are quite right to keep your own counsel. If you know who has committed this horrid crime, of course you are aware it's your duty to tell what you know."

"I *don't* know, I didn't say I *did* know. But can't a man have his suspicions? I have mine, but I'm not going to talk till I meet with somebody who thinks as I do. We'll put our ideas together, and then, perhaps, may say what we think. So good morning, sir. Your servant, sir."

CHAPTER II.

Upon reaching the Judge's residence I found a vast crowd assembled in front of it. Pushing and elbowing my way through, I rang the bell at the gate. In due time the wicket was opened, and a constable peered through. Whispering to him who I was, he immediately opened the gate, and I was promptly ushered into the presence of the chief constable.

He was a fussy sort of personage, swelling with importance at his official connection with so important a crime as *murder*. Evidently chagrined at my coming to take the case out of his hands, he began in voluble style to explain things, and then rambled off to the relation of some of his achievements in thief-catching. I cut him short by asking if anything had been disturbed.

"Not a thing, Mr. F——, not a thing."

My first care was to look for the marks of footsteps. A good deal of rain had fallen during the previous days; but on the night of the murder there had been a very white frost. Footprints could be traced from the garden wall to the housekeeper's room window, but they had not left sufficient impression in the soil to enable me to identify the shoes. I could only measure their length.

The housekeeper's room window, by which the murderer had entered, was about four feet from the ground. Marks of soil from dirty boots were evident on the paint.

The constable had locked all the servants in the drawing-room, where the female portion of them could be heard crying and sobbing quite lustily.

"I must see the servants, Mr. Constable."

"Altogether, Mr. F——, or one by one?"

"Singly. Send the man-servant first."

A staid, respectable-looking person of about fifty made his appearance in a state of great agitation.

From inquiries addressed to him I ascertained that the household consisted of the Judge, his sister (who acted as housekeeper), two female servants, and himself, who was in constant attendance upon the Judge, his late master; that the sister had last night slept from home, a very unusual occurrence. She had gone to a little farming estate she owned, about ten miles off, promising to return at nine o'clock at the latest, but she did not come back at all; consequently the room she occupied had not been secured as usual; the window looking into the garden had been left unfastened; the shutters had not been closed, thus affording the murderer easy admission. The Judge, who had become very infirm, slept on the same floor in an adjoining room. The female servants slept at the top of the house, and the man-servant slept in a room at the back of the house overlooking the kitchen garden. The Judge had retired to rest at nine o'clock, or sooner, and the servants were all in bed by half-past ten. The man-servant had heard no noise during the night except the howling of the dog in the stable. As the dog was a great favourite with its mistress, the man concluded that it was grieving at her not returning. He could *now* understand why the animal howled—"dogs always howl at a death."

Upon getting up in the morning between five and six o'clock, and proceeding to his master's room, he was first surprised at seeing the door of the housekeeper's bedroom open; next at seeing the door of his master's room open likewise. Upon looking in he saw the bedclothes in great disorder; and upon going to the bedside, to his horror, he found his master dead, with his skull beaten in.

For a moment he was overcome with terror; but he

soon recovered sufficient self-possession to ring the alarm bell. The female servants, thinking the house on fire, rushed downstairs in their night-dresses. The neighbours assembled at the gate, and rang violently at the bell: when admitted, they saw the fearful spectacle of the Judge lying in his bed murdered. Among those who first came in was a surgeon. Upon examining the corpse, he pronounced that life had been extinct some five or six hours.

"Then the murder must have been committed soon after midnight?"

"So it is supposed."

"Well, my friend, have you any suspicion as to who has done it?"

"Haven't the least idea in the world, sir. The Judge had many friends, but I do not think he ever had an enemy. Who could want to take the poor old gentleman's life I cannot imagine. He could not have had long to live in the course of nature, for he was breaking fast, although he had been a strong man in his time."

"Have you observed anything suspicious about the house lately—any bad characters?"

"None whatever."

"What company do the servants keep?"

"None of any account. They are very steady and respectable women, and seldom have any one to see them."

"Are you married?"

"I am not."

"Who visits the housekeeper, as you call her—the Judge's sister I mean?"

"No one comes here to see her but her daughter, who lives at her farm, where she went yesterday, and sometimes her daughter's husband. She did not invite her friends here, as it would have disturbed the Judge; she entertained them at her own place."

"Is any property missing?"

"I have not missed anything yet, but I have not looked very carefully. I had the plate in my own room."

"Did your master keep much money in the house?"

"Very little."

"Suppose, then, we go and examine if anything be missing."

We accordingly proceeded together to the bed-chamber where the unfortunate old man was lying dead. Everything appeared as usual; not a drawer open, not a thing disturbed. The Judge's clothes were lying neatly folded up in an easy chair, just as they had been left by his servant the night previous. I made a careful search about the room, but could detect nothing by which I could conclude the assassin's object to have been plunder as well as bloodshed. Even a valuable gold watch and appendages still remained in the watch-pocket over the pillow, and a diamond ring on the table beside the candlestick, near which lay a large Bible, closed, but with the Judge's spectacles remaining between the leaves where he had been reading. I opened the leaves, and the first words my eyes fell upon were, strangely enough, "Whoso sheddeth man's blood, by man shall his blood be shed." "Amen!" I involuntarily exclaimed, and closed the book. A search in the adjoining rooms afforded me no evidence that anything had been removed; the man-servant could miss nothiug.

During the night the corpse was watched by two brothers, Joseph and Edward Pratt, the first of whom was married to the Judge's niece.

I next proceeded to the magistrate's office.

"Well, Mr. F——, have you discovered anything of a clue?"

"No, gentlemen. The affair has a very mysterious aspect. Plunder does not appear to have been the murderer's object, and at present we cannot even surmise who could have desired to take the Judge's life."

"Do you think there were more than one engaged in the murder?"

"I cannot tell. They must have got over the garden-wall at the side of the house, climbed up to the window of the housekeeper's room, which does not appear to have been fastened last night, and that seems strange. It might all have been done by only one person; but I am inclined to think there were two engaged in it. The marks of footsteps in the garden are not very distinct, and can hardly be identified."

"Has any weapon been discovered?"

" None. The doctor thinks it was a heavy bludgeon. I have searched around the garden, but found none."

" Well, Mr. F——, we need not tell you what to do. We shall offer a reward of £500 for the discovery and apprehension of the murderer, and we have no doubt that the government will add another £250 to it. Where have you taken up your lodging, Mr. F—— ?"

" I have not taken one at present; as soon as I have done so I will report myself."

The leading gentlemen of the town and neighbour-hood formed themselves into a committee of investigation, to which everything likely to throw light on this tragic affair that came under the notice of each individual member of it was to be reported. So profound were the dismay and horror evinced by this barbarous crime, that every one felt it to be a blow aimed at his own breast.

CHAPTER III.

When I am deeply perplexed it is my practice to go to bed, and lie there till I have solved my doubts and perplexities. With my eyes closed, but wide awake, and nothing to disturb me, I can work out my problems better there than in any other place.

But as yet I had no bed to go to. I considered whether it would be better to seek a quiet lodging, or take up my quarters at an inn, and decided in favour of the latter.

I have a belief that " there 's a divinity that shapes our ends," and this faith encouraged me to think that I should ultimately bring the criminal to light, although at that moment I never had less to guide me in the pursuit of any offender. But I felt sure that this case would afford no exception. "Murder will-out;" and at the very moment when all clue appears lost, and pursuit baffled, how often has it happened that something quite unexpected has occurred to put justice on the right track !

The complete mystery within which this case was involved became my greatest encouragement for hope. It resembled, to my mind, the still, portentous calm that precedes the clap of thunder. I waited and listened, and listened and waited.

It was now past noon. While taking a short stroll through the town I carefully reviewed in my mind the things that had passed under my notice during the morning, with the intention of taking some decided course of action. But as I could form no conclusions myself as to the perpetrators of this deed, I concluded the best thing I could do would be to ascertain what other people thought about the matter ; so, upon passing an inn that had an inviting aspect, I stepped in and ordered dinner.

A good many people were assembled in the dining-room, earnestly discussing the probabilities, both as to the cause of the commission of the crime, and who had committed it. The Judge was known to be very rich, and it was also known that some of his relatives had long been waiting anxiously for the dead man's shoes.

I shall put together in a connected form what I picked up in fragments.

First as to the expectants. There was a nephew, Mr. Stephen Black, a large merchant, with a family of three daughters grown up. It was insinuated that he was living in a style that his business could not afford—living, in fact, on "his expectations." It was also whispered that he had had "losses" lately.

Next there were the sister and her daughter, married to Mr. Joseph Pratt, an idle fellow, who had often been heard to say "that it was time the old man was dead." But it was generally conceded that he was too great a coward to commit the murder.

Besides these, suspicion was not thrown upon any one. When the individual who *could* have struck the blow was named, that name belonged to a notorious character—a noted thief, and perhaps something worse, who was considered capable and willing to undertake any crime. But again, *he* could have had no possible motive to the murder. Suspicion could not, therefore, attach to him. But somehow the merchant-nephew's name was soon in everybody's mouth ; and next his footsteps were dogged by a crowd, who shouted, " There goes the murderer !"

This had such an effect upon the poor man that it nearly drove him crazy. He shut himself up in his house for ten days, without ever quitting it. The mob came and broke all his windows.

I consulted with the members of the committee as to

whether I should take measures to arrest "the suspect," but they unanimously rejected the proposal.

CHAPTER IV.

The Judge's funeral was delayed a long time, awaiting the result of the coroner's inquest, and the possible discovery of the murderer. The corpse was kept in an ice-house, to prevent decomposition as much as possible. After every effort was exhausted to obtain a clue to the perpetrators of the deed, a verdict was returned of "Wilful murder against some person or persons unknown."

The day of the funeral was blustering, wild, and rainy; but, in spite of the inclemency of the weather, the whole population turned out to witness the sad ceremony. As the Judge was greatly beloved by all who knew him, and as the office he had held was one commanding veneration and respect, his funeral would, under ordinary circumstances, have been regarded in the town as a public event. But the tragic and horrible fate he had met naturally excited public interest to the highest pitch. All the principal inhabitants of the town and the neighbouring gentry, as well as many notable persons from a distance, took part in it, forming a procession of a very imposing character, numbering upwards of three hundred persons.

First came the members of the committee, two by two, each wearing a crimson satin scarf, emblematical of the blood that had been shed. The pall was borne by six clergymen. Immediately following the coffin came his nephew, Mr. Stephen Black, as chief mourner, succeeded by the brothers Joseph and Edward Pratt; then other relatives of the deceased more or less remote, followed by private friends and a number of the neighbouring gentry.

In company with many others, I took my place at a window of the inn at which I was staying. When the corpse had arrived opposite to where I was standing I heard a voice behind me say in an audible whisper,—

"The murderer's among the mourners, or I am greatly mistaken."

Turning quickly round to look for the speaker, I asked,—

"Who said that?"

But no one answered me, or took the slightest notice. Everybody present continued to gaze at the melancholy procession impassively, and in gloomy silence.

When the procession had passed I left the inn and followed it to the churchyard. Upon its arrival there it was met by the clergymen and a body of choristers from the neighbouring cathedral town, who immediately commenced the burial service.

If the murderer were really present at this solemnity as a mourner he must have been Cain and Judas both in one, and his nerves of the strongest temper, to have acted his part without betraying himself.

"God 'a mercy upon his poor old soul!" said an aged crone standing beside me. "He'll not let his servant's death go unpunished."

The relatives and most of the friends of the deceased returned to his house after the funeral, in the expectation of hearing the Judge's will read. An attorney, who transacted business for the deceased, stated that he had made a will, which was duly executed a few weeks prior to the murder; but, although careful search had been made among the Judge's papers, no will had been found. It was known to the attorney that two wills had been made, but that the last had effected a totally different distribution of the property. In the first the bulk of his wealth had been given to his sister; in the second, to his brother's family.

Joe Pratt was taken ill during this meeting, and fainted.

CHAPTER V.

Time passed on. We did not appear to be getting much nearer to a solution of the mystery, when one afternoon (it was a Saturday, upon which schoolboys have their half holiday) the town was awoke from its dullness by a cry that ran through it like an electric shock :—

"The bludgeon's found! they've found the bludgeon!"

" Where ? where ? "

" Under the old meeting-house steps, up by the common."

Some boys were playing at cricket, when an unusually good stroke of the bat sent the ball rolling till it stopped under the wooden steps of the old meeting-house. In searching for the ball one of the boys drew

out a stout walking-stick. There could be no doubt
that this was the weapon, for blood and hair were still
adhering to it.

The stick was immediately taken possession of by the
chief-constable, and exposed for identification at the
court-house. All the town and the neighbourhood, far
and near, came to view that stout ash walking-stick,
with the hope of being able to identify it. But one
stick may be so like many other sticks that, although
A and B, down to X, Y, Z, had been seen with sticks
"just like it," no one was ready to swear to its real
owner.

But one day, when the excitement caused by the
discovery of this instrument of death was abating, a
travelling peddler looked in at the court-house, and,
examining the stick carefully, said,—

"That identical stick was mine once. I sold it to
Dick Galashiels."

"Are you prepared to swear to that, my man?" said
Mr. Constable.

"I would swear to it in any court in England. I
know it by the ferrule, which I riveted on—it's a
thimble."

The peddler was taken before the magistrate, and there
deposed to the fact just narrated. In consequence of this
development Dick Galashiels was sought out, arrested,
and lodged in prison, charged with the murder of Judge
Black.

Dick was the notoriously bad character I have already

alluded to. He had been several times in prison on various charges of larceny, and once for a burglary; in fact, when any offence of this kind was committed, Dick was the first to be "wanted"—one of the disadvantages of having a bad name.

When brought up for examination Dick maintained that the stick was none of his. It might have been; he had had a good many sticks in his time—in fact, he was a stick-fancier—but he sold them again as fast as he bought them. He had sold this one if he had ever owned it, for he had not had one like it for many months, he was sure. But he could not or would not say to whom he had sold it. The peddler positively swore that he had sold the stick to the prisoner.

It resulted from this examination that Dick was remanded for a week.

When next brought up no additional evidence was forthcoming, and several witnesses swore that on the night of the murder Dick was carousing with them from half-past nine o'clock until twelve, at which hour his brother swore they went home together to bed, and did not leave the house again till seven o'clock next morning. But this attempt to establish an *alibi* failed. A respectable inhabitant came forward and deposed that having, on the night of the murder, been too late for the stage at B——, he had walked home, and as he passed, between twelve and one, through the street that ran at the back of the Judge's house, he saw a man waiting at a corner, as if watching; that he passed along unperceived, but he was certain that this man was no other than Dick. The night was not dark, the moon being in her second quarter. Dick was again remanded.

At the next examination the wife of another inhabitant deposed that on the night of the murder she was sitting up nursing a sick child; that at about one o'clock in the morning she looked out of the open casement of her bedroom window to get a little fresh air, for the room was hot, and the child feverish; that while so looking she saw a man walking stealthily up and down before her house, which was very near the Judge's residence; in a few minutes he was joined by another man, who came hastily round the corner from the direction of the back garden of the Judge's house. As soon as the man first named perceived the second he hastened to meet him, and she distinctly heard him say,—

"Is it done?"

Upon being interrogated as to whether the man she saw waiting was the prisoner, she answered,—

"No."

"Do you think you could recognise the man if you were to see him?"

"I thought at the time it was young Pratt; for I said to my husband, 'What can young Pratt be doing about here, watching at this hour?' and my husband replied, 'After some gal, I suppose.'"

"Could you see the second man distinctly?"

"I had but a glance of him, for the other immediately joined him, and so concealed his figure. He looked like a sailor; he had on a cap and a loose pilot-coat, and carried a stick."

As this was all the evidence produced against Dick Galashiels, the magistrates did not consider themselves justified in detaining him any longer in custody. He was accordingly discharged; but I received private instructions that he should be strictly watched. He was accordingly put under the surveillance of two of my aids, whom I had previously sent for to assist me in this mysterious affair.

As Mr. Pratt's name has been mentioned I shall say a few words about him. He was the son of a respectable inhabitant of the town, and, as I have before stated, married to the daughter of the Judge's sister—an idle, shiftless fellow, who did nothing for a living, but lived upon his expectations and his mother-in-law.

I pondered over what the female witness had said in allusion to Mr. Pratt, for I considered that if he and Dick Galashiels were together on the night of the murder, a pretty good case of circumstantial evidence might be made out. I commenced making inquiries, and learned that they had been seen together frequently of late. There was nothing to justify the intimacy, for no one who had any respect for himself would associate with such a worthless fellow as Dick; therefore, if there was any confederacy between them, it boded no good to Pratt.

Remarks were freely made respecting the singular absence of the Judge's sister on the night of the murder. Many went so far as to say that she must have been privy to the deed, and had gone away on purpose to facilitate the commission of the crime. This belief became so strong that all her friends and acquaintances shunned her society.

Her connection with Pratt, who had married her daughter, both of whom, daughter and husband, were a burden upon her, seemed to lend some colour to the suspicions that were fastened upon her, while it strengthened those against Joe Pratt. On the whole, suspicion was concentrating itself around the Judge's relatives, and this conviction was a great shock to the community. Circumstances seemed to point to the conclusion that the murder was a family affair ; and, upon consideration, this seemed to be the likeliest conclusion that could be arrived at, for in that family were parties interested in the murdered man's death. Suspicion had first been fixed upon the nephew ; but, although it was devoutly believed by the *vox populi*, the members of the committee would not for a moment allow themselves to be influenced by it. Suspicion was now centring around the sister and her family; and, although it was extremely improbable that she should have been a party to the crime, there were no such doubts as to the possibility of her son-in-law's complicity. However the committee was exceedingly loath to move in the matter, both on account of the respectable position of the " suspect," and the mischief and pain that would result if there were nothing to sustain a charge.

Matters were in this state of suspense, when an incident occurred that put a new aspect on the affair.

CHAPTER VI.

Among the members of the committee was Mr. Joseph Pratt, senior. He had two sons, the Mr. Pratt, married to the Judge's niece, and the younger son, before mentioned, unmarried. The elder son was familiarly spoken of as " Joe Pratt," by which name we shall in future designate him.

It happened that almost every day a considerable number of letters containing hints, suspicions, &c., were addressed to the committee both collectively, and to individual members of it. One day a letter addressed " Mr. Joseph Pratt," was inadvertently placed in the hands of Mr. Pratt, senior, while he was in the committee-room. Glancing it over, and perceiving that it referred to the murder, he incontinently placed it in the hands of the chairman of the committee.

The chairman read it, and hastily turned it over to look at the superscription, then perused it again. Whispering to his nearest neighbour, they both perused it together, and then called a third person, who was invited to read and report his opinion.

I did not learn the contents of the letter at the time, but when the letter was subsequently placed in my hands, I took a copy of it, which I may as well introduce here.   It was as follows :—

"MR. JOE PRATT, JUNIOR.

"Sir, — I have the honour to inform you that unless you immediately hand over, or cause to be handed over, to me the sum of ten pounds in hard cash, I shall be under the painful necessity of informing the committee of what I know, and of what you know too, about the affair that happened on the night of the 2nd of April last.

"YOUR TRUE BILL."

This letter, although anonymous, coupled with other circumstances that appeared to throw suspicion upon Joe Pratt, led the committee to the conclusion that the time had come for him to be arrested.   A warrant was accordingly issued, and placed in my hands.   I executed it the same evening.

The next thing was to find out the writer of the anonymous letter.   It will be remembered that Dick Galashiels had been arrested on suspicion, but discharged for want of sufficient evidence.   I had kept him, as well as his companions, under strict surveillance. Among his most intimate associates was a certain Bill Plummer, who had married Dick's sister—an idle, dissolute fellow, who had once been tried for horse-stealing, but had escaped conviction through some technical objection.

The anonymous letter was signed, " Your True Bill." Might not this stupid signatorial conceit embody a pun on the writer's name? In a word, might not the writer be Bill Plummer ?

I tried various expedients to obtain a specimen of his hand-writing, but unsuccessfully. Determined not to be baffled, I suggested to the committee the expediency of arresting Bill Plummer, giving my reasons for advising that step.

The committee not only approved of arresting Plummer, but determined to arrest Dick Galashiels also. It was known that he had been much in the company of Joe Pratt shortly previous to the murder, and under circumstances which, although occasioning no particular remark at the time, were now regarded as suspicious.

The policy of this step soon became evident. Upon searching Dick Galashiels the following letters were found in his pocket-book.

" I have made Susan promise to invite her mother to come and spend the day with us next Monday. I 'll take care the old woman don't go back *that* night; so the coast will be clear. You now know what you have to depend upon. I will meet you to-night in Grover's plantation.   " J."

It was not difficult to interpret this. Joe Pratt's wife's name was Susan. The murder was committed on a Monday night; the allusion is evidently to procuring the sister's absence from the Judge's house that night.

Another note, in the same hand, read as follows :—

"Susan has asked her mother, who says he keeps the will in a tin box by his bedside. I would rather you did not admit Bill Plummer into the business. We can depend on ourselves, but not upon others. I have not got any money to-day, but I will try and get some to-morrow. Meet me at the usual place, half-past seven.

"J."

This explains that the murderer's object was to obtain possession of *a will*. The writer evidently objects to Mr. Plummer's being taken into confidence.

A third note was to the following effect :—

"I have an objection to meeting you in the town, as it might cause remark ; and I think it will be better that we should not be seen together. The nights are moonlight now. We can meet in Grover's plantation. I will be there to-morrow night at eight.

"J."

The following was in a different hand-writing :—

"I don't know what to make of your friend Joe, he is so shilly-shallying. Does he want to get you into a mess ? If I thought he was up to that game I would soon be down upon him. But I would not stand any of his —— nonsense. I want to know what you think, and should have come up to the Black Lion to-night to look for you ; but I have got such an infernal black eye that I don't care to come out and show it. Some of Lucas's doings, larking—I call it spite. Can't you screw something out of Mr. Joe *now* ? I 'm hard up, and s'pose you 're ditto.

"Yours, BILL."

Upon comparing this note with that sent to Mr. Joe Pratt, I found the hand-writing identically the same. It was evident to my mind that all three were "foul;" but as yet no clue to the actual murderer. I was inclined to think it was Dick Galashiels; and my reasons for thinking so were, that he was a reckless, dare-devil sort of a fellow, while Joe Pratt was notoriously a coward. Bill Plummer was evidently an accessory, but most probably after the fact.

If Joe Pratt and Dick Galashiels were the actual murderers it was hardly likely they would say anything to criminate each other. It was, therefore, extremely desirable that one, the least culpable, should turn king's evidence.

Great excitement prevailed in the town when it became known that three suspected persons had been arrested. They were brought up for examination, and a certain amount of evidence, entirely circumstantial, produced against them. Thereupon they were remanded.

I had no hope of a conviction on the external evidence that would be brought against them. My hopes were chiefly centred in Mr. Bill Plummer. If he would only do what we wished, the result appeared to me tolerably clear. I resolved to go and make the proposal to him. There was a reward of seven hundred and fifty pounds offered for the discovery and apprehension of the murderers, and, to a man in Mr. Plummer's needy condition, I thought this would be no slight temptation.

But I was to some extent forestalled in my project.

Next day another of those convulsive throes occurred to agitate a community wound up to the highest pitch of excitement. I was sitting at my dinner at the inn when I became aware, by the confused murmur of voices without, that something unusual had happened. Soon I heard distinctly,—

" Joe Pratt's confessed ! "

" What has he confessed ? "

" To the Judge's murder."

" Did he murder the Judge ? "

" No ; but Dick Galashiels did."

" Ah ! Well, let us hear all about it."

It appeared that Joe Pratt, after passing a sleepless night, requested early in the morning to see a certain clergyman whom he named. Upon his arrival Joe stated to him that his mind was so troubled, he could not rest until he told all he knew about the murder. The following is the substance of his confession :—

"Some time ago I learned that Judge Black had made a will, in which he bequeathed the bulk of his property to his sister, my wife's mother. Recently I learned that he had made another will, giving most of his money to his nephew, Stephen Black. As I could not endure the thought that my wife should lose the property, and I my large expectations, I determined to get this last will and destroy it. I did get it, and burnt it without reading it. Dick murdered the old man. There were three others in it besides Dick."

As Mr. Pratt's connections were exceedingly anxious to be spared the ignominy of having a member of their family hanged, they made every effort to get him admitted as king's evidence. His counsel endeavoured to put his statement into proper form, but Joe prevaricated so much, and so contradicted himself in every particular, that his legal adviser cautioned him to hold his tongue altogether, and say nothing; for, as sure as he spoke, he would criminate himself.

Upon hearing of this I resolved to see what could be done with Mr. Bill Plummer. I therefore obtained the necessary authority to visit him in prison in the character of a member of the committee.

"I don't want you to say anything to your own prejudice," said I; "but you probably know that there's a reward of seven hundred and fifty pounds offered for the discovery of the murderer, and any one turning king's evidence would be likely to get it, and a free pardon also, unless he were the actual murderer."

"A great inducement," he answered sneeringly, "a strong temptation, to any one in want of money, which I am not."

"It's probable," I replied, "that your friend Joe will avail himself of the offer, especially after showing your letter to the committee, which he has done."

"The —— scoundrel!" said Mr. Plummer, turning white with rage. "I'll be even with him. But he knows better than to blab."

"But he's arrested, and who knows what he may do to get out of prison?"

"Arrested, is he? and Dick too?"

"Dick's all right," I replied.

"So, then," I said to myself, "Dick's one of the party, is he? I'll take a note of that."

"Better say at once what you know of this affair," I continued. "You'll be up to-morrow for examination, and so will Joe, and the first that splits will stand the best chance."

"The first that splits will forfeit his life," said Mr. Plummer, with much warmth; "that's the understanding."

I was startled at this inadvertent speech, but said nothing. Plummer had no sooner uttered the words than he saw that he had made a false step. He looked confused, and gave me a glance that said distinctly, "I have put my foot in it." Upon my moving towards the door of the cell he lifted up his finger, as much as to say, "Not yet; wait a bit." I waited.

"I don't know you," said he, "and am not sure I may trust you. I 'll have a lawyer to get me out of this —— scrape."

"Do so. You have no time to lose," I replied.

Musing awhile, and pacing up and down the floor of his cell with his fists clenched, and grinding his teeth, he muttered,—

"I 'd give a thousand pounds, if I had it, to see Joe just for one minute."

"No doubt, my friend; but you know that cannot be. Next time you meet it will doubtless be at the bar, and you 'll certainly be committed for trial for that murder. You will have to explain away, if you can, that letter you sent to Joe Pratt."

"Oh, that was only a bit of fun! I only wanted to frighten him. He is such a cowardly fool."

"And you 've pretty well succeeded. The consequence is, that you are here, and he is close by, both under lock and key. Do you see any fun in that?"

"I see that I am a bigger fool than I thought I was."

"You know best; but we are losing time. Have you anything more to say?"

"Will you come and see me again in the afternoon, after I have seen a lawyer? Then we can have some more talk."

"There 's no time for talk; we must think of business."

"Well, never mind; only come, that 's all."

CHAPTER VII.

As I proceeded from the prison back to the magistrate's office, I became aware that something unusual was going on, from the excited state in which persons were hurrying to and fro, and gathering together in knots at various corners. Stepping up to one of these groups, I inquired if anything was the matter.

"Oh, nothing! Only Dick Galashiels has blown his brains out!"

"Nonsense! he's in prison. How could he get a loaded pistol?"

"Nobody knows; but he did get it, and shot himself with it."

"Dead?"

"Dead as a door-nail! He was terribly put out when he heard that Joe Pratt had confessed. His wife was allowed to visit him in prison; and it's my belief she supplied him with the pistol."

"So, then," I mused, "Mr. Dick Galashiels has cheated the gallows!"

At a meeting of the committee this day orders were issued for the arrest of Joe Pratt's brother, Edward. I lost no time in executing the warrant.

Late in the afternoon I returned to the prison for another interview with Mr. Plummer. I found him very downcast, at which I was not sorry, for I thought he would be the more easily impressed by good advice. He was deeply moved at the suicide of his friend Dick Galashiels, and for a long time sat deeply buried in thought. At length he rose up and looked at me.

"Well, Mr. Plummer, I have come again as I promised. I hope I have not come in vain."

"I see there is but one chance for me, and that is to tell all I know. But you must understand that I had nothing to do with murdering the old man."

"So much the better for you; then you can speak the more freely."

"Him as did the murder has gone to his account. I had rather not have been him. But I know nothing except what Dick told me himself."

"And what did Dick tell you?"

"Well, this was it. Joe Pratt came to him, and asked him if he would not like to make his fortune. Of course Dick was quite agreeable. Joe said something about a will which he wanted to get: would Dick get it? How was that to be done? By breaking into the old man's house. Joe would tell him where to find it. Dick was willing. Next time Joe saw Dick he said the will would be of no use if the old man was alive. Would Dick mind killing the old man? Joe would get the will himself. Dick had no objection. Thought the old man had not long to live at any rate, and a few weeks or months could not make much difference to him anyhow. Joe planned it, and the night was fixed; but it had to be put off because he had not got the will. But on the 2nd of April the thing was arranged. Joe, to avoid all suspicion being thrown upon him, slept out at the farm, and so did the Judge's sister. Joe's brother, Ned, and Dick managed the business. Ned watched. They saw the man-

servant go to bed, and they waited about for a couple
of hours, when Ned helped Dick over the wall: he got
in at the window. French window, made no noise. It
was soon done. Ned had brought up a horse and
chaise from the farm, which was concealed in a gipsy
lane. They both got into it and drove down to the
farm, and waited in the stable until Joe joined them
there, and then they told him what they had done.
Dick was to receive a thousand pounds as soon as Joe's
wife got the legacy, and a thousand a year for life. It
was agreed that the first who told should forfeit his life
at the hands of the others."

Plummer's confession was put into writing. It
tallied in every important particular with that which Joe
had made to the clergyman.

Ned Pratt was put upon his trial. There really
appeared to be no direct evidence against him. Never-
theless, the jury were so satisfied in their own minds of
his complicity, that they found him "guilty," and he
was forthwith hanged.

I could never understand why he was tried alone,
and not with his brother. There seemed to me an unaccountable aversion to deal with Joe as he deserved,
and a very strong desire that he should be admitted as
king's evidence. I think that the sister's complicity
had something to do with the matter. It was generally
supposed that she had abstracted the will; but I do
not think, even if it were true, that she could have
known of Joe's diabolical intention.

Joe was brought to trial, found guilty, and hanged.

I believe that Joe Pratt's wife endeavoured, by every means in her power, to supply her condemned husband with a weapon wherewith he might take his own life, rather than he should suffer an ignominious death on the scaffold. But the authorities, suspecting as much, were on the alert; their vigilance had been aroused by the manner in which Dick Galashiels had slipped through their fingers. Therefore Joe had to meet his fate like any other felon; I cannot say manfully, seeing that he was so great a coward, for he was half dead with fear and terror when brought out to suffer, and fainted away. While held in the arms of two strong men the fatal noose was applied, and in this state of unconsciousness he was launched into eternity.

There was a sale by auction of the Judge's household property. Among the articles sold was an elaborately-contrived escritoire. The cabinet-maker who had constructed it attended the sale, and opened a *secret drawer,* which no one else had discovered. A sealed envelope, endorsed " MY WILL," was found within it. Upon opening it a will was found, in which the Judge bequeathed the bulk of his property (after paying a legacy to his sister) to his nephew, Stephen Black. Joe Pratt *had stolen the wrong will,* and destroyed it without reading it—the will in which the Judge had bequeathed the greater part of his property to his sister, Joe's wife's mother !

CHEATING THE GALLOWS.

" £100 REWARD.   Whereas Oliver Holman, Printer, of
" 21, New Street, left his home on Saturday, the
" fifteenth instant, and has not since been heard of ; and
" whereas it is suspected that the said Oliver Holman
" has been murdered, any person giving information that
" will lead to the discovery of his body, and the detection
" of the murderer, will receive a reward of One Hundred
" Pounds upon application to Messrs. Fisk and Perry,
" Solicitors, Godliman Street, Doctors' Commons."

A bill, of which the above is a copy, was placed in
my hands one morning as I entered the —— Street
station.   Turning to two or three of my staff who
were warming their backs at the fire, I addressed
them :—

" This can't be a very difficult case, boys.   Suppose
we go in for it ? "

" With all my heart," replied Pike, who had a scent
like a bloodhound.   " Things are very slack just now,
and the hundred pounds will come in very handy, for
my wife presented me with twins yesterday, and——"

"Wish you joy, Pike. Take the matter up by yourself, and if you find you want any help, let me know."

Pike thanked me, and buttoned on his coat.

"New Street, Bishopsgate?"

"Yes, No. 21."

In about a couple of hours Pike returned.

"Well, what news?"

"I have been to New Street, and inquired about the missing man. They say he left his office on Saturday forenoon, about eleven o'clock, for the purpose of calling on several of his customers to collect some money due to him. Several of the persons upon whom he called—some of whom paid him what they owed him—have come forward and stated at what hour they last saw him. I have traced his movements up till one o'clock on that day, but not later. At that hour a person left him at the entrance to —— Chambers, where Holman said he was going to call upon a rascally accountant of the name of Tupling, who owed him some money. After this all clue is lost."

"Have you seen this Tupling?"

"I have not. I called at his place, but not at home."

"Well, it is early yet. Suppose we go together about twelve o'clock?"

"Very well. Meanwhile, I'll just go and make some inquiries about this Tupling."

"Do. Well thought of, Pike."

Shortly before twelve Pike returned. I "made up"

as a baker—white coat, &c. Pike, in a nice suit of
black, was to introduce me as a "tradesman in difficulties," who wanted his accounts squared up.

Tupling's office was a back room on the second floor
of an old house that must have been erected immediately
after the great fire of London. Up a dark heavy staircase we groped until we arrived at a door upon
which was painted,—

> JOHN TUPLING, *Accountant.*

I was about to knock when Pike, with a keen
knowledge of human nature, stayed my hand. *He*
thought that *if* so be Tupling had committed the crime,
he had best be taken unawares; his conscience would
then be visible in his countenance.

Firmly seizing the handle of the door, in an instant
we were in presence of a sneaking-looking rascal
sitting at a desk facing the door, with a pen in his
hand, the motion of which our presence had rather
suddenly arrested. The penman was visibly nervous,
for underneath the point of his pen was a huge blot on
the paper upon which he had been writing.

If a man may be judged by his looks I should have
at once sentenced the penman to be hanged. It was
easy to perceive that the fellow had habitually screwed
his visage into a sanctimonious mould, in order to
deceive the unwary.

" Mr. Tupling ? " said Pike.

"That's my name, sir. What—what may—may be the—nature of—of your business—with me, sir?"

"Oh, professional! You're an accountant. My friend here, Mr. Cooke, a baker, is in difficulties; his creditors are rather pressing, and he wants to arrange with them."

"*We'll* pull him through. You want protection, I suppose?"

"Well, that we'll see about. See how his affairs stand first, and then, if it should be necessary, apply to the court."

"Any fear of arrest, Mr. Cooke?" inquired Tupling.

"Not exactly; still I cannot say what may happen."

We conversed on the subject for a few minutes, he having asked us to be seated near the fire. I wanted to turn the conversation on Holman's mysterious disappearance, and was casting about for an excuse, when, strange to say, my eye fell upon his name on a large printing card, such as printers present to their customers, nailed up on one side of the mantel-piece.

I gave Pike a quiet signal, by which he understood that he was to keep a sharp eye on Tupling. Fortunately we had managed to get him opposite the window, where his face was in full light. Seeing that Pike took the hint, I leaned over against the mantel-piece to which the card was nailed.

"Holman!" I said. "Why, that's the name of the man who is so mysteriously missing," turning sharply round, and looking Tupling hard in the face.

"Y—e—s, very singular, isn't it? Very shocking!"

"Yes, very singular and very shocking. Did you know him, Mr. Tupling?"

"O yes! He did some business for me; printed this little book for me."

"Seen him lately?"

"Not since he was missing."

"Did you see him on that day—the Saturday he was last seen, I mean?"

"No. He might have called when I was absent, for I was out all day."

We then discoursed further on our business.

"Well, Mr. Tupling, my friend, Mr. Cooke, will know where to find you when he wants you. You think you have leisure to undertake his business?"

"O yes! Things are very slack just now, and I could devote all my attention to his affairs."

"You can give us a reference, I suppose, Mr. Tupling?"

"Certainly. I can refer you to Mr. Rutt, the eminent cheesemonger, in the Strand, or to Mr. Lugner, the carpet dealer, in Cheapside, both of whom have employed me for several years."

"Very well, Mr. Tupling. I dare say all will be satisfactory. I have some little points to argue with my friend Cooke. You shall hear from us again soon. Good morning, sir."

"Good morning, gentlemen—good morning."

I felt considerably relieved when I got out into the

street, for there was a very sickening atmosphere in the dark, dingy hole where Mr. Tupling held his audience; and the fellow's hypocritical face made me feel so disgusted, that I had become rather nervous.

"Well, Pike," I said, turning to my aid, "what is your opinion of that gentleman?"

"A sneaking scoundrel, every inch of him—one who would stab his best friend in the dark for half-a-crown. He is as much likely to have murdered Holman as anybody. Did you notice his confusion when we spoke of the missing man?"

"I did, and put it down for what it was worth."

"Well, I am determined to satisfy myself about this fellow, for I must confess I am ready to think the worst of him. I shall go to Holman's office, and make some inquiries about the transactions that have taken place between Tupling and Holman."

Pike resumed his inquiries at Holman's office, and ascertained that Tupling owed about two-and-twenty pounds for printing, and that it had been standing on the books for a couple of years. Holman had made up his mind to sue Tupling for the amount, and before leaving his office had mentioned that he was going to call once more (it should be the last time) on that "d——d scoundrel, Tupling."

Pike also sought out the person who had parted with Holman outside the door at Tupling's chambers. He gave it as his decided opinion that Holman proceeded up the staircase. The next step was to inquire of

Tupling's neighbours and of the old housekeeper if anything had been remarked of an unusual character on the preceding Saturday. The person who occupied the adjoining chambers to Tupling's stated he knew that the accountant was at home during the forenoon, and that about one o'clock he heard the voices of persons talking loudly, as if in altercation, and of something heavy falling, but beyond this he had seen or heard nothing.

In all this there was not enough to warrant the arrest of Tupling; so we resolved to keep dark, and wait patiently for what might turn up.

There appeared to be no clue to the discovery of the murder. In fact, at present we did not know that there had been a murder committed at all. The man was missing—missing in a most mysterious manner; and that was all. But as no motive or reason could be assigned for his absence from business and his family, the fair conclusion was that the missing man was an unwilling absentee.

Time wore on, but still no development of the mystery. I began to think either that there had been no murder at all, or that this was an exception to the general rule, that "murder will out," when one day a custom-house officer called at the Station, and stated that a very mysterious affair had come to light, begging that an inspector would step down on board a ship which had just returned from Trieste.

It appeared that some months previously the ship

had sailed for the port of Trieste. Among the cargo
was a large packing-case, addressed to certain parties at
that place, but who could not be found ; and as no one
came forward to claim the package, it was brought
back in the same ship.   Before storing it, and previous
to advertising for the owner, it was decided to open it
to see what it contained, lest its contents might be
perishable.   To the horror of those engaged in opening
the case, they found that it contained a quantity of
coarse salt, from amid which a human hand protruded.

I immediately ordered the removal of the salt, when
a human body was gradually brought to light.   It was
in a complete state of preservation ; the salt had
effectually retarded decomposition, so that it was as
easy to identify the unfortunate victim as if he were
still alive.

Upon examination of the body—which wore the
clothes of the living—a large wound was observed just
above the temple, apparently inflicted with an axe, or
some sharp heavy weapon.

The body was removed to a neighbouring public-
house, there to await identification and the coroner's
inquest.   Informing Pike of what had occurred, I
directed him to go to Holman's office, and fetch some
one acquainted with the missing man to ascertain if the
corpse were his.   I also gave instructions to have
Tupling's movements watched.

One of the men employed by Holman instantly
identified the body as that of his lost master.   The

inquest continued for three days, at the expiration of which a verdict was returned of "Wilful murder against some person or persons unknown."

Of course the discovery of the body caused great excitement, and the government offered a hundred pounds reward, in addition to the hundred previously offered by the family of the murdered man, for the discovery of the murderer.

I had ordered that Tupling should be strictly watched, for I strongly suspected that, in case he was the murderer, so soon as he learned of the discovery of the murdered man's body, he would think it prudent to bolt

Of course one morning an account of the singular discovery of the body appeared in the newspapers Tupling's shadow saw him step into a little shop where the *Times* was lent to read. Obtaining a copy, he walked slowly along towards his chambers, reading i meanwhile. Presently he stopped : something interest ing appeared to completely absorb his attention. In a few moments he hastily folded up the paper, thrust i into his pocket, and, glancing nervously right and left hurried up the staircase to his den.

My man waited a few moments, and then quietly followed him on tiptoe up the staircase to his room Arrived there, he applied his ear to the keyhole. H could hear Tupling pacing up and down the room, ex claiming,—

"My God ! what's to be done ? What shall I do ? Shortly afterwards a rumbling noise was heard, the a sound as of rummaging papers; then the locking as of a desk or cupboard; next a pause. My man thought it prudent to beat a retreat. He easily concealed himself in the recesses of the dark staircase. Presently Tupling came out with a carpet bag in his hand, and proceeded downstairs, followed at a discreet distance by his shadow.

Arrived in the street, Tupling made his way to London Bridge. At the station he took a ticket for Tunbridge Wells; the shadow did the same. Arrived at the Wells, he took up his quarters at a private lodging-house. His shadow communicated with me, and waited for orders.

I waited the result of the coroner's inquest. It was an open verdict. I lost no time, however, in obtaining a warrant against Tupling, proceeded with it to Tunbridge Wells, and arrested the " suspect," while he was enjoying his supper.

Any one who has been long in the habit of arresting suspected persons gradually acquires a faculty of deciding upon the guilt or innocence of the parties arrested, from their demeanour on such critical occasions. As to the signs and tokens of guilt and innocence I shall say nothing; they are not strictly infallible, but they influence a detective's treatment of a prisoner materially.

As I had pretty well made up my mind that Tupling was guilty, I acted upon that conviction; and considering I had a crafty customer to deal with, I took my measures accordingly.

First I consulted with my aid. He did not suspect Tupling was armed, and thought the arrest might be made without much difficulty, especially if we made it in company.

Next I had a private communication with the land-lady. I informed her that she was going to lose a lodger, but that I would pay what was due. She was a poor widow woman, and I did not wish to see her wronged. I led her to suppose that her lodger was to be arrested for debt.

The kind-hearted old lady seemed very much grieved. She shed a few tears, which she wiped on the corner of her apron, and assured me that her lodger was a very quiet, inoffensive man, who gave no trouble.

"But I think he be very unhappy, miserable like; he talks dreadfully in his sleep, and as his room is next to mine, I hear it all; and he keeps me awake o' nights. I dare say the poor man has got his troubles."

"We have all got our troubles, Mrs. Grove. I dare say you have had your share."

"Indeed I have. Ever since my poor dear hus-band——"

I thought it best to nip that story in the bud.

"Just so, Mrs. Grove. We want to get back to town to-night; so now do you just keep out of the way. We wish to do things quietly, else we may alarm the town, and you will have a mob round your house for a week."

"Oh! not for worlds. Do just as you like, sir, but pray don't be rough with him."

"Not at all, ma'am, if he be quiet. Be sure we shall not raise a disturbance—it is against the rule in such cases."

Having settled matters with the landlady, we proceeded to the room where Mr. Tupling was partaking of his frugal supper—bread and cheese, and a pint of ale.

I knocked at the door.

"Come in, Mrs. Grove." Without raising his head from the newspaper he was reading, he continued, "I don't feel very well to-night; I should like a little brandy and water. Will you be so kind as to send for some brandy?" and he put his hand into his waistcoat pocket to take out the money.

"Mr. Tupling," I said.

He started, raised his head quickly, and was on his feet in a moment. His hand felt for the knife he had been using. I took no notice of that.

"Mr. Tupling," I said, "resistance is useless. You are my prisoner. I have a warrant for your apprehension on the charge of murdering Mr. Holman."

At hearing these words he sank into his chair, pale as death, and uttered not a word. I sat down opposite to him, to give him time to recover. Meanwhile Pike quietly entered the room, and took a pair of bracelets from his pocket. I gave him a sign to wait a bit.

"We don't want to hurry you, Mr. Tupling, but

we must return to town to-night, and we cannot go without you."

"I'll be ready in a few minutes, gentlemen. I just want to pack my carpet-bag that's in the next room."

"Oh, certainly, Mr. Tupling. Here, Pike, show Mr. Tupling a light."

In a few moments the carpet bag was packed, and Tupling and Pike returned to the sitting-room. Pike slipped one handcuff over his own wrist, and quietly taking Tupling by the hand, slipped the other over *his* wrist, and prepared to start, linked together in a loving embrace.

We reached town without any particular incident, and lost no time in lodging our prisoner in a place of safety. Next day he was brought up for examination. The evidence against him was purely circumstantial, and very inconclusive. Considering that the ends of justice would be best served by the prisoner's remand, I obtained it.

Of course I examined the prisoner's apartments and office. Upon turning up the carpet of the latter I observed several large stains on the boards, which looked as if they might have been *blood*. The boards had, however, been washed, and in some places scraped. I immediately obtained the assistance of a chemist, who, by dint of much ingenuity and care, satisfactorily ascertained that the stains were of blood—of human blood.

I must confess that my admiration of the chemist's art is very great. How often it leads to the detection of crime! By his wonderful skill he can not only tell, from a drop of dried blood you may give him, what animal it belonged to, but also whether it was shed while the animal was living or dead. Then again, in cases of poisoning, how sure are the means by which the detection of the minutest particle of the deadly drug is arrived at! Many's the wretch that has had to swing through the evidence of the analytical chemist.

There was a closet in Tupling's office, which was used as a coal cellar, in which was a considerable quantity of coals—nearly half a chaldron—together with some bundles of wood. These I thought it advisable to remove. In doing so, a small hatchet was found on the floor, peculiarly rusted and stained, both on the blade and the handle. This was also submitted to the chemist's examination; and he pronounced the rust and stains to be human blood.

I next examined the walls of the room : on one side, next the fireplace, I perceived the wall was whiter than on the other sides, as if it had been newly whitewashed. Upon applying the light of a lantern with a large bull's-eye, I could discover a dark tint beneath in several spots. Before touching these I thought I had better consult my friend the chemist.

Upon examining the spots he took an old razor, and commenced scraping the whitewash very cautiously off the wall over the spots. In a very short time the peculiar red stains of blood became visible. Some of this red substance was carefully scraped off into a piece of writing paper : this was analysed, and found to be human blood.

My attention was next turned to Tupling's papers. These I very carefully examined, and among them I found Holman's account against Tupling. It was very much crumpled, and on it was the mark of a thumb *in blood!* Upon submitting this document to the inspection of Holman's clerk, he positively stated that it was in his master's possession on the day he was last seen.

The evidence these discoveries afforded was deemed sufficiently conclusive to warrant the prisoner's committal to Newgate to take his trial.

A man never knows how many friends he has got till he gets into trouble. The chances are that he then finds he has not got any : so Tupling found it. No one came forward to speak a word in his behalf.

The defence set up was, entire ignorance of the whole affair. Tupling had never seen Holman on the day of his disappearance, nor for some time previous. He knew nothing whatever about him.

But, on the other side, there were witnesses who came forward to testify to Holman's avowed intention of calling on Tupling on the morning of his disappearance. One stated that he parted with the murdered man at the foot of the stairs leading to Tupling's chambers, since when, no further traces of him could be found.

Then there were the stains of human blood on the floor and walls, and the condition of the hatchet.

While I was standing in the court, watching the trial, a policeman forced his way through the crowd to where I was standing; he was followed by a man who had expressed a desire to speak with me.

He proved to be a cartman—the one Tupling had employed to carry the packing case, containing the body of the murdered man, down to the wharf, for shipment on board the vessel bound for Trieste. He had only just learned the particulars of the case going on, and thought he might be able to throw some light on it.

The court adjourned till the next day. I employed the interval in accompanying the cartman to where the packing case was lying. On comparing the marks upon it with those in his memorandum book, he immediately identified it as the packing case Tupling had employed him to convey to the ship on the Monday succeeding the murder. He remarked upon its weight, and on the trouble he had had in getting it downstairs, and into his cart.

Upon this man's testimony the chain of evidence seemed complete and conclusive. It was quite circumstantial it is true, but no more so than in many cases of like nature. The summing up of the judge was against the prisoner, and the jury, after a very short consultation, found a verdict of GUILTY! Sentence of death was passed upon him in the usual form, and he was left for execution on the following Monday.

I had some commiseration for the guilty wretch, as

he seemed deserted by all mankind; so I visited him in the prison, to see if there was anything I could do for him. I found that a brother who resided in a distant part of the country had been to see him, and promised to stay by him till after the execution.

The fatal day at length arrived. It was a cold, gloomy, gusty day in March. The preparations for the execution had all been made. The prisoner had taken farewell of his brother on the Sunday evening, and retired to rest soon after twelve o'clock. At five o'clock in the morning the attendants proceeded to rouse the unhappy wretch, but without success. Upon further inspection, they found that with the smallest of penknives he had severed the JUGULAR VEIN, AND WAS A CORPSE.

A written paper was found neatly folded and placed under his pillow. It was indorsed,—

" STATEMENT IN JUSTIFICATION
of the crime
for which I am about to
SUFFER."

In this document he gave an account of the murder, and the circumstances which led to it.

He stated that Holman called upon him on the fatal Saturday, and demanded payment of his money. As he was not prepared to pay, Holman abused him, and called him opprobrious names—swindler, scoundrel, &c.

Excited by his language, Tupling seized a small hatchet that he had just been using for some trifling purpose, and threw it at Holman, without any intention of inflicting bodily injury. Unfortunately the hatchet struck Holman on the temple, and caused almost instant death. Horror-struck at this dreadful issue of his anger, he was quite bewildered. As there were no witnesses, he did not suppose he should be able to justify himself; so he hit upon the expedient of making away with the body as described above. He never thought it would come back, and when he saw the account of its discovery in the newspapers he felt that it would soon be brought home to him, and it was his intention to surrender himself into the hands of justice. Delay in so doing was fatal. Had he done so, and pleaded the facts as stated by himself in extenuation, he might have escaped the sentence of capital punishment.

How he became possessed of the instrument of his death was an impenetrable mystery. It is supposed that it was supplied to him by his brother. At any rate, Tupling had succeeded in

CHEATING THE GALLOWS.

THE INNKEEPER'S DOG.

THERE had been queer doings in Yorkshire that winter, what with rick-burnings and a murder or two. I was sent down by the Home Office to see what I could make out of it all, when the following adventure befell me. Romantic as it may appear, you may rely upon the truth of it. The facts are well known to many reliable persons now living, who could add their testimony to mine if it were necessary.

I have a great respect for the intelligence and sagacity of dogs. I had a dog once, the only sincere friend I ever could lay claim to ; but he is gone the way of all dogs.

But to my story. As I was saying, I was ordered down to Yorkshire. It was in the month of February : what with the thaw and the rain, half the country was under water. When the mail-coach put me down at S—— I had some seven miles to walk, and every step of the way the water was over the tops of my boots. I could obtain no sort of conveyance ; the Yorkshiremen I found very churlish; they seemed to enjoy a stranger's dilemmas exceedingly.

How I groped my way to the village of M—— I never could make out. It is true I kept to the turnpike road, and followed my nose and the curt directions of the innkeeper at S——. At length, by the light of a crescent moon, I perceived I was approaching what I hoped would prove an inn or ale-house, the Rising Sun, the goal of my destination. Soon a faint light, glimmering through a casement window, came in view, and in a few minutes I was drying myself before a huge fire in the kitchen of the Rising Sun.

How the boors eyed me! They sadly wanted to know my business—where I came from, and so forth. I was a *grazier* for the nonce, looking out for a nice lot of sheep, and choked them up with that pretence well enough.

I was hungry enough you may be sure, and the landlord managed to provide me with a good hot supper. Sleeping before the fire lay a large mastiff dog. The smell of the cooking supper roused the animal into a state of activity. He seemed to understand perfectly for whom the supper was being prepared, and endeavoured to cultivate a friendship with me, which I encouraged, and treated him to a few tit-bits. He evinced his gratitude by placing himself by my side, rubbing his head against my knee, and looking up in my face.

There were some very rough, ill-looking fellows hanging about the room, drinking their beer. I fancied I was the subject of conversation with one

group, for they conversed in whispers, and sent some
very sinister, furtive glances at me across the room.   I
half regretted having given myself out as a grazier, lest
they might conclude I had a good sum of money about
me ; but reflecting that I was at an inn, I did not
suppose that I should be in any danger.

The landlord got into conversation with me after supper,
and related to me the news of the neighbourhood—all
the harrowing particulars of the murder of Mr. Perry,
and the details of the burnings, which had been so
numerous in that quarter of late.   I was glad he had
taken up these subjects himself, as it put me in full
possession of all that was then known about these
incidents, which enabled me to draw my own conclusions.

I remarked that while this conversation was going
on my ill-looking neighbours became silent, and
listened attentively to all that was said, without making
any observation.

It grew late, and my stiffened, aching limbs
demanded rest ; so I requested the landlord to show
me my bedroom.   As I mounted the old creaking
staircase to the upper storey, the guests assembled in
the kitchen took their departure.

Following my host along several long passages,
through which the cold wind blew and whistled fitfully,
he at length halted before a whitewashed door, which
opened into a bedroom : handing me the candle, he
wished me " Good night."

I was about to ask him what part of the house I was in, and whether I had any neighbours sleeping in the adjoining rooms; but I checked myself, and, taking the proffered candle, entered the room, responding to the landlord's " Good night."

I heard his footsteps retreating along the dark passages while I placed the candle on the table, and I then turned to close the door, when, to my great amusement and surprise, I saw the dog which had partaken of my supper in the kitchen standing outside wagging his tail, and looking up in my face, saying, as plainly as dog-language could express it, "I'll come in if you will let me."

" Come in, old fellow," I said ; and in he walked.

I was not at all sorry to have a companion, although but a dumb one. It was company anyhow. Whether it was the fatigue of my journey, or what not, I felt myself rather depressed in spirits, and a companion I looked upon as a real God-send.

The dog placed himself in the middle of the apartment, wagging his tail and looking at me as if he was waiting for orders. Considering that to be his view of the case, I pointed to a piece of ragged carpet lying on the floor at the foot of the bed, and said, "Lie down there, doggy ; " and he laid down.

When I sleep in a strange bed I never take off my under garments; so, quickly slipping off my coat, waistcoat, and trousers, and removing my neckerchief, I lay down fearless of damp beds. I did not lie awake very long. I think I must have fallen asleep within five minutes. I sleep rather heavily when I am fatigued. Once in the course of the night I was awoke by a strange noise, as of a scuffle, and something falling. I spoke to the dog :—

"Are you there, doggy ?"

A low whine was my answer. I turned on my side, drew the blanket over my ears—for I thought the wind whistled rather coldly about them—and in a few minutes I was asleep again.

I was awoke in the morning by the rays of the sun shining full on my face. I raised my head, and was surprised to see the window open. It was fastened when I retired on the preceding night.

Stepping out of bed, I was proceeding to the other side, when, to my infinite surprise, I saw a man lying on his face full length on the floor. The dog was crouched beside him, with one paw resting on the man's head.

I called out, "What do you want here ?" but received no answer. I then applied my foot gently to his body ; but he heeded me not. Stooping down, I turned the fellow over, when, to my horror, I saw the man was dead !

But how came he by his death in that place ? Upon closer examination I perceived a wound in his throat, evidently caused by the dog's teeth.

The fellow had entered my room by the window, with the intention of robbing and murdering the *grazier*. A life-preserver lay beneath his body, and in one hand was a large hog-knife, such as pig-killers make use of in their business. I called the landlord, but I called in vain; my voice echoing along the passages, met with no response. I stepped to the window: it looked out upon a large field of turnips. A ladder had been placed against the window, by which the intruder had obtained access to my chamber.

Hastily dressing myself, I groped my way down to the kitchen, and then raised the alarm. The landlord and some other inmates of the house hurried back with me to the bedroom. As soon as the landlord saw the man's body he exclaimed,—

"Whoy, that's Dick Shawler! Be there any more on 'em?"

The body was removed to a room downstairs. Soon the story spread around, and numbers of persons flocked in during the day to hear the news, and see the man who had met with so singular a fate.

I questioned the landlord as to who Dick Shawler was, and who his companions were.

From him I gathered that Dick was one of a gang of four idle fellows, who got their living no one could tell how—partly by poaching, partly by stealing.

I learned enough to justify me in taking steps to have the gang arrested; and it came out quite unexpectedly that they were the perpetrators of the murders in that quarter, and guilty of many other crimes, which I shall tell you of some other time.

THE GALLANT SON OF MARS.

EVERY fool has his folly. Major Brownlees had his.

"Ah, Mr. Inspector! I have been wishing to see you for some time past; but it is so difficult to catch you when one wants you."

I was walking up the shady side of Pall Mall one hot day in July, in the year ——, when a respectably-dressed gentleman descended the steps of the —— Club, and addressed me as above. Although I remembered his face, I did not identify him at the moment; so I replied, —

"Have you? I am always to be found, you know, at——"

"Yes, I know; but I should not like to be seen coming there, it would give rise to awkward suspicions. There are always some busybodies about, who are sure to be spying where they are not wanted."

"Quite true—quite true. But what, may I ask, is your business with me, Mr. —— ?"

"Mr. Steel, that's my name."

"O yes, I remember; you are the secretary of the —— Club."

"Just so.   One of our members has got himself into a confounded snare, and wants you to get him out of it."

"What! Major Brownlees?"

"The deuce!   How did you know it was him?"

"Oh! I've known all about it a long time; but what does he want done?"

"Why, the major is being awfully bled, and wants it stopped, and he wishes me to make some arrangement with you to that effect."

"I never do things second-handed, Mr. Steel.   I deal only with principals, not with agents.   If the major wants my advice or assistance, he knows how to obtain it."

"You are mighty particular, Mr. Inspector; but I suppose you must manage things your own way.   It won't do to dictate to you, I know.   I'll go and tell the major what you say."

"I'll walk up to the palace, and you can come to me there."

I proceeded up the Mall as far as Marlborough House, and was about to turn back, when I perceived Mr. Steel approaching, followed by a tall, portly gentleman of about fifty-five years of age.   Upon coming up to me, Mr. Steel stopped till the gentleman came up also; then he introduced us.

"Inspector F——, Major Brownlees."

"Mr. Steel has informed you, I believe, of the nature of the business I have with you, Mr. Inspector?"

L

"No, sir, he has not. I preferred having it from yourself."

"Well, Mr. Inspector, the facts are—— Confound it! here comes that bore, Colonel Waddle, and he has clapped his glass eye upon me. Could you make it convenient to come and dine with me this evening at Vercy's —half past six, say? We can have a quiet chat there."

"I shall be very happy to wait upon you there, major."

"Oh! no ceremony, my dear fellow. Be sure and come. Ah, Colonel Waddle, good morning. Good morning, Steel."

Walking along with Steel, he informed me that the major was a real gentleman, in the truest and noblest sense of the word, who had seen long and arduous service in India, and won high honours for his bravery and generosity. He held as high a position probably as any officer in his corps who had preceded him. The major had, however, one little weakness, like most mortals. When the tempter was a pretty woman he could not resist; and if he yielded it was his warm heart that suffered, not his honour.

Well, I dined with the major, and he entertained me with a long story of his troubles. I was amused to think how one who could baffle the stratagems of an Indian chief could be outwitted by a crafty chit of some twenty years.

"The fact of the matter is," said the major, as he tossed off his Hock, "I have been awfully bitten, and I begin to think myself an old fool."

" Never too late to mend, major."

" It was too late for me to begin such pranks, though: never in my young days did I get caught in such a confounded scrape. There was that affair with Lady ——, it is true."

" Better to keep to the business in hand, major," I suggested, deferentially.

" Well, to make a long story short, some months ago a young Irishman enlisted into our regiment, of whose anteeedents, of course, I knew nothing, and eared less. As he had evidently reeeived a good edueation, and was greatly superior to the class that usually enlist, I took some interest in him. He wrote a very good hand, and was a elever aeeountant; so after he had eompleted his drill I had him placed in the orderly room, and promoted him to the rank of eorporal. He beeame a sort of seeretary, and was employed in drawing up reports, &e., and was a general favourite among the officers. I had occasion myself to employ him in his new eapacity, and in the course of time drew from him the information that he was deseended from a good Irish family, and would, in the natural eourse of events, inherit a considerable fortune. He gave me the names of his relatives, some of whom I knew. Through some youthful indiscretions and follies, and perhaps something worse, his family had disearded him; and smarting under the disgrace he had brought upon himself, he had enlisted. It appears that one of his follies had been that of getting married to a beautiful

but penniless girl—one of two sisters; and the trifling
allowance he received from his family contributed to
her support. The sisters partly supported themselves
by keeping a school; but the recruit, having been
brought up to no profession or trade, soon exhausted
what little resources he had brought with him to
London, and had no alternative to save him from
destitution and beggary but enlistment.

"But you don't drink, Mr. F——. Come, fill your
glass. Capital wine, this.

"As I have said, his superiority to his position was
soon remarked; and, with the exception of drilling, he
had none of the routine duties of a soldier's life in
garrison imposed on him.

"One day—it was after I had drawn from him as much
of his early history as he chose to tell—we were at
Portsmouth then—he asked of me permission for his
wife and her sister to visit him, which of course I
granted; and then, for the first time, to my great
surprise, I learned that they were as yet ignorant of
his whereabouts or position, and probably thought him
dead.

"How do you like that wine, Mr. F——? Vintage
of '24."

"Excellent, major. Never tasted better—not even
at the old Duke's."

"Well, as I was saying, a day or two past, I was
looking out of the mess-room window after dinner,
when I saw two stylish-looking young ladies coming up

the barrack-yard. The sight of a petticoat in such a place was, of course, sufficient to put the whole garrison in a flutter. As they passed by the window where I was standing, I could see their faces; and certainly one of them was the most beautiful woman I had ever seen. Fine features, brilliant eyes, raven hair, and a figure such as any sculptor would have coveted as a model for Venus."

"And the other, major: what was she like?"

"As different from the other as possible, yet still very beautiful. But she was of the fair type; golden hair, light blue eyes, clear complexion, and such rosy cheeks and lips."

"Which was the recruit's wife, major?"

"The dark one."

"O'Donnell—for that was the recruit's name—was engaged writing at the time, so I just strolled into the room where he was busy. Presently a man came in, and informed him that two ladies wished to see him, O'Donnell looked at me inquiringly. I understood what he wished to say.

"'Show the ladies in by all means,' I said.

"The meeting was cordial and sad; sunshine and tears. I pretended to be busy looking over some papers, but I could not resist the temptation of looking out of the corners of my eyes at the weeping beauties. After the first emotion was over I thought I would sacrifice dignity to feeling, so I left them alone.

"In about an hour, thinking they had probably

gone, I returned to the room, but, to my surprise,
found the ladies still there, not exactly in tears, but
having evidently just passed through that crisis, for
their eyes were red and swollen, and their countenances
plainly indicated that they had gone through some
painful emotions.

"The moment I entered, the dark-haired beauty,
Mrs. O'Donnell, sprang forward, and throwing herself
on her knees before me, and raising her clasped hands,
begged me, in Heaven's name, to liberate her husband
from the captivity to which he had voluntarily, but in a
moment of desperation, committed himself.

"I raised the weeping beauty, and endeavoured to
soothe her grief; but of course had to tell her that I
had no power to grant her request, however much
inclined I might be to do so. Then the other young
lady joined her entreaties, and amid sobs and tears
implored me to release 'her dear brother.' I may tell
you, Mr. F——, that for a moment I wished myself
Secretary for War, or Commander in Chief; but I was
not, and neither could I be; so I had to stand against
the sharpest, the hottest battery I ever faced, and cry,
'No surrender.'"

"But you got wounded I suppose, major?"

"Well, as for that, you shall judge for yourself by
the sequel. So far, all well enough. I felt for the
sufferers, and did my duty. The ladies seemed in no
hurry to part from the recreant husband and brother,
and used the permission I had given them to visit him

very liberally; they became regular and constant visitors every day.

"Of course I could not avoid encountering them on many occasions when they came, and I began to suspect they selected the hour for their visits when they would be sure to find me with the young recruit. Mrs. O'Donnell never lost an opportunity of imploring my intercession in her husband's behalf, backing her entreaties by the assurance that they would soon be reduced to destitution unless he was restored to them."

"I do not see, major, how he could have helped them much, incapable of earning his livelihood, as it appears he was."

"Nor I. Well, things went on in this way for many weeks, perhaps months, the ladies being frequent visitors, and invariably appealing to me with their prayers and entreaties for O'Donnell's release. I could not but feel a deep interest in them, for they, like himself, appeared far above the position circumstances had placed them in; and so selfish is human nature, I really think that if I could have released O'Donnell I would not have done it, for I took so much pleasure in seeing the ladies come to visit him."

"You *say* so, major, but I do not suppose you mean so."

"Well, I had no opportunity of testing my disinterestedness. I see by your looks," continued the major, "that you are jumping to conclusions; but hear me out. One evening I had been dining-out, and perhaps had taken a little too much wine, when, as I was wending my way to the barracks along High Street, who should I meet but 'the ladies' attached to my young recruit. The wine, or the devil—I don't know which—prompted me to stop and salute them, and I turned and walked along the way they were going. Turning down a little by-street, they halted before the door of a neat-looking tenement:—

" 'This is our humble abode, major,' said Mrs. O'Donnell. 'We are sorry it is not worthy of your reception, but our circumstances——'

" 'Don't mention it, ladies,' I replied ; ' any place that is graced by your presence needs no other attraction. Fate is cruel to prevent fortune being more kind to you than she is. Let us hope for better days.'

" While saying this the door had been opened, and before I knew where I was, I found myself seated in a comfortably furnished apartment, but with no attempt at display.

" The fair young lady retired, to take off her bonnet, I suppose. Meanwhile Mrs. O'Donnell renewed her entreaties for her husband's release, which, of course, I was obliged to pacify as I best could.

" 'Can you give me no hope, major? I am nigh broken-hearted ; and if O'Donnell is not soon restored to me I am sure it will be the death of me.'

" I stammered out something about the sad necessity, &c., when the door opened, and the fair lady, radiant in her beauty, made her appearance.

"Mrs. O'Donnell rose, and proceeding to the door, said to her sister, 'Here, Amelia, do you try if you can soften the major—he will not listen to me;' and without saying another word she went out of the room, leaving Amelia and myself alone.

"I know what I should have done had I been in my sober senses; but the wine was in, and the wit was out.

"Amelia did not follow her sister's mode of pleading, but pursued a system of tactics entirely her own. She made no use of sighs and sobs, groans and tears, clasped hands and kneeling attitudes, but——"

"Ha! ha! ha!"

"But plumped right into my lap, threw her arms around my neck, and smothered me in kisses."

"Ha! ha! ha! Oh! oh! oh!"

"You laugh, Mr. F——; but what could a man do? You know St. Anthony was tempted, but all are not so proof against temptation."

"I suppose I can guess the rest, major?"

"You may if you choose," replied the major, colouring-up as he raised his glass to his lips to hide his confusion, draining it at one gulp. "But the worst of it was that confounded wife of O'Donnell's——"

"What! the lovely brunette—the charming——"

"Just so. She caught me *flagrante delicto*, as the lawyers say, I believe, when a man has allowed himself to be caught in a scrape."

"Well, and what did she do?"

"Why, stormed and raved, called me an old villain,

vowed I had ruined her poor dear virtuous sister!
She did not know what the consequences would be
when her dear husband came to hear of the insult done
to her sister; that he was terribly hot-headed; and
that she was sure there would be murder, and so forth.
So, to pacify her, I was obliged to promise that I would
get her husband's discharge."

"And did you, major?"

"Why, of course, bought it and paid for it."

"And did that satisfy them?"

"Not a bit. Every day Mrs. O'Donnell applies to me
for money upon some pretence or another, threatening,
if I do not give it to her, she will tell her husband. It
has cost me many hundreds already, and I don't see
where it will stop. I think I have paid dearly enough
for a drunken folly, and have got quite tired of this
' bleeding.' I never can keep a sovereign in my purse.
Mrs. O'Donnell is sure to come 'a-borrowing' every
time I draw a cheque. I really think she must have
some friend at the banker's, who gives her information
whenever I draw money out."

"Not at all unlikely. They are all in London now,
I suppose?"

"O yes; they came up the very day I did myself.
I don't know but they came by the same train, they
stuck so close to my heels."

"Do you know where they are living?"

"In Great Pulteney Street, No. —."

"Well, major, leave them to me for a few days. I

think I have no need of an introduction. I believe, from your description, the party is well known to me. If so, I have no doubt that I can relieve you from their importunities."

"If you can, you will be my best friend. Here, take another glass before you go. Success to you!"

Next day I selected Brookes, an officer upon whose judgment and discretion I could rely, and directed him to institute inquiries as to who the O'Donnell family were. It did not take him long to find out that the ladies were both of easy virtue, and that the "discharged recruit" had taken up the profession of begging-letter impostor, pretending to be a school-master stricken with blindness, with a young wife, &c. That they were a set of confirmed rogues, there could be no sort of doubt, their sole occupation being, it seemed, to prowl about seeking whom they might devour.

I then directed Brookes to contrive to form an acquaintance, somehow or another, with the party, leaving it to his own discretion and tact how to manage it. He was not idle, for in two or three days he reported the result of his labours. His face wore an expression which led me to conclude that I had put his virtue to a very severe test.

Next day I sent a polite, but pressing invitation to Mrs. O'Donnell and her sister. Upon seeing them I was forced to confess (mentally, of course) that the major had been sorely tempted. Such a Venus as

Amelia, with her voluptuous form, brilliant eyes, pearly teeth, combined with a lavish bestowal of ardent kisses, must have been more than a match for the gallant son of Mars.

However, putting on my official sternness, I laid before them the discovery I had made as to their mode of obtaining a living, and produced the threatening letters they had sent to the major. It was these letters that had induced the major to apply to me. I pointed out to them the certainty of the punishment they would render themselves liable to by pursuing such a course; and, finding themselves completely cornered, they promised never to molest the major again, or to give me any further official trouble.

But Mr. Brookes had an account to settle with them : nothing would pacify him but that they should quit London without delay. I had thus the satisfaction of relieving the major from a set of harpies who had been preying upon him so long. What became of the ladies I never knew ; but Mr. O'Donnell was implicated in a certain forgery case that made a great noise a few years ago, and was sentenced to fifteen years' penal servitude.

ROBBING THE BANK.

"TALKING about the Bank—did I ever tell you the story about a plot that was laid to rob the Bank of England?"

"No, John, but I should like to hear it. Something bold in that idea."

"So you 'll say when you 've heard the particulars. I know of but one scheme that will compare with it, and that's the Cato Street Conspiracy. Dare say you 've heard of that."

"Yes; I have heard that story over and over again. But what about robbing the Bank?"

"Well, that was a foolhardy plot, I must say; but sane men sometimes take very wild notions into their heads. I dare say *you* could not think of any feasible plan for robbing the Bank, and making off safe with the plunder."

"A feasible plan has never occurred to me yet, it is true; but the fact is I never entertained the notion, else I do not know what scheme my ingenuity might suggest. But come, let 's have your story."

" Well, at that particular time—I mean the time when
that mad project was entertained—I was in the habit of
visiting a certain public-house in Lower Thames Street,
where I was in hopes of meeting a sea-captain, who was
' wanted ' for trying to sink his ship and defraud the
underwriters.   I made-up as a working-man, and used
to spend the evening in blowing a cloud, and reading
—I should say spelling—the newspaper through and
through, from beginning to end.   Sometimes, if the
company was sociable, I would get into an interesting
conversation on the Canning ministry, and such-like
topics.   Great man, that Canning, sir !   No such men
now-a-days, sir.   Why, Pam and Lord John are mere
children to what he was.   Such a head !   Ah, poor
George ! he and I were good friends.   Many 's the bit
of good advice I 've given him ; and he had the sense
to take it too."

" But what about the Bank, John ? "

" Oh ! thank'ee for putting me in mind of it.   When
I think of those good old times, so many things rush
into my mind that I soon lose myself.   But I 'll go
back to that public-house in Thames Street.   It frequently happened, when I went in there of an evening,
I disturbed the cogitations of a party of three, who
seemed to be in deep consultation on some subject of
very engrossing interest.   I did not pay any particular
attention to them, as there was nothing remarkably
suspicious about their proceedings ; but I noticed that
they always broke off their conversation when I en-

tered, and made some common-place remark about the weather, &c.; but even this did not excite my suspicions. After meeting them there several evenings, I ventured upon a ' Good evening, gentlemen,' to which they made a curt reply, but never attempted to maintain a conversation.

"What did they look like? Oh! nothing in particular—German clock-makers, it might be, or something of that sort. As I was saying, they were quite mum after I entered the room, so that I could make nothing out of what was going on amongst them.

" Thus matters went on for several evenings, when one night they broke up rather earlier than usual. After they were gone I happened to look under the table for a bit of paper to light my pipe with, when I picked up a piece near where one of the men had been sitting. I attempted to read what was written upon it, but as it was scribbled all over, crossed and recrossed, at first I could make nothing of it. At last, with some ingenuity, I contrived to hit upon a method of reading it, and had no sooner done so than every hair of my head stood erect."

"Was it so dreadful, then?"

" From what I could gather it was a plan for robbing the Bank, but so daring and extravagant that it looked like madness. Still I thought it worth my while to look into it, notwithstanding."

"A very absurd project, certainly, and one that could never be carried into effect, I should suppose."

"So you would say if you knew all; but these fellows, like most knaves, were too clever by half in their own conceit. Well, to continue my story, I took very good care of that bit of paper, you may be sure, and spent half the night sitting up, trying to write it out fair, and I succeeded in making a tolerably coherent story out of the fragments. Before I left the public-house I had a private interview with the landlord, and inquired if he knew anything of the party that I described to him, and who were in the habit of frequenting his parlour.

"He, however, knew nothing of them further than this—that first two of them came together, then a third and a fourth joined them, and sometimes there were as many as ten or eleven. He thought some of them were Germans, as they spoke a lingo he did not understand. They did not spend much money at the house, but they took up a good deal of room, and the publican had thought that he should be better off with their room than with their company.

"I pondered in my mind what I should do. Go to the Bank authorities, and warn them of the impending plot? They would have laughed in my face, and I should have lost in their estimation my character of being a shrewd officer. Tell my superiors at the Mansion House? They would have thought I had been troubled with the nightmare. So I resolved to keep the discovery to myself, and work it out alone.

"Of course I was at the public-house next evening

in good time, but I waited and waited hour after hour
—not one of the party came. This appeared very
strange, and could only be accounted for on the sup-
position that, having discovered their loss of the
slip of paper, they were fearful it might have fallen
into the hands of some person who might connect them
with it.

"Well, I waited till half-past ten, and then gave
them up for that night, at least. Next day I took a
turn into the Bank, thinking that by chance I might
stumble upon some one or other of the party on the
look-out. But no ; I was at a dead lock.

"Still I could not get the thing out of my mind.
Everybody else might have considered it absurd and
improbable, but I have always found that it is the
improbable things that are most sure to happen. I
resolved to keep a good look-out, and I never passed
the Bank without giving a look in.

"It happened one evening that I was in the neighbourhood of Bishopsgate, looking for a gentleman I
wanted, when in a by-street I dropped into a quiet
public-house to smoke a pipe and see the evening paper.
Upon entering, to my great astonishment, there I saw
my gentlemen all cozily seated, blowing great clouds of
smoke, and drinking beer, &c.

"The recognition was mutual ; and, I think, so was
the surprise.

"' Good evening, gentlemen. Glad to see you again.
Missed you from the old shop.'

"'Vy, yees; ve likes this moosh petter, ve does, 'cause tish quieter. Vat you doing here, mein goot freend?'

"'Oh! nothing particular, mynheer. Happened to be in the neighbourhood, and feeling thirsty, have come in to take a pint of ale.'

"'Yah! ver' goot ale at dis plashe.'

"'Is it? Then I shall come often.'

"'Vat you do for living, my ver' goot freend? Ish you in de bus'ness?'

"'Not doing anything now, I am sorry to say. Out of luck, as the saying is.'

"'Then you voud be glad of a nice leetle job, eh?'

"'Of course; anything to turn an honest penny.'

"'Vell, mine freend, I tink I can give one clever fellow a ver' good job.'

"'What is it?'

"'I'll speak to you by and by. Vill you have some ale?'

"He called for a pot of ale for me, and I kept a sharp look-out upon it, I can tell you, for I was not altogether sure they did not intend to hocus me. But I got the pot into my own safe keeping, and had my eye on it. The spokesman paid no more attention to me, but turned to his companions and conversed with them in German."

"Do you understand German?"

"A little; enough for ordinary purposes. At any rate I understood what the present conversation was about, and I assure you it was so interesting that, although my eyes were fixed on the evening paper, I did not see a word on the page. I was 'all ears.' In the course of an hour the party separated, leaving the spokesman and myself alone together.

" 'Take a glass of branty, mein freend ?'

"I declined the proffered civility in spite of his earnest solicitations. Seeing me resolute, he at length desisted, and we left the house.

" 'Vich vay you go, mein freend ?'

" 'Towards Cheapside.'

" 'Ah ! then ve vill valk togeder, and we can talk business as ve go along. I can troost you, mein freend, eh ? You look fair.'

" 'Oh, certainly. Anything you say to me will be quite safe. I never tell secrets.'

" 'Vot, not to your vife ?'

" 'No, sir.'

" 'Vell, you vould like to make some money ; goot lot, eh ? goot lot of money, eh ? Make money very easy, eh ? Vat you say ?'

" 'Why do you ask me such a question ? Do you think me such a fool as to refuse a good chance ?'

" 'But vat if there be some danger ? You onderstand ? No ? Eh ?'

" 'Do you mean robbery ? Murder, perhaps ?'

" 'Ah ! now, mein freend, you 'fraid. If you vere in big room full of money, and nobody to see you, vould you be fear to help yourself ?'

" ' Well, that depends.'

" ' Depends ? Ah ! to be sure, it *depends*. I onderstand, my goot freend. Yah ! yah ! it depends ! Ver' goot—yah ! yah ! Well, now, shwear me one big oat that you will keep my secret, that you vill nevare tell nobodies.'

" ' What shall I swear ?'

" ' So help your Gott !'

" ' But you have not told me what it is I am to do.'

" ' Ah ! true, I forgot. Vell, mein freend, we go to rob a big place full of money. You fill your pockets vit gelt, as mush as you can carry. Tink of dat—*as mush as you can carry*, and mush more !'

" ' But what do you want with me ? Can't you help yourself, or do you want me to rob for you ? '

" ' Ah, now, don't be angry, mein goot freend. It will take a good many prave men to do de business ; for perhaps dere will be some resistance, you see ; and some must get de money, while some must do de fight.'

" ' Oh ! I can fight, if that will do. I can fight better than I can steal ; but if I fight, who is to pay me for it ? '

" ' Ah ! mein freend, we all share de same ; those who do de fight help as mush as those who do the tief. You shall have goot share if you do de fight. You shall have goot share if you do de steal.'

" ' Well, I will do the fight for you ; but where is the job to be ? '

" ' Ah, den, mein freend, would you like to know ?

Then I shall no tell you—not till you prove me you are prave man.'

" ' How can I do that? '

" ' Meet me to-morrow night at twelve o'clock in the churchyard, and sit on big tombstone till I come.'

" I could have laughed outright at the Dutchman's test for bravery, had not discretion counselled me to keep serious; so putting on as sober a face as possible, I replied,—

" ' Well, I will do that if you require it; but I assure you it is not necessary. I am afraid of neither ghost nor devil.'

" ' Vell, mein freend, I vill trust you. You look honest countenance, but I want to see you to-morrow. Come to me at eight o'clock, and then I speak more.'

" I promised to keep the appointment, and we parted; but I had not proceeded many steps before it occurred to me that I should like to know something of the whereabouts of my arch-conspirator; so I turned cautiously round, and taking advantage of the screen afforded by a man and woman in advance, I followed, and soon came in sight of ' mein freend.'

" I cautiously kept him in view, and followed him to a dark lane somewhere in Shoreditch, and could, on account of the darkness, follow very closely on his heels unobserved. Presently he halted at a place that looked like a stable with a loft over it. He took out a key and quickly let himself in, and locked the door behind him.

"I reconnoitred and carefully noted the spot; then, concealing myself on the opposite side of the street in a doorway, I waited to see what would turn up. In about half an hour two men, carrying what appeared to be a heavy load, stopped at the door and let themselves in. Presently another man arrived, and he also let himself in.

"I now had some doubts if the door was locked, so I crept cautiously over, and looking first right and then left, to see if any one were coming, I applied my hand to the latch, but the door would not yield.

"I then tried a way of opening doors that was taught me when a boy by a gipsy. The door gradually yielded. Hurrah! I was in the enemy's camp.

"But softly. Look before you leap. Where are you, friend John? You are doubtless in the strong-hold of desperate men, and although you have got on so adroitly, look out for a safe retreat, in case the Philistines come upon you. I turned to the door, and forced the bolt of the lock back, then shut the door quietly. I endeavoured to discover what sort of a place I was in, but the den was dark as pitch. I could hear voices, but they appeared to be overhead, and I could see a faint glimmer of light through a crevice in the floor; but I could not see my own fingers, even if held up to my nose.

"Of course I concluded that there was a ladder, or some such means of access to the upper loft, and I proceeded to feel cautiously round the walls for it. As stealthily as a cat I lifted my feet, and put them down again as quietly as if I trod on a velvet pile carpet. I stumbled against several articles, and had a difficulty in making out what they were. In the farthest corner I found a gun leaning against the wall.

" ' So this is the rogue's armory,' I thought to myself.

" I had made the circuit of three sides of the place and come in contact with what I concluded to be a heavy ladder, when just at the moment I heard a key applied to the lock of the outer door by which I had entered. After considerable rattling the latch was suddenly lifted, and a man entered, swearing angrily.

" ' D—d careless,' said he, upon reaching his comrades upstairs ; ' d—d careless, I must say, to leave that door open. Who came in last ?'

" The last comers protested that they had locked the door after they came in, which was true ; but they did not know that I had tampered with the lock.

" One of the party proposed that they should take a lantern and search the stable, to see if any one was secreted there ; but the proposition, fortunately for me, was overruled.

" I was now at a loss what to do. I could not hear much where I was, so I concluded I had better beat a retreat, although I had listened with all my ears I could not distinctly make out the subject of the conversation. To let myself out, however, was a delicate manœuvre, that could hardly be executed without being overheard; but a heavy, lumbering cart happening to pass along the street, I took advantage of the uproar it made to escape.

"I am no coward; but I may confess to you that I breathed much more freely when I reached the open street. Had I been caught in the stable, there is no doubt the villains would have made short work with me, and probably buried me under the floor.

"Next evening I met 'mein Herr' according to appointment.

"'Well, mein freend,' says he, 'I have made up my mind to trust you. The great Lavater says you have a ver' honest face. You know Lavater?'

"I had the humiliation to confess my ignorance, for I supposed he alluded to one of his confederates.

"'Vell, you should make de acquaintance of de great Lavater.'

"Had I done so, it is probable that I should have discovered 'mein freend' to have been an arrant scoundrel, had I not known it from his own confession.

"'I shall troost you, mein freend, wid a very grand secret. You shall be mein confederacy, mein right-hant man, shall you?'

"'I should like first to know what the business is that you wish me to engage in.'

"'Dat you shall, then, ver' soon; but you must come long vays vid me to de rendezvous. Dere you shall see some prave shentlemens, like yourself—goot, prave men, who vants moneys, as everyboty vants moneys.'

"Leading the way, he quickly threaded the crowded streets till we reached the very place I had watched him to on the previous night.

"He quickly opened the door, and when we both were inside he locked it very carefully behind him, and then tried if it would open. I fully appreciated this excessive caution.

"'It is ver' dark for you dat do not know de ways,' he said, taking out a lucifer match and striking it. 'Look you dere—dere ist de ladder. Mount up quickly.'

"I obeyed with alacrity, and soon found myself in the presence of nearly a score of hairy-visaged rascals, every one of whom looked an eligible candidate for the hulks.

"'Yah, yah!' said my friend. 'I must introduce you to these shentlemens ; and, mein Gott, I never know your name. Vat is it, mein freend ? Pray, vat is your name, I peg ?'

"'Norval, sir, Norval. My name is Norval.'

"I could not resist the temptation if I had died for it.

"'Hah! Mr. Norfoll ? Ver' goot name—ver' goot name. I like dis name, Norfoll ; but you haf anoder name, Mr. Norfoll. Vat did your mutter call you ven you vas leetle boy, eh ? Vat did she call you ?'

"'John.'

" 'Ah ! dat is ver' goot name, too.   So, Mistar John
Norfoll, I introduce you to dese mein freends.   Never
mind dere names now; you vill find out by and by.
Dey all know *your* name now.   You know deres by
and by.   Take your seat dere, Mr. Norfoll, at de
corner, next mein seat.   Now, Mr. Norfoll, let us to
pusiness.   Ve are going to troost you vid a matter of
ver' great importance.   If we succeed you will be the
richest man in England.'

"I smiled—the prospect was refreshing ; for I was
not overburdened with cash at that time.

" 'Mr. Norfoll, ve tink we can empty the Bank of
England into our pockets, but it requires mush courage.'

" 'I should think so.   But allow me to ask how you
propose to bring it about.'

" 'Pring it apout ?   Ve do not vant to bring it
about ; ve vant to do it, as in dis way, Mr. Norfoll.
Now you listen.'

"Of course I pricked up my ears, and was all
attention.

" 'It is in dis way, Mr. Norfoll—I like your name
so much, it sounds so full in de mouths.   Norfoll !
Norfoll ! now you listen.   Ve go to de Bank at quarter
before four ; ve go in one by one ; some get by each
of the doors of de room vere dey pay out all de
moneys, to prevent people from coming in to help ;
when all our freends are in, ve seize de gate-keeper,
kill him, shut the door ourselves, and keep it safe for
de exit of our freends inside, who vill kill all de

peoples in de room, and fill de bags with gold, and retreat before any alarm can be given.'

" 'Capital ! excellent ! the best plan I ever heard of in my life—sure to succeed. When is it to be done ? I wish it may be to-morrow.'

" 'Stop, stop, Master Norfoll. You too quick ; dere is mush precautions to be taken. Ve must go many times first to see how many peoples are dere at dat hour, and if dat be de best time to do the business. Dere may be too mush public. We must use precautions, Mr. Norfoll.'

" I was next favoured with all the minor details of the plot. Each conspirator was to be armed with a strong dirk and a brace of pistols. The latter were to be carried in side-pockets, and not used unless absolutely necessary, as the report might cause alarm outside. It was considered best not to use them at all except to prevent pursuit.

" 'What part do you wish me to play in this business ? '

" 'Oh ! you are young and strong man; you must kill de gate-keeper, and shut de gate, and hold it for us to pass out.'

" I considered this the post of honour, and expressed myself perfectly satisfied and willing.

" The loft was dimly lighted by a smoky lamp that hung suspended from the rafters. I cast a furtive glance around, and on a shelf behind observed a quantity of pistols and dirks — I should say nearly a hundred of each. *That*, I thought, looked like business.

"'Now, Mr. Norfoll, ve has admitted you into our secret, but ve do not know but you vill go avay and betray us ; derefore you must remain wid us. Ve shall not let you go out of our sight; and if you resist, ve kill *you*.'

"I was, I must confess, taken rather aback at this arrangement; but I expressed myself quite satisfied with the precautionary measure.

"The company at length rose to depart. I was handed over to the watchful care of a red-haired ruffian, and he took me with him to his lodgings, and I had to sleep in his bed with him—a sort of contiguity I by no means relished, but needs must on the present important business.

"I had a large pocket-book with me, in which were some blank sheets of paper. Watching my opportunity next morning, I hastily penned a few lines to my Chief, narrating the circumstances in which I was placed, and leaving it for him to take such measures as he thought fit. I informed him of the locality of the stable, and suggested it would be as well to make a capture there. As for myself, I was fairly hooked in.

"I managed to drop this note into a letter box unperceived as we passed along a narrow street to an eating-house. I patiently waited the result.

"I did not expect that this wild project would be carried into execution immediately; so I made myself as comfortable as circumstances permitted. As we proceeded to the stable in the evening I saw two or three of my men planted on the way, in close proximity to the place of rendezvous. One of them managed to slip a note into my hand unperceived. It ran as follows :—

" 'We have taken measures to arrest the gang to-morrow night at ten o'clock. A file of soldiers will form part of the attacking party, under the direction of Sheldon. Take care of yourself.'

" I could now smoke my pipe tranquilly, so I gave way to the humour of the farce that was being enacted, and in which I was so unexpected and unwilling an actor. Next afternoon we all rehearsed our parts. Little did they think the catastrophe was so near.

" At night, with somewhat elated feelings, I accompanied my guardian to the stable about eight o'clock. Never did the time lag so slowly as with me on that occasion. Nine struck, then the quarter, the half-hour, three-quarters !

" Now look out for squalls !

" The neighbouring church clock had just concluded its task of striking ten, when I heard the outer stable door smashed in with the butt end of a musket, as I supposed. My confederates were at once alarmed, and all were on their feet in an instant.

" ' Teufel, vat is dat ? '

"I tried to look as scared as the rest, and hope I succeeded.

"In a moment I saw Sheldon enter the loft with a pistol in his hand, followed by some half a dozen other officers. Mynheer drew a pistol from the shelf, and presented it at Sheldon. I expected as much, and was prepared; so, seeing his movement, I knocked the muzzle of the weapon upwards, and the ball wended its way through the roof.

"'It's of no use,' said I, 'we are all caught; don't let us commit murder for nothing.'

"In less time than it takes to describe it, the gang were handcuffed together in couples. It was difficult for them to descend the steep narrow ladder linked together as they were; and one couple made a very precipitate descent, much to the injury of their noses.

"The troop of Grenadiers had remained in the stable below. They now formed the escort of the conspirators, who were safely lodged in Giltspur Street Compter.

"The authorities kept the matter very quiet. The Quixotic scheme was never divulged. The fellows had broken the laws of their own country, and they were handed over to some Berlin police, and quietly shipped on board a steamer bound for Hamburg. In this way the government was spared the expense of prosecuting these foreign rascals.

"I often reflect upon the enormous sum it must cost this country for prosecuting foreigners. Our hospitality cost us very dear."

THE BEGGAR'S RING.

I HAVE observed the world from many different points of view, but think none so amusing or instructive as that which is taken from under a lamp-post.

My favourite stations are at Charing Cross, close by Northumberland House, and at Regent Circus, Piccadilly and Oxford Street. These are busy corners, where the omnibuses stop to set down and take up passengers. If you happen to be looking for anybody in particular, ten chances to one but he will come along if you plant yourself in readiness to meet him, of course selecting the most likely spot of those I have named, or of others that I have not. Men have their particular haunts and walks in London. It would be of no sort of use looking for Brown at Oxford Street, whereas you would be pretty sure to see him pass by at Charing Cross some night in the week between ten and twelve o'clock. On the other hand, Jones is never to be seen at Piccadilly corner, but frequently at Oxford Street.

So I take up my station at one or other of these busy points when I am not looking for anybody in

particular, just for the amusement and adventure that
may chance to turn up ; and strange revelations have
been made to me at times, I assure you.   I have sometimes thought myself a public confessor, for many an
overburdened heart has poured its tale of sin and
sorrow, error and repentance, into my patient ear.

Will I tell you one ?   O yes !   Let me see.   Ah !
there's that one I call the BEGGAR'S RING.   That is a
good sample of the largest class of misery-stories I have
listened to.

It was a cold night in November.   At about half-
past nine I stood propping up the lamp-post at Piccadilly Circus, opposite corner to Swan and Edgar's.   It
was a good night for picking pockets, and as I thought
some active operations in that line would be carried on
among the people who wait for omnibuses at this
corner, I took up a position as a casual observer, but
with a keen eye to business.

The fog had come on rather suddenly.   A change of
wind from the south-west to the opposite quarter during
the day had blown all the smoke from the eastern
district of the metropolis to the West End.   Many
persons, strangers to the quarter where I was stationed,
appeared bewildered, and for some time I had to serve
as a direction-post to people in search of the Hay-
market, Strand, Pall Mall, &c.   One of the bewildered
was a delicate-looking young lady, elegantly dressed,
with a small travelling bag in her hand, who inquired
of me the way to London Bridge.

I was a little bit surprised at this question, especially as the lady appeared excessively nervous. I intimated to her that London Bridge was a very long way off, too far for a lady to walk there alone, at such an hour, and in such a night. I recommended her to take an omnibus.

She appeared to approve of the suggestion; still she did not avail herself of it, although several omnibuses passed by bound for that destination. I was puzzled, and my curiosity became excited. Turning her head, so that the gas-light shone full on her face, I saw the tears rolling down her cheeks.

"Why do you not take an omnibus if you really wish to go to London Bridge?" I again inquired.

"Yes; but I——I should like to; but——"

"But what?"

I began to suspect that she had not enough money to pay her fare, and I concluded she had had her pocket picked.

"What shall I do? I got into the wrong omnibus. It should have taken me to the Bank. I have come from Chelsea, and the 'bus goes to Islington. I am a married lady, living at Sydenham; and if I should not reach home to-night what will my husband think? I have been to see my sister, who is in great trouble, and I have 'gone further' than I ought; for I gave her all the money I had with me, except just enough to pay my fare to the Bank. You tell me," she continued, sobbing, "that I am three miles from London Bridge.

N

What shall I do ? If I walk I shall be too late for
the train."

Now, I am not a hard-hearted man, although you
might think I am. Who could see a woman in distress,
and not wish to relieve her ? Yet I know some
scoundrels, considering themselves gentlemen, who,
meeting a female under such circumstances, would have
insulted her with the most infamous proposal that can
be made to a virtuous woman. But such mean dogs
shame the mother who bore them.

Well, as I was saying, my heart was touched at the
artless manner in which the distressed lady told her
troubles. She was one of those quiet, delicate, sensitive creatures, quite incapable of encountering the
thorns and briars of this rough world. She might have
sat for a portrait of Desdemona—so gentle, so timid.

Come, John, you forget the lady is left standing in
the cold and fog all this time. How did she get to
London Bridge ?

Why, I put my hand in my pocket and felt for a
sixpence. I then hailed the next 'bus bound for London
Bridge and helped her into it, and sent her on her way
rejoicing.

She had not been long gone, when a new actor
came on the scene. This time it was a girl about
eighteen years of age—fine dark hair, and black eyes—
a pretty, intelligent face, that had once been happy.
Rounded and dimpled, it needed but the sunshine of

favouring fortune to light it up to be what men call beautiful.

She carried a heavy burden in her arms, covered by a thin, dingy shawl. I took it for a bundle of linen, or "work," or something of that sort. The few clothes she had on were black, and so was her bonnet. She appeared to be in what was intended to pass for "deep mourning."

When she had approached near to where I was standing, she stopped, and looked beseechingly in my face, but uttered not a word.

"Well, young lady, what have you got there?"

"A child."

"A child! Out on such a night as this! Do you want to kill it?"

"Kill it! God forgive you! It is a heavy burden to me, but I would not part with it for all the world."

"But why are you out at this hour with it? This fog will certainly kill it or cause its death. You were both better at home."

"Yes, if we had a home."

"No home! Where's its father?"

"I wish I knew."

"Has he run away and left you?"

"No."

"Does he let you come out, then, such a night as this? Is he a drunkard? Are you searching public-houses for him?"

"O no! *I don't know who he is!*"

"Nonsense! To tell me such a story as that!"

"But it is true. I wish it wasn't."

"Is it a girl or a boy?"

"A boy, bless his heart."

"And not to know who is his father! You are not an idiot; but you must think I am one."

"O no! Perhaps you would not believe me if I were to tell you the truth."

"I can always believe the truth; but lies don't go for much with me."

"He is very heavy, and I have been carrying him ever since seven o'clock. Would you mind holding him for a minute or two while I hook my dress?"

I held out my arms and took the boy, and he *was* heavy. I should not have liked the job of carrying him about the streets four or five hours at a stretch, I can tell you.

"Look at him—doesn't he sleep beautiful?"

I looked at him by the light of the gas-lamp. He was the image of his mother. He did sleep "beautiful." Poor child, I thought, never to know the author of its being—never to know its father! What stuff are *men* made of? Had it been the offspring of a baboon or a hyena, it might have met with a little natural sympathy.

"Now tell me all about it. You say you don't know who is the father of this child, and yet you are the mother. How am I to understand that?"

"Of course I know its father; but I mean I don't

know his name, nor where to find him. You look a kind gentleman, and perhaps you won't speak harsh to me, or blame me, when I tell you my folly and my troubles."

"Say on. I have no wish to be harsh, but tell me the truth."

"My father and mother are both dead. Father has been dead a long time; but——poor mother——she died broken-hearted when she knew of my trouble. Oh, how foolish I have been! But don't think I was wicked?

"I lived with my mother. I was acquainted with a girl who lived next door. She went away to a situation. After a year she came back, dressed so beautiful, with a gold watch, rings, and bracelets. She invited me one evening to go to the theatre. I never told mother, for I knew she would not let me go. We went to the boxes: there were two gentlemen there. We left, and went somewhere to supper. They made me drink a deal of wine. I didn't know where I was. When I woke up next morning I was a ruined girl."

"Did you ever see the gentleman again after that?"

"O yes, frequently. I used to meet him, and he used to write to me; but after I told him I was in trouble he never wrote to me again, nor have I ever seen him from that day to this."

"And did he never tell you his name?"

"He said his name was Robert. His initials were

W R. on the seal of his letters. He said he was a lawyer, and lived in the Temple. I have often looked for him there, but never could see him."

" Did he give you any money ? "

" Very little."

" How did you manage to get through your trouble ? "

" When poor mother died she left some furniture, but I had to sell it for little or nothing to pay the doctor, and the nurse, and the rent. Everything is gone; the landlord seized upon everything. Oh, if I could have kept my little home I could have got along very well; now, when I have not money enough to pay for a room, I am obliged to go to a common lodging-house, and there the people are so dreadful. They swear so, and use such awful language."

" And what do you expect will become of you ? "

" God knows. I can work, but there's my baby, he won't let me; and if I put him out to nurse they ill-use him, and it takes all the money I can earn."

" Have you no friends ? "

" I have an aunt, but she has a large family and cannot do anything for me."

" And how do you support yourself now ? "

" People give me a trifle sometimes. It don't take much to keep me and my darling boy, bless him."

" Then you are a beggar, I suppose."

" You may call me *that*, if you choose, but I never ask anybody for anything. If they give it me I take it, if they don't I don't. But I never beg; not I, indeed ! Anybody that looks at me will see I am no beggar."

" I did not intend to hurt your feelings, child. I meant you have nothing to depend upon but charity."

" Nothing else."

" And have you never thought of what you would like to do ? "

" I wish to find my child's father first and foremost. I wander about the streets all day in the hope of meeting with him ; but I never do."

" And what would you do if you were to meet him ? "

" Show him his boy, and ask him if he were not proud of such a son."

" I do not think the son has much reason to be proud of such a father. Have you enough to pay for your lodging to-night ? "

" I have but twopence, and, perhaps, you know how far that will go towards paying for a lodging."

" I don't know what 's to be done for you. I am a very poor man myself, and cannot help you if I would. I am afraid you will have to go to the workhouse."

" Never ! I will die in the streets first."

" But your boy ? "

" Ah ! the dear child—what shall I do with him ? Will they take him into the Foundling when he grows bigger ? "

" Not unless his father be rich, and will give you a recommendation."

"Is there no school where they will take and bring him up?"

"None that will take him, unless you can get good —I mean respectable—recommendations. Christian charity is meant only for the virtuous, not for the erring child of misfortune."

"What is a poor girl like me to do, then?"

"Trust in God. He tempers the wind to the shorn lamb."

"But how He punishes me for my disobedience! Oh, have I not been a foolish girl? See what I have brought myself to. God help me!"

"But what is that you have got on your finger? It looks like a ring."

"It *is* a ring."

"Let me see it."

"I cannot part with it. *He* gave it to me. I shall never part with it. Many's the meal and the bed it would have given me, could I have made up my mind to part with it. But I never shall."

I lifted up her hand more into the gas-light to examine the ring. It was of antique form, massive gold, set with emeralds, evidently of great value. It looked like an heir-loom.

"How did you come by this ring?"

"He lent it to me; but I would not give it back to him, although he was very cross with me about it. I said he should have it again when baby was born; but that did not satisfy him, and I do think sometimes that it was on account of the ring that he has not written to me or seen me. Don't you think so, too?"

"Very likely. I should like to examine it in my own hands. Take it off for a minute."

"You won't run away with it, will you, now?"

"Not likely. Here, hold my stick. I think as much of *that* as you do of your *ring*. That stick was made out of a piece of Nelson's ship, *Victory*."

"Was it though? Then it must be valuable."

I took the ring into my hands and examined it very carefully. It was of a very peculiar make. It resembled a cable in the interweaving, and it was a complete circle of fine large emeralds. Inside there was engraved, in old English letters, "H. S. to W R. 1811." These were quite legible, as they were black—probably, from constant wear.

An idea came into my head, while scrutinising the ring, that I might be able to do the poor girl a service.

"Suppose I want to see you again, where can I find you?"

"Wherever you like."

"Well then, come here to this place every Tuesday and Friday night, at nine o'clock, till you meet me. I may be able to do something for you. What is your name?"

"Maria Morris."

"Very well, Maria. I shall expect to see you again very soon, and I hope I shall bring you some good news. Here, take this; it will get you a lodging and a breakfast for two or three days at least."

"God bless you, sir! How kind you are to a poor girl. Tuesdays and Fridays—I 'll be sure to come."

I wended my way to my solitary crib, musing as I went on the best plan I could adopt for bringing the poor young waif into *rapport* with her betrayer.

In a day or two the readers of the *Times* were entertained with the following advertisement :—

"Found, an old-fashioned emerald-ring, with initials, and the date, 1811, engraved on the inside. The owner may obtain the same by sending an accurate description, by letter, to J. F., Post Office, 186, Strand."

On the following day a host of letters poured in, most of them evidently mere speculations, on the possibility of hitting the description by chance. From among the number I selected the following :—

"KING'S BENCH WALK, MIDDLE TEMPLE,
               "*Wednesday.*
"SIR,
        "Some months ago I lost a ring, which, from the description given in your advertisement in to-day's *Times*, must, I think, be the one you have found. The ring I lost is chased like the strands of a rope, set

round with twelve large emeralds. Inside is engraved in old English characters—'H. S. to W R. 1811.' If this should correspond with the ring you have found, I will thank you to send or bring it to the above address, when a suitable reward will be given upon its restoration.

"Yours obediently,

"WALTER ROSS.

"*To J. F.*,

   "*Post Office*, 186, *Strand.*"

This was just what I wanted. The fish was hooked; I hoped to land him safely.

I returned him a polite note, stating that the ring corresponded exactly with his description, and that I looked upon him as the rightful owner. I further stated that I would wait upon him next day, at five o'clock in the afternoon.

Next day I made myself up as a gentleman of the old school. Blue coat and gilt buttons, drab kerseymere small clothes, frilled shirt, diamond breast - pin, two diamond rings on my fingers, powdered hair, gold-headed cane, silver buckles in my shoes. A regular Sir Peter Teazle. I got into a hackney-coach, and punctually at the hour named I made my appearance at the chambers of Mr. Walter Ross, Barrister.

I knocked pretty loudly with my cane, and presently the door was briskly opened. Mr. Ross was startled at the apparition; he evidently expected to see quite another sort of personage; perhaps a butcher, or a cheese-monger.

"Ah! Mr. Ross, I presume. You see I am punctual," said I, taking out a gold repeater and making it strike five. "Always been punctual all my life, Mr. Ross. It is the only way to get along in the world, Mr. Ross; but people are not nearly so punctual as they used to be, Mr. Ross. Do you think they are?"

Mr. Ross did not deem it advisable to differ from me in my opinion of the punctuality of the present generation.

"Will you be pleased to take a seat, sir? I have not the pleasure of knowing your name."

"My name is Forbes, Mr. Ross; John Forbes. I dare say you have heard the name before."

"Perfectly well. The Forbeses——"

"Just so, Mr. Ross. My time is rather precious. We will proceed to business, if you please. Of course you know what I have come about."

"Have you brought the ring with you?"

"No, I have not."

"You have not! But——"

"It is not in my possession at all. I have seen it, it is true, and I make no doubt of its being yours. But it is in the possession of a lady, and it is in her interest that I have sought this interview with you, to arrange about the reward you are disposed to give for the recovery of so valuable a jewel. Money is an object to her, I can assure you."

Upon my uttering the word *lady* I could easily see that Mr. Ross winced a little, and his pale face became slightly, *very slightly*, flushed: an abortive attempt at a blush, I imagine.

"I am disposed to be liberal, sir, for the ring belonged to my father, who obtained it under peculiar circumstances, and did not wish it should ever go out of the family."

"How did you lose it, Mr. Ross, and *when*, may I ask?"

"Well, I did not exactly lose it. I lent it to a friend."

"And that friend has lost it probably."

"Very likely. But you say it is now in the possession of a lady: may I presume to inquire her name?"

"Oh yes, sir; there is no concealment. Her name is Maria Morris."

"Maria Morris! I have not the pleasure of her acquaintance. I do not know any one of that name."

His looks and manner were so confused that they quite belied his words.

"Strange," said I, "that you should not know the mother of your child."

"The mother of *my child*, sir! I do not understand you. Really, sir, I think this is a most unwarrantable liber——"

I was getting angry at the gentleman's cool assurance, so I rose from my chair, and addressing Mr. Ross in a loud, firm tone, I said:——

"Mr. Ross, look at me, sir. Do I look like a fool? Do I look like a man to be trifled with? I am not an actor in a farce. I am a man of the world, sir, and I hope a gentleman, and a man of honour. If you aspire to that distinction, you will drop the part you have assumed, and deal candidly with me. You have foully wronged a poor silly girl, and, if you are not a brute, you will certainly make some effort to rescue her and your own offspring from a most cruel fate, such a fate as must make a Christian gentleman shudder to contemplate."

"I was not aware, sir——"

"Of course not. You wreaked your lust upon a poor helpless girl, whom probably you could not have seduced. But, to compass your foul purpose, you drugged her, or by some foul snare made her incapable of protecting her honour, and, in that helpless condition to which you brought her, effected her ruin; and, when she told you of the consequences of your foul treachery, you basely deserted her, not caring to what extremity she might be brought through her shame. You caused the death of her mother, sir, and you have consigned this poor helpless creature and her babe—*your child*, sir—to the tender mercies of the streets, sir—of London streets, sir—where she has now to beg her bread. Is this gentlemanly conduct, sir? Is it *manly?*"

"But she need not have been in want with that ring in her possession."

"Very likely not, sir. If she had wished to sell it, to whom, let me ask, could she have disposed of it at anything like its value? If she had attempted to pledge it, sir, would it not have been stopped? How idle your remark is."

"What would you have me do, sir?"

"*Your duty* as a man. Remove this poor girl, whom you have condemned to a life of shame and misery, from her present cruel condition. Provide honourably for your offspring, else he may live to become a thief, or worse, perhaps, and curse you in his hour of trial. You have money, doubtless, if you have no feeling; give your money, and that may salve your conscience. Now you know the result of your baseness you are fully responsible for the consequences; you can plead ignorance no longer."

"You have her address, I suppose."

"I know where to find her."

"Can I not see her?"

"Not at present, and yet I wish you could. A sight of the wreck and ruin you have caused, of the fair life you have blasted, might excite some remorse in your heart."

"Enough sir. May I trouble you to convey this to her?" said Mr. Ross, handing me a sovereign.

"I will, sir; but you must be aware that this trifle will not go far towards relieving even her most urgent necessities. She is destitute, sir. Her home is the streets. She cannot reckon upon her next meal; and her child, *your* child, sir, derives its nourishment from her poor body. She wants clothes, sir, shelter, food, everything. Why, sir, ten pounds would be more like the thing."

" Well, that will do, at least, for the present. I will see her as soon as you will permit me, and endeavour to make her position comfortable."

" It is only your duty, sir. Notwithstanding the foul wrong you have inflicted upon her, she bears you no ill-will; she loves you, I may say, as the father of her child."

There is nothing like having to fight in a good cause. Right is might in that case. I stood up for the poor girl, and the justice of my cause made me bold.

Taking leave of Mr. Ross, I promised to see him again in a day or two.

Next day was Friday. I was at the appointed place at nine o'clock. Soon my bright-eyed *protégée* came in view, bearing her heavy burden.

" You see I 've come, although I did not quite make sure of meeting you."

" How 's the boy ? "

" Oh, he is very well, bless his heart! He begins to take notice, and wants to sit up."

" He wants to rise in the world, I have no doubt. Well, I have some good news for you."

" Good news for *me ?* What *can* you mean ? "

" I have found your boy's father. Is not that good news ? "

This news was too much for her. She was speechless for some minutes, looking quite bewildered. Hope deferred had made her young heart sick.

At length her eyes sparkled through her tears. Many times she attempted to speak, but her words were inaudible. At length she gasped : —

"You don't mean it."

"But I do, though ; and he has sent you this," and I handed her the sovereign.

"Well, this looks like it, indeed ; but how did you manage to find him so soon ? Why I have been looking for him for weeks and months."

"It's my business, child. I can find anybody I want to."

"And you've seen him ? And what did he say ? "

"Oh, nothing in particular; he wants to see you immediately."

"And doesn't he want to see his boy, too—his beautiful boy ? "

"Yes, he will see *him*, too, and provide for you both."

"I thought he would when he knew."

"Well, take care of your money; make yourself comfortable ; and when you have you shall see Robert. You must meet me again to-morrow night. Come here at nine."

When she made her appearance next evening there was an evident improvement in her condition. Her face was clean, her hair neatly brushed, and shining like a raven's wing.

" Have you got a lodging ? "

" Yes, a clean and comfortable room. I am so happy ; but when shall I see him ? "

" I 'll tell you to-morrow."

I had another interview with Mr. Ross. I cannot say that he was very cordial in his manners, or that he appeared at all elated at my interference in his poor victim's behalf. However, I arranged an early meeting between him and Maria, at which I took care to be present, provided with an agreement properly drawn up, in which Mr. Ross undertook to pay to Maria a guinea a week until the boy arrived at sixteen years of age. Mr. Ross also undertook to be at the expense of the boy's education.

The meeting of the injurer and the injured was rather a painful one. There was evidently no *love* on Mr. Ross's side ; but poor Maria, her heart was full. She expected some signs of affection from the father of her child, and was ready to fly to his arms had they been opened to receive her ; but she was doomed to a bitter disappointment. A cold, formal shaking of hands was all that he vouchsafed to her. She put her little rosy mouth towards his cheek, but the cold-hearted wretch turned his head away. He kissed the boy, however, and praised it, and that pleased Maria as much, nay, even more, than if these tokens had been bestowed upon herself. She had to give up the ring— I do not say reluctantly, but she looked very wistfully at it after Mr. Ross had put it on his finger. He gave her ten sovereigns to make herself comfortable with, and then the interview, alike painful and perplexing to both, came to an end.

Whenever business or pleasure takes me towards Millbank, I generally meet Maria taking her darling boy out for a walk. She keeps him very clean and neat, and he looks a strong, healthy, intelligent child. She looks very neat and tidy herself. Her bright eyes sparkle brighter than ever, and her cheeks are plump and rosy. If any honest, good-tempered, sober, hard-working fellow, wants a kind-hearted, thrifty, industrious girl for a wife, he might do much worse than take Maria for the partner of his joys and troubles.

THE LOST PORTFOLIO.

It was during the —— ministry. Ah! you need not open your eyes so wide; I am not going to divulge any state secrets, although I know a good many. Discretion, sir! I hope I do not lack discretion. Everybody's secrets are safe with me—quite safe, I assure you.

Late one evening I was sent for by a certain prime minister, whom you know very well, I am sure. He was in a very excited state when I entered his study, and seizing my hand, he said :—

"Ah, Mr. F——, I am very glad to see you. I never needed your services more than I do at the present moment. Most unfortunate affair. Cannot imagine how it happened."

"What is it, my lord, may I ask?"

"Well, you must know I have been down to Windsor to-day; came back by rail, bringing with me a portfolio of very important papers, which I wished to look over on the way. It grew dark some time before I reached the station, and I laid the portfolio down on the next seat to that upon which I was sitting, but when I reached to take it up again it was gone."

"Any other person in the carriage with you, my lord?"

"Only one, a very gentlemanly-looking person—I should say a foreigner, a German, from the character of his face."

"Did he quit the carriage before you did, or afterwards?"

"I really did not notice, but I think he got out first."

"Then he took your portfolio with him."

"I very much fear he did. What's to be done? It is of the utmost importance that I should recover it; and I need scarcely tell you that there are papers in it which I should not like to fall into the hands of an indiscreet or unscrupulous person, least of all into those of a German."

"Can you describe this person to me? Were there any peculiarities about his features? Was he marked in any way by which you could recognise him?"

"He looked, as so many foreigners do, like a military man. I remarked that he had a scar under his left eye; his hair was light, yellowish, with a full curled moustache. I did not take any particular notice of him, still I could recognise him if I were to meet him."

"And the portfolio—anything peculiar or remarkable about that?"

"Yes, fortunately, it is a very remarkable one—quite unique, I have reason to believe. It is patented, and the inventor informed me, when he brought it, that it was the first and only one that had passed out of his hands."

"Then I must see him immediately. It is probable that he has another like it. His name and address is—— ? "

"Harvey, 15, Rathbone Place. The name is on the lock of the portfolio."

"Enough, my lord. I shall first endeavour to see a duplicate of the lost portfolio; and as to the gentlemanly foreigner, I think he is well known to me. I believe he is a German spy. I know his haunts."

"You relieve my mind very much, I assure you. But I am so annoyed I cannot rest here while I must wait to hear what success you meet with. Would there be any objection to my accompanying you?"

"None in the least. I do not anticipate much trouble; and it would be more satisfactory to you, I am sure, to receive the portfolio intact, without being submitted to unwarrantable inspection."

"Very thoughtful of you, Mr. F——. I need not tell you that it is of the utmost consequence that its contents should not be divulged. They might find their way into the newspapers, and then—why, then the whole course of history might be changed."

"Well, my lord, time flies. Delays are dangerous. Do not let us lose another moment."

Putting on a " shocking bad hat " and a grey paletot, his lordship announced that he was prepared to accompany me, and we sallied forth. A cab quickly transported us to Rathbone Place. Fortunately, although the portfolio-maker's shop was closed, the ingenious inventor himself was at home. His lordship introduced me as " a friend," who wished to make himself acquainted with the peculiarities and merits of the " patent portfolio." The task of inspection was rather a long one, but still interesting. I had had no idea until that moment how capable this very useful article was of improvement.

Whatever the hand of genius touches is transformed.

Here, what was originally merely an empty bookcover was transformed into a safe receptacle, amply secured from dust and inquisitive inspection. But as it was portable, of course it was not free from the casualty of being " boned " by German spies. I saw a duplicate of the lost portfolio; it was of so marked a character that it would have been impossible to mistake it. I ordered one exactly like it, upon which his lordship requested that Mr. Harvey would send the bill to *him*.

Armed with this acquired intelligence, we next directed our steps towards that questionable territory, Leicester Square.

Entering one of the *restaurants* that invite the hungry passer-by to comfort his inner man, we seated ourselves at a table at the upper extremity of the room, and quietly surveyed the guests scattered about, as well as the clouds of vile tobacco smoke would permit. We called for coffee.

When the *garçon* brought it I gave him a shilling, and refused to take the change. This unusual liberality

won the youth's heart. In a whisper I inquired if Herr
Trübner had been there that night.

"No, m'sieu, he is very late this evening; but I
expect him every minute.''

We waited, and pretended to drink our coffee; but it
was impossible to swallow the vile compound of chicory,
horse beans, and roasted carrots : the mawkish liquid
was perfectly innocent of the fragrant berry.

Ten o'clock struck, but no Trübner. His lordship
had become very nervous and fidgety.

"*Garçon*, do you know where Trübner lives ? "

"No, m'sieu, but I think Hans does. Hans! Hans!
hi ! "

A comical-looking individual responded to this summons. He appeared to be the "drudge" of the establishment : rough flaxen hair, face begrimed with grease and
soot, and such hands! What if he proved to be the cook?

"Hans, do you know where Herr Trübner lives?"

"Yah ! Number —, Bedford Street. Shall I show
de shentlemans?"

"No, thank you, Hans ; here's sixpence for you."

"Dank you, m'sieu. You go up von pair, two pair de
stair, den anoder stairs, and you vil come to Herr
Trübner's chamberen. Knock once—twice—den you
go in.''

Thanking Hans again for his information, we bent
our steps towards Bedford Street, and soon reached the
number indicated. From the opposite side of the
street I reconnoitred the house. It appeared in total

darkness—not a glimmer of light at any of the windows. Crossing over, I found the door ajar. Leaving his lordship outside in the street, I crept softly up the dark staircase.

I had to grope and feel my way at every step. A more crooked affair I never encountered than that staircase. I would lift my foot, expecting it to alight upon an ascending stair, when it would prove a descending one, and down I would go, with my head against a partition, with force enough to split it or my head. I grew tired of this kind of sport, and drawing my match-box from my pocket, I lit a vesta, and by its light made an easy ascent.

Just as I came within sight of the door of what I concluded to be the German's room my light went out, and I did not think it advisable to renew it.

Arrived at the door, I knocked, but no answer.

Next I tried the handle; the door was locked. I had no alternative but to beat a retreat, and I had just turned to do so, when I heard the sound of voices and footsteps ascending the stairs.

I drew myself up in one corner of the landing, out of the track of the way to the room, and made myself as small as possible. The voices and footsteps gradually ascended. The discourse was in German, and the invisible speakers appeared in high glee.

They unlocked the door and entered the room.

I could hear the snapping of a lucifer-match, followed by a glimmer of light shining under the door.

It was necessary that I should make up my mind quickly what course to pursue. I was not long about it. In another moment I had passed the Rubicon, and stood in the presence of a couple of hairy-visaged Deutschmen, who were busily engaged with a pair of pliers endeavouring to break open the lock of a port-folio—*that* portfolio.

" You have stolen that," I said. " I will thank you to give it to me."

The sound of my voice seemed to restore them their wits, somewhat scattered by my sudden intrusion. In an instant the fellow who held the portfolio blew out the light, and, at the same moment, his partner, a powerful rascal, rushed at me, seized me by the throat, and nearly garotted me.

" Hands off, you villain !" I growled, as soon I could get breath; and then I showed him a gipsy trick that I learned when a boy, and he would have measured his length on the floor, had he not come in contact with a large trunk that intercepted his fall. He managed to pull me down with him, and by some means I found myself prostrate on my face and hands, and before I could recover myself the other rascal was upon me.

But I did not lose heart. I was determined to die game. I was only afraid that the cowardly villains might use knives upon me, according to foreign custom. The thought made me desperate. I strained every muscle to free myself from my assailant, but in vain. He had taken me at disadvantage.

I was on my back. My foe had inserted his fingers in my stock, and I found my breath going, when luckily the buckle gave way. He then commenced pommelling my face with his clenched fists : all I could do was to kick the air.

What was the other rascal doing all this while ?

I had enough to do without minding him ; but I managed to observe that, upon receiving some hint from my antagonist, he quitted the room.

The room, you will remember, was in total darkness, except the faint light from the gas-lamp in the street. I managed to get one arm free, and partially raise myself. Having accomplished this, my strength returned, and I was soon able to hit right and left. One blow I am sure did execution, for I felt hot drops of blood trickle down on my face. I grappled my foe by his coat collar, and with a sudden spring regained my feet.

Now Richard was himself again !

I felt for my adversary, but he did not come within arm's length. I thought he had beat a retreat, so I made for the door as well as I could in the darkness. I then discovered that my gentleman was sneaking downstairs. I quickly followed, and had just passed the first flight when I became aware of an altercation going on lower down, followed by cries of—

"Help ! help !"

It was his lordship's voice !

I do not like fighting in the dark—you cannot tell friend from foe.

I lost no time, you may be sure, in making my way down the staircase; but I got my matches out as I went along, and before I reached the scene of action I was in a position to throw some light on the business.

On the lower landing I could see his lordship grasping one of my adversaries by the collar, the fellow with the portfolio under his arm, who was endeavouring, with might and main, to free himself. Midway between myself and this animated group I could see Trübner hastening to the rescue of his friend. There was no time to lose. I made a spring, and came down full weight on the back of the spy, and quickly brought him to his knees, then gave him a blow that completely knocked the wind out of him.

I was now enabled to hasten to his lordship's assistance; but before I could reach him the other villain had managed to break loose, leaving the collar of his coat in his lordship's hands. I quickly followed in pursuit; but the fellow, in passing out at the street door, pulled it violently after him and closed it. Some time was lost in finding the latch, and, upon re-opening the door and getting into the street, the fugitive was nowhere to be seen.

"How very unfortunate! The rascal has got my portfolio!" exclaimed his lordship impatiently.

It was raining very hard when we emerged into the street, and as we passed into the Strand we were very glad to take shelter under a gateway.

"I am afraid we must give it up as a bad job. How very provoking !"

"I shall not give up the game yet. Fortune may do more for us than we can do for ourselves."

We were not the only occupants of the gateway ; the sudden shower had driven in a motley crew of way-farers, some of whom were quite concealed in the darkness. We had waited about ten minutes, and then the storm had begun to abate. Just as we were about to quit our shelter a fellow sneaked out of the darkness into the street, and made off down the Strand at a very rapid pace. My eyes followed him mechanically. In about a minute the thought flashed into my mind that this was my late adversary, although, as I had not seen the fellow's face, it was but the merest surmise.

Communicating my suspicion to his lordship, we both immediately started in pursuit, avoiding, as much as possible, any movement that might attract public attention.

We gradually gained upon the fugitive, although his pace was very rapid. He appeared to suspect he was followed, and looked over his shoulder two or three times.

We passed Somerset House and the Strand Theatre, where we began to lose ground. I whispered to his lordship to keep me in view, for I was going to give chase ; when, upon arriving at Arundel Street, the fugitive suddenly turned the corner, and took to his heels.

He probably did not know that locality so well as I
did.   At the bottom of that street runs the river.   A
low parapet wall crosses the end, in which is an opening
to a flight of steps for the convenience of those who
hire boats at this place.

The fugitive reached this wall before finding out in
what direction he was going.   Seeing his onward
progress stopped, he rushed headlong down the steps.
It was high tide.   By the time I reached the wall he
was struggling in the stream.

"*Hilf ! hilf !*" he shrieked ; but the tide bore him on,
and his voice was soon inaudible.

You know the Thames police station is moored close
by Arundel Street.   I shouted :—

"Police !   Man overboard !"

In a few moments a boat pulled up at the stairs where
I was standing.   I jumped in, and, briefly explaining
what had occurred, we pulled into the stream.

It was very dark, and I doubt very much if I could
have perceived any floating object, let alone a drowning
man ; but the policemen who rowed the boat were
keener sighted.   They named several objects as we
passed along which were quite invisible to me.

Arrived at Blackfriars Bridge, we lay to.   Search
was made with the aid of a lantern into places where
the body might have been carried by the eddies.   But
the search proved fruitless.   We resumed our progress
down the stream.

Shortly before reaching London Bridge we encountered another police-boat. Upon hailing and pulling alongside, we found the crew busily engaged in lifting something heavy into their boat.

"What have you got there, mate?"

"A croaker, I should say!"

When their burden was hauled in, and laid in the bottom of the boat, I took the lantern, and held it to the drowned man's face, and instantly recognised the German, my adversary. His features were frightfully convulsed. One hand was crossed over his breast withinside his paletot. It grasped the LOST PORTFOLIO!

He had stuck to it to the last, even in the moment of extreme peril and death.

We landed the body at Blackfriars, and lost no time in obtaining the assistance of a surgeon; but when he arrived he only shook his head, and announced that the patient was beyond the reach of human help.

I next rowed back to Arundel Street, and landed there. I found his lordship walking up and down waiting for me. He had no idea what kind of a voyage I had taken. I placed the dripping portfolio in his hands. He looked at me for a moment in silent astonishment.

"It's wet. How is this?"

"The thief rushed into the river with it. He has met an untimely fate. Your portfolio was saved by a miracle. It has been in the river, and but for the tightness of the drowned man's grasp would have been lost. We recovered both."

We adjourned to a tavern in the Strand, where his

lordship opened the portfolio, expecting to find the papers it contained saturated with water. They were scarcely soiled.

What became of the spy I left on the stairs? Why, he made himself scarce for some time; but I kept a good look-out for him; and upon his first appearance in public he was arrested on another charge I had against him, duly tried, and convicted. He is now working out his sentence at Bermuda.

Look on that *what-not,* and you will see a *fac-simile* of the LOST PORTFOLIO.

His lordship made me a present of it. When I unlocked it I found inside a bran new one-hundred-pound note.

I feel myself greatly indebted indeed to the German spy, Herr Trübner.

THE GOLDEN-HAIRED WIG.

You remember that very long cold winter of 18—, when the frost continued from November to the end of March?

We got so accustomed to it that we never expected it would change. A good many curious adventures happened to me while that cold weather lasted, some of which I have already related to you. I shall now tell you my adventure with the GOLDEN-HAIRED WIG.

It was about the middle of December; the night was dark and stormy, and the cold intense. A dismal storm of sleet and snow was driving on the wind like spiteful mischief; but, notwithstanding the inclemency of the weather, I was out braving it in a horse and chaise on a very long journey. I had been down into Hertfordshire to inspect the traces left by some villains in a daring burglary committed at a nobleman's mansion, and having completed my task, was hastening back to town, where my presence was urgently needed on another affair no less important.

You know that every noted burglar has his own peculiar style of carrying on his operations. By an

P

inspection of the premises it is easy for a detective to tell whether Bandy Bill or Bosky Bob be the artist. In the case I had been inspecting I was sure that Bandy Bill had been at work.

The burglars had been disturbed while engaged at their work, and made a precipitate retreat, not without carrying off considerable plunder, however. The butler had fired a blunderbuss, loaded with swan-shot and slugs, at the retreating burglars; and it was supposed that the charge had taken effect, for traces of blood were distinctly visible on the gravel-walk, along which the robbers had hastily retreated.

Bandy Bill was pretty well known to me. He had often been in trouble, and I had frequently been his guardian. You never would have taken him for a desperate burglar. He was a little active fellow, slightly made, with hair of a peculiar golden brown colour, smooth visaged, with no beard, nor a particle of hair on his face, although he must have been at least seven-and-twenty years of age. I believe he was a Welshman; but that's neither here nor there. I only know that he was a daring, desperate fellow, who stood at nothing in accomplishing his designs.

Why was he called Bandy? Well, he *was* rather queer about the legs, it is true; but, as he usually wore loose sailors' trousers, this defect of nature was not so very conspicuous. Had he been a woman, why, of course, nobody would ever have known of his peculiarity.

But to return to the road. About nine o'clock I found

myself approaching the neighbourhood of Waltham. My fast mare seemed quite exhilarated by the storm, and dashed along "light and swift," imparting some of her own dash to my drooping spirits; and the prospect of a good supper and a roaring fire soon rose as a bright vision to my mind's eye.

The village—or town I think they call it—was about a couple of miles in the rear, and we were bowling along at full speed, when suddenly my mare shied—so suddenly, in fact, as nearly to jerk me out of the chaise. Looking out into the darkness to ascertain the cause of this very unusual conduct on the part of the faithful animal, I discerned a dark object in the snow, lying a little on one side of the road, which I imagined to be a human being.

I well knew that no man or woman could survive exposure to the cold on such a night as that, so I jumped out of the vehicle to see if it really were some poor creature whom it was my duty to save from perishing.

I found my surmise realised. The form was that of a woman, but of what age or condition the darkness prevented my discerning. I could feel the bonnet and woollen shawl, and that decided me. My duty was clear, for the person, whoever it might be, was apparently benumbed with cold, and fast sinking into that torpor from which there is no awaking.

I raised her—she was rather heavy—and lifted her into the vehicle, intending to convey her to the nearest inn, where she could receive proper aid and shelter. I wrapped her in a large horseman's cloak upon which I had been sitting, and, propping her up as well as I could, drove on, musing on the pleasing theme of my own philanthropy.

Before long, however, this comfortable feeling of self-complacency gave way, and was succeeded by a less satisfactory feeling. I remembered that footpads frequently disguised themselves as women, and being treated to "a lift," by generous and unsuspecting travellers, turned suddenly on their benefactors and robbed them of their money, sometimes making a pretty good haul, when the victim happened to be a country farmer returning from market with his pockets filled with the proceeds of his sales of produce or stock.

This suspicious feeling gained upon me every moment, and was in no respect diminished by my companion pressing very heavily upon me. All things considered, my situation was far from enviable. Here I might be sitting cheek by jowl with one of the greatest villains in the kingdom. I would gladly have got rid of my anonymous companion, but as yet there was no excuse for dropping her in the road. I resolved to stop at the first inn we came to, and leave her there. Soon one came in view, and I attempted to rein in the mare; but when I endeavoured to do so, found, to my amazement and horror, that the reins were no longer between my fingers: the cold had so benumbed them that the reins had slipped down. I was afraid to stoop to feel for the reins, lest my companion might take advantage of my position; so, after a moment's reflection, I resolved to rouse my equivocal travelling companion, and at once commenced the operation. I took off my glove, and put my hand to her cheek—it was *warm*. I then felt her hands—they were warm too. I had a flask of brandy in my breast coat pocket. I put it to her lips, and she sucked down the cordial with remarkable avidity. I had hopes now of a speedy and complete revival. I spoke a few words of inquiry, but gained no response except a groan, followed by a deep sigh.

It *must* be a woman after all!

Meanwhile the mare continued to dash along at her own free will with unabated speed. I had no control over her, but every confidence in her sagacity. At this rate, I thought, we shall soon reach a turnpike, and then we *must* stop. And in a few moments, in fact, the mare came to a stand-still.

"Gate! gate!" I shouted.

The toll-keeper came out with a lantern. Now then, I thought, I shall see what sort of a companion I have got.

I turned to look at her. The head was drooping, but I could see that it was covered with a profusion of curly hair—long ringlets of a very peculiar colour. Some envious people might have called it *red*; but I, who have some taste in hair, especially woman's hair, pronounced the colour to be golden brown.

I nudged my companion gently.

" Wake up, if you please, ma'am. Wouldn't you like to get out and warm yourself by the toll-keeper's fire ? "

No answer—only a groan and a sigh, as before.

" Better drive on to town, Mr. F——," said the toll-keeper; " the road's not very safe at this time o' night. Got your pistols, sir, I suppose ? "

At hearing this my companion slowly raised her head, and, with widely-opened eyes (I could see no more of her face), took a keen survey of *mine*, but said nothing. I picked up the reins, and started afresh, in the hope that another half-hour would put an end to my very uncomfortable state of suspense.

But I did not feel myself at all reassured in thinking over matters, so I made up my mind to prepare for the worst. I turned to drop my whip into the rest, spoke a few words to my mare, and began to whistle to keep up my courage.

" Steady, Polly; steady, old gal."

I wore on this occasion an overcoat made of thick box-cloth, not over-long in the skirts, but long enough to reach to my knees : there were pockets in front, in one of which I carried a pair of bracelets, and in the other a pistol.

As I slightly turned to deposit the whip into its receptacle, my companion suddenly struck my left hand, by which I held the reins, and, with his other hand, gave me a blow on the head, sending my hat spinning into the road.

The sudden jerk on the reins caused the mare to stop

and rear, and I very nigh lost my balance. This, together with the blow on my head, had nearly sent me tumbling into the road; but I am rather solid in the flesh, and therefore quickly regained my seat.

At the same moment my companion leaped from the gig, and, on reaching the ground, struck my mare a blow on the haunch. The mare started, and doubtless would have made off, had I not fortunately retained a firm hold of the reins.

Whatever doubt I might have previously entertained as to the character or sex of my companion, it was now pretty evident that she or he "was no good." The thought flashed into my mind that it was Bandy Bill, and the colour of the hair strengthened my suspicion.

There was a reward of £250 offered for the apprehension of this rascal, and I felt that I must use every effort to capture him.

But I was in an awkward fix. Upon leaping from the chaise, the rascal scrambled over a gate into a field, where, of course, I could not follow him with the mare.

Generally speaking, the intelligent creature was obedient as a dog; but as she had been somewhat flurried by the unusual treatment she had received, I could hardly make up my mind to leave her alone in the high road at that hour. But there was Bandy Bill almost within my grasp. I felt that I must run all risks to secure *him*.

I drew the chaise as close to the side of the road as possible, and fastened the reins to the wheel, patted the

mare on the neck, and spoke a few soothing words to
her.

" Steady, Polly; steady, old gal."

She showed her impatience by pawing the ground
furiously and champing her bit. As I turned to cross
into the field, she looked after me and neighed.

" Steady, old gal, steady."

All this was but the work of a moment. I had no
time to look for my hat, so I bounded over the gate in
double-quick time. I could see the dark figure of Bandy
Bill relieved against the white snow about a hundred
yards ahead. Supposing him to be incumbered with
petticoats, I reckoned that I should soon overtake him.
But he began to throw away his incumbrances : first
came the bonnet and wig, next the woollen shawl, then
a skirt that served, I suppose, for gown and petticoats
in the disguise he had assumed. Of course I did not
stop to pick up those articles *then*.

Bandy Bill was an active little fellow, as I have told
you, and he made his way across the field with wonderful
agility. I can skim the ground myself at a very good
pace ; but I soon found that I should have hard work
to overtake Bill. He seemed to know the ground
thoroughly, for he struck diagonally across to a gate,
bounded over it, and before I reached it was half way
across the next field. My blood was up. I gave hot
chase. He reached another gate, cleared that, and was
out of sight. When I reached that gate I found that it
opened, not into another field, but into a narrow lane.

I could see nothing of Bill; he might have turned to the right, or he might have turned to the left. I was completely at fault. I paused to listen, but could hear no sound except the whistling of the wind through the trees. He might be within a few feet of where I was standing: I should have been none the wiser. If he were armed I was completely at his mercy; for, sheltered as he was by the darkness of the lane, I should have proved an easy mark for him, while I was powerless to act either on the offensive or defensive.

I was anxious about my mare, which I had left standing in the road. Bill might double and make off with her. I at once attempted to retrace my steps—a task of no little difficulty, on account of the blinding storm of snow and sleet. Besides, I had no Bill now to guide me to the gates.

I blundered along, trusting to "fate and metaphysical aid," and soon reached the first fence. I looked for the gate as well as the darkness permitted; but not finding it, I forced a passage through the hedge, and in this way I managed at length to regain the turnpike road.

But there was no mare and gig in sight. As I had not returned by exactly the same path as I first crossed the fields, it was probable that I had emerged somewhere above or below the spot where I had fastened the mare; so I wended my way along the road, hoping soon to come upon her.

I plodded on for, I should say, at least half a mile

without seeing anything of my mare. I was then forced
to conclude that I had started from a point in advance
of where I had left her; so I retraced my steps in no
very amiable mood, I can assure you.

I had not proceeded far before I became aware of the
approach of a vehicle. I could hear, but not see it.
As it came nearer I drew on one side of the road.
Presently it dashed past me at a furious rate. The
glance I had of it was but momentary, yet I made
no doubt of its being my own mare and chaise;
nor was I less sure that they were driven by Bandy
Bill.

I had heard him lashing the whip—my whip—as he
approached and passed by. He had goaded the mare
up to a pace of at least fourteen miles an hour. For a
moment I was confounded with rage and indignation.
To be done in that manner by such a rascal! I felt
my character was gone. I should be the laughing-
stock of my brother officers. The thought was un-
endurable.

I had my hands in my pockets while I was walking
along the road, retracing my steps, and at the instant
the chaise and mare passed me, driven as I had no doubt
by Bandy Bill, I drew out my pistol and fired in
the direction he had gone. It was too dark to take
aim, and there was little probability that the bullet
would take effect; but I did not consider my ammunition
wasted, as the report, I hoped, might bring me assistance,
if any happened to be near.

A minute or two after I had fired my pistol I heard the report of another shot in the direction the chaise had gone. I did not know what to make of this, but I immediately hastened along the road, and in a few minutes came upon a saddle-horse standing in the middle of the road, but without his rider, who was lying on the ground at the animal's feet, with the reins tightly grasped in his hand.

I stooped down, and addressing the prostrate man, inquired of him what was the matter.

"Oh, that villain has shot me ! I am badly wounded. I 'm very faint, but never mind me. Take my horse, and pursue the villain."

I gently removed the wounded man on to the pathway skirting the road, and following his advice, mounted his horse and started in pursuit.

Giving the animal the rein, I soon urged it into a fast gallop. Its pace was splendid. My mare, harnessed to the gig, could but trot. At the pace I was now hurrying along, I had no doubt that I should soon overtake her. I hoped that at least a wheel would come off, or some other accident enable me to come up with the object of my pursuit.

I knew that there was another toll-gate within a mile or so, and I had every hope that it might be the occasion of either impeding or altogether stopping Bill's progress.

Soon I observed a moving light at some distance in advance. This I had no doubt was the toll-gate. In a few seconds I was there. I found my mare and chaise in the custody of the toll-keeper, but Bandy Bill was missing.

A few words of explanation informed me that the toll-keeper had been roused by the cry of " Gate." Upon coming out he found the mare with the chaise at the gate, but no driver.

I concluded that Bandy Bill, hearing the sound of the horse's feet, knew that he was pursued, and had thought it wise to make off.

I informed the toll-keeper of the wounded man I had left on the road, and having seen him and his son set off on horseback to the poor fellow's aid, I proceeded to the nearest inn, whence I dispatched a messenger to town with information of what had occurred, and requesting that assistance might be immediately sent to me. I concluded that Bandy Bill would conceal himself in the neighbourhood somewhere, and not dare to venture into London.

As soon as day broke I repaired to the scene of the previous night's encounter. My hat I found lying in a ditch, and in the field where Bandy Bill first entered I found his shawl, bonnet, wig, and the skirt that served him for gown and petticoats. These I brought away with me, as a matter of course.

We examined the ground around the toll-gate, to discover, if possible, the traces of Bill's footsteps after he got out of the gig. The snow had ceased falling about the time of his arrival at the gate, and we could not only trace footsteps into a field upon the snow, but there were also drops of blood on the track. My random shot at Bill had hit him, although the wound did not appear to be very serious, for he seemed in no way disabled. Seeing these spots of blood in the snow prompted me to examine my chaise: there I found some little blood on the seat and bottom. I therefore concluded Bill had been hit in the arm.

We followed the traces of the footsteps and blood for a considerable distance across several fields, until we came upon a by-road or lane, where we encountered some difficulty, for the snow had been trodden down by passengers. Still with diligence we were enabled to follow up the traces for nearly three miles, till they stopped at a cattle-shed in a field some little distance from the road.

Beyond this all traces of blood were lost; the marks of the footsteps we had first seen at the toll-gate were no longer visible, having been trodden out by way-farers. We continued along the road, however, passing several humble cottages, at which we made inquiries, but with no result. At last we reached a little ale-house, and there we concluded to halt, and hold a council of war as to the next move to be taken.

We called for refreshment, and inquired of the land-lord, "What news?" He had none to tell. We then told *him* some, and informed him of the object of our pursuit.

"Bandy Bill, you said, I think? If so be he is wanted, I suppose there's a reward offered for him?"

" Two hundred and fifty pounds."

" Paid when ? "

" On his conviction."

" And no mistake ? "

"And no mistake.   I 'll give you my word for it."

" Well, I dare say it 's all right, but you 're strangers
to me, gentlemen. Now, suppose I show you where
Bandy Bill is, what security will you give me that I
shall get the reward ? "

" I 'll give you a writing, to the effect that it is upon
your information we are enabled to discover and arrest
Bandy Bill, *alias* Joe Lee, *alias* William Barlow, and a
dozen other *aliases*."

" Agreed, give me the writing."

I wrote out the agreement, with which the landlord
expressed himself satisfied.

" What 's Bandy wanted for this time, I should
like to know ? "

" Oh ! for a burglary, and an attempt to murder."

" Well, gentlemen, that individual is in my house.
You will find him in bed upstairs."

" Then show us the way, if you please."

Opening a door at the end of a passage, he pointed
with his hand up a narrow crooked staircase. We
understood.

" Second door on the left. You won't want me, I
suppose ? "

" We can do without you."

As quietly and as cautiously as possible I ascended

the stairs, and, having reached the landing, awaited the
ascent of a brother officer. I did not think it necessary
to knock at the door; so putting my shoulder to it,
and seizing the latch at the same time, I was soon in
the presence of Mr. Bandy Bill.

He had evidently been awoke out of a sound sleep.
He slowly raised himself in bed, displaying a blood-
stained shirt.

"Good morning, sir," said I. "Sorry to disturb
you, but——"

"What the —— do you want?"

"Want you, Mr. Lee; so rouse up, quick."

"I'll see you —— first!"

And he threw himself back in the bed again. We
had much difficulty in rousing him to a proper consciousness of his situation. Loss of blood had probably
weakened his intellects a little.

The sight of the ruffles, however, convinced him of
the real state of things; but he obstinately refused
to get up, and as he seemed much exhausted, we
humoured him, and let him have a good sleep.

About noon we prepared to start. A butcher's cart
was hired, and in the course of that evening Bandy
Bill made his fortieth entrance through a prison gate.

Of course he was tried, and found guilty. Sentence
of death was commuted to transportation for life.

The wig? Oh! I had forgotten that. Of course it
was produced at the trial, and caused much amusement

and curiosity. It was certainly a very remarkable head of hair, and no little curiosity was excited to know how Bill came possessed of it.

After the trial a fashionable hair-dresser at the West End called upon me about that wig. He believed it was one that had been stolen from him in a very mysterious manner. It was so peculiar in colour that the hair-dresser set great store by it ; he regarded it as something quite unique, and said he would not have taken a hundred pounds for it.

When I showed him the wig he identified it instantly. His joy knew no bounds. I was quite loath to part with it; but he made me a very handsome present.

I asked him if he knew the owner, and he told me the following story :—

" Some two years ago I was sent for to Mivart's hotel, to dress the hair of a young lady who was going to the opera. I was particularly struck with the colour and fine texture of her hair. Both qualities were very remarkable ; so much so, that never in the course of my long practice as a hair-dresser had I seen so beautiful a head of hair, either in colour, quality, or profusion.

" I was called several times to attend professionally upon this young lady, who appeared to be about twenty years of age, exceedingly beautiful, and accomplished. From what dropped from her maid I gathered that the lady was a Hungarian of noble family : she was accompanied by her mother. There was some mystery connected with them, which of course I took no trouble to penetrate. My attendance upon the lady continued several months, and suddenly terminated without any notice being given to me.

"About two years afterwards I was surprised one day by a visit from the young lady. She was accompanied by her mother. My professional services were put into requisition, during which she asked me what such a head of hair as hers was worth.

"The question surprised me, and I had an inkling of the probable motive of her asking it.

"I replied that upon a head of hair of such singular beauty it would be difficult to fix a proper value. I would be glad to obtain it for twenty-five guineas.

"She exchanged some words in a foreign tongue with her mother; then addressing me, she said,—

"'Doubtless twenty-five guineas is as much as it is worth. I would part with it for fifty.'

"When I had named five-and-twenty guineas, it was at a mere venture, for I did not suppose money would buy it. Now I saw it could be obtained, I would have bid a hundred, and willingly have given it.

"'If it can be had for fifty guineas, mademoiselle,' I replied, 'I will give that sum for it.'

"'Then take it,' she replied.

"I hesitated; it seemed desecration, almost sacrilege, to rob that fair head of its beautiful ornament.

"'You hesitate,' she said; 'but you need not. Circumstances of a very painful nature compel me to make the sacrifice. We are strangers in a foreign country, and cannot make our necessities known even to those who would gladly relieve them.'

" This was spoken in very good English, although with a foreign accent. I could sympathise with the ladies in their distress, and was upon the eve of offering to lend her the sum she required ; but, upon reflection, I did not.

" She seated herself again in the chair, saying, ' Why do you not take it ? '

" I could see but one solution to the question ; so I took my scissors, and commenced, I must say reluctantly, to perform my profane task.

" I gave her the money. She seemed exceedingly gratified, and took her departure.

" I had the hair made into a wig, and in due season it was placed under a glass shade in my shop-window.

" It had not been exhibited there many weeks, when one day a tall, military-looking gentleman came in, and eagerly inquired where I had obtained that wig.

" ' I know of but one person to whom it could have belonged,' he observed, taking out a pocket-book, and removing from it a piece of folded paper. Opening this, a lock of hair of exactly the same colour as that of the wig was displayed.

" ' You see it matches exactly.'

" ' It does indeed.'

" ' Can you tell me how you came possessed of this hair ? Was it from the owner ? '

" ' It was. I cut it from her head with my own hands.'

" ' Then you can tell me where I may find her ?'

" ' I regret to say I cannot. Two years ago she was staying at Mivart's ; but I do not suppose she is there now.'

" A few weeks afterwards I was one morning passing St. George's, Hanover Square, while a grand wedding was going on. I was prompted to pass under the portico just at the moment when the newly-married couple were proceeding to their carriage.

" Judge of my astonishment when in the lady I recognised the original proprietor of the golden-haired wig : the gentleman was the same who called upon me with the lock of hair that so exactly matched the wig."

That was the hair-dresser's story. You see even a wig may experience many vicissitudes in its career.

MONEYBAGS AND SON.

CHAPTER I.

ONE morning—it is a good many years ago, before the alterations were made in that quarter—I received a hasty summons from old Moneybags, the wholesale grocer of Eastcheap. I promptly obeyed the summons, and upon entering the counting-house I saw a feeble old man, with palsied head and hands, seated before a long desk, covered with piles of gold, silver, bank notes, cheques, bills, &c., which he was counting and assorting.

It was a melancholy spectacle to see this frail piece of humanity, for whom the grave must have been yawning, so deeply absorbed with the dross of life. All his faculties—and they were not many—seemed centred in the contemplation of his money. He was so deeply absorbed in his idolatry that he did not perceive my entrance. I paused, without making a noise, to contemplate the singular spectacle of an old man, verging on eighty, gloating over that for which, perhaps, he had sacrificed everything a rational being would prize in life, and from which he must, however reluctantly, so very soon be called upon to part.

I made a slight noise to arrest his attention. He looked up, at the same moment spreading out his arms so as to cover and embrace his treasures, and in agitated voice inquired,—

"What do you want here? Mr. Barton," calling to his managing clerk, "why do you let people come in here?"

"This is Mr. F——, sir, whom you desired me to send for."

"Oh, Mr. F——! Ha! yes; I think I *do* want him. I think I do, indeed. Take a seat, Mr. F——. I will attend to you directly. O dear me!"

I took a seat as directed, and the old man resumed his task. It seemed a mortal struggle with him to tear himself away from his favourite occupation of counting his money, and he very soon appeared to forget my presence altogether.

Growing impatient, I made a shuffling noise with my feet.

"In a minute, Mr. F——, in a minute."

It was a very long minute. However, he managed at last to tear himself away from his darling occupation, and came and seated himself in a chair opposite to where I was seated.

"Would you mind shutting that door and locking it?"

I did as he desired, and resumed my seat.

"You must know, Mr. F——, I have been robbed."

"Very sorry to hear it, sir. What is your loss?"

"Impossible to tell, sir. It has been going on a long time."

"What have you lost, sir?"

"Money, sir, money! You see that iron chest outside there? Well, sir, as I thought lately that the banks were not over safe, I have kept a deal of money there, all in gold, to provide for a rainy day. I locked up one drawer full, and was filling another; but to-day, when I opened that drawer to see if it was all safe, I found it nearly empty. I shall be ruined, sir! I always said I should die in the workhouse, and now it is inevitable."

I could hardly repress a smile. Crœsus in the workhouse—that would be a sight worth seeing.

"Not so bad as that, sir, I hope."

"Ah! you don't know all. I must have lost twelve hundred pounds. Isn't that enough to ruin any man?"

"It would ruin me, sir, without doubt; but as for you, Mr. Moneybags, the world knows you are very rich."

"The world's a fool, sir; the world's an ass, sir; it knows nothing at all about it."

"Well, sir, what do you wish me to do in the matter?"

"Get me my money back, and punish the rogue; that is all I ask of you. Can you do that?"

"That depends, sir, very much upon who is the thief. Will you show me how the robbery has been effected?"

"There's the iron safe, and there's the drawer in

which the gold was kept. They have been opened, sir, but without violence."

"Perhaps with your own keys, Mr. Moneybags."

"That's impossible. I always lock the safe up, and take the keys home with me, and never let them out of my sight."

I carefully examined the safe and the locks, and then observed,—

"It must be somebody in the establishment, depend upon it, sir. No one could have opened that safe while you are here, nor while you are absent except with your key, or its duplicate."

"But do you think so, Mr. F——? Do you really think so?"

"It must be so, sir, as no burglary has been committed."

"But some one may have had false keys to the outer door."

"That is true; but, as no violence has been employed, I must think it is some one belonging to the establishment."

"Impossible! Mr. Barton, only think—Mr. F—— says this robbery must have been committed by some one in the establishment."

"I think so myself, sir."

"You do, do you? Then why didn't you say so before?"

"I did not like to encourage my own suspicions till they occurred to another person. Since Mr. F—— is of that opinion, I have now no hesitation in saying I think as he does—it is some one in the establishment."

"That is really very dreadful.   Only to think——But you have not told me whom you suspect."

"Nor shall I, sir.   That will be Mr. F——'s business to find out."

"Well, Mr. F——, lose no time in finding me the thief, and do not fail to bring me back my money. Bring me the money, remember."

I had a little confidential talk with Mr. Barton, upon which I formed my plans.

"Of course, Mr. Barton," I said, "you will keep this robbery quite secret for the present.   My success depends entirely upon things going on as usual in your establishment, without the slightest suspicion that the robbery has been discovered."

That night I was on the watch.   The house opposite being uninhabited, I took possession of it.   The rats resented the intrusion.   Nothing unusual transpired that night, nor the next.

Sunday night came.   At about a quarter-past twelve o'clock, as I was looking through the window, I saw a tall, gentlemanly young man walking slowly up and down in front of the premises, and then let himself in.

I let myself out quietly, and took up my position in the dark recess of the doorway, patiently awaiting the re-appearance of the visitor to old Moneybags' warehouse.

In about half an hour he came out, and locked the door after him; then proceeded towards Cheapside, followed at a prudent distance by your humble servant.

He took a cab. I did the same. Passed along Cheapside, Holborn, Oxford Street, to the corner of Rathbone Place. There he alighted, and I followed his example. Proceeding up the Place about half way, he stopped and knocked at a door. A panel was opened by a porter to reconnoitre; a pass-word being given, the door was then opened, and the gentleman admitted. I was so close upon his heels that I passed in with him unchallenged, being taken, I presume, for an associate.

I found myself in a very strange place. The inmates were mostly foreigners, engaged in smoking, drinking, fiddling, and dancing. Such a pandemonium I have rarely seen. It was Sunday night, remember, or rather Monday morning.

My gentleman seemed quite at home there. He was " hail fellow " with most of the company, and seemed to be a great favourite with the ladies present, most of whom were of a very slippery sort. He was liberal withal, and treated the company all round *ad libitum*. It was very easy to see that he had never worked for the money he spent so freely.

The debauch was kept up till five in the morning. My gentleman had much ado to free himself from the drunken embraces of the two or three ladies who were not helplessly intoxicated. It was only by ordering them fresh liquor that he managed to get into the street unattended by them.

He staggered a little upon attaining the open air. In Oxford Street he called a cab, and ordered it to drive to Notting Hill. Of course I stuck to his heels, and, to my utter astonishment, I saw him, after he got out of the cab, go up to the door of Moneybags' private residence and let himself in.

"So, then," I thought, "this is a family affair after all. Moneybags, senior, is robbed by Moneybags, junior." There could be no mistake in this affair; the prodigal son was only squeezing the senior's sponge, helping himself to what he probably thought his own by right of inheritance.

Had it been a mere matter of feeling, I should have proceeded no farther in the business; but I had a duty to my client to perform, and I resolved to discharge it.

My first step was to communicate with Mr. Barton, and ascertain his views as to the course I ought to adopt. He was not in the least surprised when I informed him of what I had seen.

He thought I ought to see more, and suggested that I should follow up the junior for a week or two.

"At present," I said, "I cannot say that he is actually the thief, as I have not seen him in the act. He *might* have visited the warehouse with other objects than that of plundering the iron safe."

"Very true; then perhaps you had better be quite

satisfied. Conceal yourself in the warehouse next
Sunday night. I will arrange to let you in."

" That 's the plan. I think about ten o'clock will be
the right time."

I consequently arranged to be concealed in the warehouse on the following Sunday night ; for that, I concluded, would be the night selected for the prodigal's
next visit.

Accordingly, the next Sunday night saw me duly
ensconced behind a tall pile of chests of tea, where I
could have a clear view of the iron safe without any
risk of being seen myself.

Very shortly after the neighbouring church clock had
struck twelve I heard the door of the warehouse opened,
closed again, and locked. Then a match was struck,
and a wax taper lighted, the light being shaded by the
hat of the intruder—young Moneybags.

He walked straight to the iron chest, applied a key,
and opened it. Then he opened one of the drawers
containing gold, looked in, then opened the other.
From this latter he took a handful of gold, and dropped
it into a little canvas bag. Judging from the sound,
I should say there were forty or fifty sovereigns. He
then relocked the drawers and the safe, and prepared to
retire.

I don't know how it happened—never could tell ;
but perhaps, in my eagerness to survey every movement,
I pressed too heavily against the lofty pile of tea-chests.
They reached to the ceiling, and were rather top heavy ;

but over they went, and three or four of the top ones
came down with a crash on the floor —down on the
floor, just within a few inches of the iron safe, as
suddenly and with almost as loud a report as if a
gun had been fired.

Out went the light, of course. I heard the hat fall
upon the floor, accompanied with a sudden exclamation
of fright and terror—then a silent pause.

"My God! what can that be?"

All was then as still as death for at least fifteen
minutes. I scarcely breathed, but waited patiently for
the *dénouement*.

I concluded young Moneybags was more frightened
than hurt, for I could hear his loud breathing, mingled
with an occasional sigh. His fright I could not
wonder at; for I was frightened myself—never more
so in my life.

After the lapse of about a quarter of an hour—
certainly the longest fifteen minutes I ever passed—I
heard a slight movement on the part of young Moneybags.

"What a villain I am! If that's the devil it just
serves me right. I deserve it, I do. To rob my poor
old father! Might have waited till he was in his grave
—couldn't have had to wait long, at all events."

This soliloquy was uttered in a tremulous voice,
occasionally interrupted with sobs. Mr. Moneybags
junior, was in a repentant mood.

"What had I best do? I suppose the d—d police

is alarmed, and listening at the keyhole, and when I go out he 'll take me into custody ; and to-morrow I shall have a public audience with the Lord Mayor, and the papers will be full of a case of 'Shocking Depravity.' Very respectable, really ! Well, I am in a d—d scrape ! It was a good job the whole warehouse did not come down on my head. I should have been buried in the ruins; and then—coroner's inquest—how puzzled they would have been—thought me a second Samson—pulled the old warehouse down on my own head—capital."

By this time young Moneybags had recovered his composure. He sought his match-box, struck a light, and, pulling out his cigar-case, coolly commenced blowing a cloud.

I was half afraid he would commence an investigation among the tea-chests, so I crouched down behind some that had not been overturned. Those that had fallen formed a sort of barricade between us. I could see him seated on a chair, calmly puffing his cigar, soliloquising:—

" By Jove, though, only think if one of those d—d things had come down on a fellow's head ! Narrow escape, I must confess ! Well, I dare say I deserved no better fate. This ought to be a warning to me. I 'll take it as such, and be a good boy for the future. Curse the gold, I say ! What good have I ever done with it ? and what good has it ever done me ? All squandered away upon a set of reps. What could I have been thinking of ? "

Thus the hours passed away in puffing and soliloquising till the clock struck five.

"Five o'clock!" he said. "Well, I think it is about time I made a move."

He then got up, and cautiously let himself out.

After waiting about half an hour I followed his example. Next day I sent a message to Mr. Barton, requesting that he would meet me at the Guildhall Coffee-house in the evening.

Before I related to him what I had seen he informed me of the *great fall in tea*, expressing his astonishment at so unusual an accident. He eagerly inquired what was the state of things at the time of my visit to the warehouse.

When I told him of the scene that had taken place at young Moneybags' visit he laughed immoderately.

"I hope it will have the effect of reforming him," said he. "His nerves are shaken by dissipation, and are not over strong ; and I have no doubt this accident has shaken them still more, for he has not been at business to-day. The old man is in a dreadful way, in consequence of losing the key of his iron chest."

A day or two afterwards I received another summons from old Moneybags, who, thinking that enough time had elapsed to enable me to discover the depredator, was getting impatient. I did not consider it advisable to inform him of what I then knew, as I was desirous of learning a little more of young Moneybags' pursuits. I satisfied him, however, by telling him that I thought I was on the track of the thief, but that to succeed in my efforts it would be prudent not to divulge anything at present.

"Do you know, Mr. F——," he said, "I have lost the key of my iron safe. What shall I do? This is very unaccountable, very mysterious. What had I best do?"

"I think, sir, you had best have your iron safe opened, and your money removed to a bank. Don't you consider the Bank of England safe enough for you, sir?"

"I must consider what you say. Oh, this loss will be the death of me!"

CHAPTER II.

It was summer time. In the evening I strolled up Pall Mall, and into the park. In passing one of the seats I observed it was occupied by two persons, male and female, engaged in earnest discourse. The woman appeared to be making a very strong appeal to her companion's feelings. I do not commonly play the eavesdropper, but here was something that instinctively roused my curiosity, for I felt convinced a scene in a domestic tragedy was being enacted; so I leaned against a neighbouring tree, where I could hear and see without being seen.

"Oh, Edward, consider the shame you will bring upon me—on me, who have sacrificed everything for you. Do have some pity, some feeling of honour."

"Don't be a fool! What would you have a fellow

do? Comply with your whims, and offend the old man, who will then leave all his money to charities, and cut me off with a shilling? Nonsense! preposterous!"

"But, Edward, consider my family—my father—my brothers. What must be the consequence when the truth becomes known! I dread the hour, and it cannot be long. Even now I suspect that my mother's suspicions are aroused."

"Can't you go away for awhile? Go on the Continent—anywhere till things are right again."

"But how can I? You know I should not be allowed to go away alone; and then if I am accompanied by whoever it may be, why of course the truth will become known; and then what difference will it make whether the discovery be made here or there? The consequences will be just the same."

"Well, it's an infernal mess, and I don't know what's to be done. Can't you think of something yourself? You women are always fertile in expedients."

"There is but one way, as I have often told you."

"Impossible! Don't mention it again, or you will make me angry."

"Then you have no honour—no feeling! Were I a man, I would sacrifice every prospect of gain to sustain a woman's reputation. You know, when that is lost, all is lost for her."

"Fiddle-de-dee! if you were a man you would do as a man does."

"You are young—have health, strength, talent.

Many men have begun the world penniless, and risen to fortune and distinction. Why should not you?"

"I wish to spare myself the trouble. My nest is feathered: why should I build another?"

"This discussion is idle. You know what risk I have run to meet you here. I will not go away unsatisfied. The suspense is killing me. Oh, Edward! if you loved me as you have so often said you did, you would not treat me thus."

"Love! That sort of thing is all very well in its place; but when it stands in the way of half a million of money, why then it's quite *another* thing."

"I see what it is; you will leave me to my shame—to brave the anger of my father—the revenge of my brothers, and—my mother. O, God! what a fool—what a wretch I have been!"

"You should have thought of all this before."

"I did; but I thought too much of you. Well, I deserve this punishment. The scales have fallen from my eyes. I now see that I have thrown myself away upon a man who cares nothing for me, who cannot see the value of such a sacrifice, but weighs his filthy gold in the scale against the honour, the happiness of her he pretended to love, but only to betray. I have heard that the warmest love turns to the bitterest hatred, and I feel it now—the poison is creeping through my veins. Think, Edward, think again, before it be too late."

"Hush! Consider where we are. Don't get up a scene here in public, for heaven's sake."

"A scene! What do you mean? Can I be as cold-blooded as you are? A scene! Ah! there will be scenes yet, such as I dare not contemplate. Now, Edward, let me ask you once more—it shall be the last time: will you be honourable and act like a man? You know my father is rich—not so rich as yours, it is true; but he will give us enough to begin the world with, and what need we fear? Oh! do not cast me away to shame and misery—to shame worse than death! I cannot endure the thought, Edward. *I* am the suitor now, not *you;* and I sue—for what? For the fulfilment of a promise so often made unsolicited. There is no time for dallying. I expected you would have come to-night prepared to act. I told you what I expected; but you seem inclined to do nothing but leave me to my fate."

The man rose to his feet.

"There is no use continuing this discussion. You had better go home; you will be missed, and then——"

"No, Edward, I will never return to that home until you have given me your solemn promise to make me your wife within one month."

"Impossible! Come away, it's getting late."

"Too late for me. You can go; I have nowhere to go to."

"Haven't you a home, foolish girl?"

"No home for *me* any longer, but a hell, where I suffer every torment of the damned. Go, Edward; you had *better* go. I shall never trouble you again."

"Well, I really must go. I have an appointment, and if you won't come along, why I must leave you here, which I am loath to do."

"Loath to leave me here? Is it worse to leave me here than to leave me to the shame and scorn of the world? No, here no one will harm me; but when I walk into the daylight——Oh, villain! go! go! go!"

"Well, if I must, I must; so good night, Henny."

Saying this, the gentleman coolly walked away, leaving the lady motionless on the seat. In a minute or two she raised her head to see if he were really gone.

"Cold-hearted villain! Cursed fool, I, to believe him!"

My indignation was roused. I followed in the footsteps of the recreant wretch to see if I could recognise him. Under the full glare of a gas-lamp I saw his face.

It was that of young Moneybags.

Upon making this discovery I turned slowly back to the seat where he had left the lady sitting, and I seated myself at the opposite end.

She sat unmoved. My proximity seemed to make no impression upon her.

I could sympathise with her feelings at that moment. I knew full well that no consolation I could offer would avail; but still I lingered on the seat, as much to protect her from insult as anything.

Thus we sat for nearly half an hour, when she uttered a suppressed groan, and gave a convulsive shudder. Lifting up her head, she seemed for the first time to be aware of my proximity. Straining her neck forward to catch a nearer view of my face, she exclaimed,—

" Edward !"

" It 's not Edward," I replied.

" Ah, no! I forgot : he 's gone. Curse him for a villain !"

" Shall I call him back ?"

" No ; let him go. I have done with *him* for ever, and with everybody. Oh, my poor heart, how it burns! Ah me !"

As well as the darkness permitted I endeavoured to look in her face. Suspicion flashed across my mind that she had probably taken poison. The shudder was repeated again and again, intermingled with groans.

" Are you ill, madam ?" I asked.

" Past all cure. Oh, if I could but see my poor mother !"

" Where does she live ? Shall I call assistance—a doctor ?"

" Nothing. I want nothing more in this world but to die in peace. God forgive me! I 've been very sinful."

A labouring man passing by at the moment, I beckoned him.

" Run !" I said. " Tell the first policeman you meet to bring a stretcher here—a lady 's dying."

The man hastened away, and in a few minutes returned with what I required, accompanied by a couple of policemen.

We laid the now helpless lady gently on the stretcher, and went out at the gate at Spring Gardens, where we found a cab. Putting her into it, we drove to Charing Cross Hospital.

Here she received every attention. The stomach pump was applied. It then became evident that she had taken laudanum.

There was no clue on her person by which we could discover who she was; consequently it was impossible to communicate with her friends, and in her state of unconsciousness it was useless to question her. As she was in good hands, and my presence of no avail, I quitted the hospital; somewhat cut up by this tragic feature in the Moneybags' case. I strolled listlessly down the Strand, and dropped into a certain notorious house in —— Street, thinking I might find something to divert the current of my gloomy thoughts, and perhaps pounce upon some of my black sheep.

The room was nearly filled with the reckless and dissolute of both sexes. Wishing to avoid observation, I quietly seated myself in a corner, from whence, unobserved, I could see what was passing.

The scene was not very edifying. It served but to show what a beast human nature can make of itself by "a base abandonment of reason." Drunkenness, profanity, thinly-disguised indecency, blasphemy — such were the talents displayed by these wanton imbeciles, who, under the flimsy plea of "seeing life," were grovelling in a sewer of moral filth.

My attention was directed, by the noise they made, to a group behind where I was seated, whom I had not noticed when I entered the room. I did not wish to turn my head, lest I might attract their attention; so I listened.

Their table was liberally supplied with the usual paraphernalia of debauchery—cigars and brandy. Their conversation was at first carried on in low tones, heightened occasionally with a blasphemous oath. Gradually they became excited, and their talk grew louder, till it became quite audible to me where I was seated.

"Don't spare the liquor, boys; the gov'nor pays."

I thought I recognised the voice that uttered this: it was like the one I had so lately heard in the park. Placing a newspaper before my face as a screen, I was enabled to make a survey of the party without my design being observed.

I soon recognised among the noisiest of the trio the actor of the scene in the park—young Moneybags. He appeared labouring under a degree of excitement which I could not attribute entirely to the drink he had imbibed.

"Come, fill your glass, Ned, and give us a toast. Of course it will be the incomparable Henrietta."

"Hush, for God's sake! Not to-night—don't breathe her name! I feel wretched about her, as if something serious were going to happen to her."

"Whew! what's up, my heart of oak? Has little

Henny grown jealous? found out your poaching tricks, Master Ned? Oh! fie, true blue in courtship, say I."

"Cheer up!" said another; "cheer up, Neddy, boy: though Venus frowns to-day, she'll smile again to-morrow. Fickle, fickle toys—source of all our smiles and joys! Take another pull, Ned, and cheer up. Here's a toast for you, if you won't give us one yourself—'Absent friends.'"

"Curse your tongue!" growled young Moneybags. "Do I need to be reminded of absent friends, think you? Villain as I am, I cannot drink that toast. Absent friends! Were they present, they would make cowards of us all. There's poor Isabella and Marianne! Absent friends—absent, but not forgotten: wish that I could forget *them*—one in a madhouse, the other an outcast. There's—— "

"What do you propose doing with little Henny, friend Ned? Is she to swell the list of your vic—I won't say that — your conquests, eh, my invincible charmer?"

"Your remarks sound like insults, sir," exclaimed young Moneybags. "I will thank you to use less freedom with me and my actions."

"Oh, to be sure, my dear fellow. No offence, of course; we know each other—have done so a long time; and many's the d—d scrape we've helped each other out of. You remember that little affair with Julia and Lizzie up the New Road, don't you, Ned?"

"Ah, what was that?" chimed in number three.

"Why, you must know that Master Ned and myself, eager for a night's spree, called upon Julia and Lizzie, expecting to be invited to supper. We were very jovial and merry, when all at once we were informed that the house was on fire. The cook had been too liberal with the coals, and the chimney was blazing away at a fine rate. We rushed out into the garden in front of the house, but when we reached the gate we could not open it: some rascal had fastened a chain round it to the railings, and locked it, and there we were exposed to the jests of the mob which had assembled in front."

"And what of Julia and Lizzie?"

"Sly jades, both."

"With an enormous appetite for diamond earrings, coral necklaces, moire antique dresses, and such-like trifles."

"Ay, and deuced expensive all that, as you must have found out to your cost, Ned."

"Oh, d—n the expense: what's the odds to us?"

"I must confess myself puzzled, Ned, to know who's your banker; your drafts must have been very heavy."

"And I, for my part, have often wondered by what process you raised the wind to supply your expensive divertisements. Give us your secret, Ned; it may be useful to both of us, provided the process be safe, and the law does not make us accessories."

"As for that, why, you know, we sometimes have rich uncles."

"Oh, as for that, why, so have I, and be hanged to them!"

"No, I do not mean those with the golden balls, but real uncles by kindred, fellows with their plums, who will relax their purse-strings sometimes to save the credit of the family, in case of a nephew's making a wrong calculation or a slip of the pen, taking other men's names in vain, or other financial errors of that sort. Family honour or family pride might melt even old Moneybags himself."

These words were scarcely uttered when I heard the sound of falling glass. I involuntarily raised my head, when I saw that a conflict had arisen among this estimable trio. Young Moneybags was on his feet in a defensive attitude, while one of his companions was crouching under the table, amid the glass which had been aimed at his head and got broken.

"Come out of that, you scoundrel!" roared young Moneybags. "Let me punish you for the insult you have offered to me!"

The gentleman thus forcibly addressed slowly raised himself into view. As he did so, young Moneybags seized another tumbler, and would have hurled it at the head of his companion, had not his arm been seized and forcibly held.

The offending party, upon regaining his erect position, looked a picture of flaming wrath. Mad with drink, he rushed upon young Moneybags, and they were soon engaged in a deadly struggle, in the course of which the latter fell among the broken glass, striking his head against the corner of a chair as he fell.

There he lay, apparently senseless; those around lifted him up; his face was covered with blood, and he was also bleeding profusely.

The uproar was very great. I stepped forward, and authoritatively demanded that a cab should be sent for, and the wounded man be conveyed to the hospital.

In a few moments a cab arrived, and the man, still senseless, was lifted into it. It was not until we arrived at the hospital that I recognised it was the same to which, a short time previously, this patient's victim had been also carried in a state of insensibility.

Being there, however, I thought I would ascertain how the fair patient was getting on; so I proceeded, in company with one of the nurses, to the ward where she had been placed.

A large room, that looked gloomy in the feeble light by which it was illuminated, was filled with beds, most of which appeared tenanted. Near one bed there was more light than at the others: towards this we directed our steps. The occupant seemed in the last agonies of death. The doctors and nurse looked on in silence. I approached nearer, until I could scan the features of the unhappy creature. She seemed aware of my approach, and fixed her eyes steadily upon me, and made a slight motion with her hand, which was extended outside the bedclothes; the motion of her lips showed that she desired to speak words, which she vainly endeavoured to articulate. I interpreted the motion as an invitation to approach nearer, and the nurse and others who were standing around the bed made way for me.

I drew near to the bed, and knelt down so as to place my ear close to her mouth. Her struggles to speak were fearful. She raised her hands to her throat, pressed them on her chest, as if she would widen the issues of life to enable her to utter her last wishes. The effort seemed fruitless, till at length she lay passive, as if completely overcome with the exertion. In a short time she appeared to rally, and anxious to renew her attempt to speak, and looked earnestly in my face.

I again placed my ear close to her mouth, so that I might not lose a syllable of what I felt sure would be her last words. Her lips frequently moved when no sound was audible, and I feared that death would triumph in the struggle, and bury her wishes with her in the grave.

Suddenly, as if by a convulsive effort, she put her arm round my neck and drew herself up in the bed, and heaved a deep sigh, and again essayed to speak.

"My mother, my poor mother!"

"Tell me who is your mother," I said. "We do not know who you are, and cannot communicate with your friends, and it is proper they should know."

"Ah! you know ——, do you not?"

"I do, well."

"That's my father. I am—his lost—daughter."

Saying this, she fell back on the pillow, as if exhausted

with the effort. It had cost her the little spark of life
that remained, and she was now silent for ever.

All present were painfully affected by the simple
scene they had witnessed. Even the nurses, whom
familiarity with such scenes of death must have
hardened—whose feelings must have become somewhat
blunted—dropped a tear of sympathy at the fate of their
unhappy sister. I withdrew from the room, with the
doctors and the nurse; and after a short conversation
with them, in which I carefully refrained from mention-
ing the name the poor girl had whispered into my ear,
I quitted the hospital, and betook myself to the residence
of her parents in Russell Square.

Upon entering the house I could at once perceive
that a commotion prevailed in the establishment. The
head of the family was absent, and the lady was in deep
affliction—so I was informed.

I urged that I had very important business, which
must be at once entered upon. Being asked my name,
I inclosed my card in an envelope, and handed it to the
servant to convey to her mistress. She soon returned
with a message.

"Will you be so kind as to wait, sir, till master
comes in? He will not be long."

It was now past twelve o'clock, and I had business
elsewhere at that hour. I wanted to fall in with a very
clever artist in the precious metals, who I was given
to understand had been in Birmingham, making large
purchases of base coin, and was expected to return to

town that night. I was in hopes of meeting with him at one of his usual haunts, and could not afford to lose my chance. One o'clock struck. The maid-servant, upon some excuse, came into the dining-room where I was seated.

"Do you know where your master is gone?" I inquired.

"Gone, I believe, to look for Miss Henrietta."

"Is Miss Henrietta lost, then?"

"She went out at six o'clock this evening to go to the circulating library, as she said, and has never returned. Master and missus are very anxious about her. They are afraid something has happened to her."

"What do you suppose can have happened to her?"

"I really do not know what to think. She has been very low-spirited lately, and I fancy she may have made away with herself."

"Do you know the cause of her trouble?"

"I suspect it is owing to a worthless fellow she has been in love with. I am sure he means her no good. I have told her as much. I am quite certain he does not care for her a bit."

"What makes you think so?"

"Why, he don't act like a gentleman at all. I know the difference, although I am but a poor ignorant girl."

"But what makes you think ill of him?"

"Oh, he is not open and straightforward; he does things clandestine-like—things he does not want master and mistress to know, and wants to bribe me not to tell. But I won't touch his filthy money—not I; it would do me no good."

" Does Miss Henrietta think much of him ? "

" She thinks *too much* of him—idolises him; and *he* does not care a straw for her, I am sure."

" Can't you give me your reasons for thinking so ? "

" I can. Why, she has to sue to him—what for I don't know; but isn't it shocking? "

I was about to assent to this opinion, when our conference was cut short by a loud knock at the hall door.

" There 's master ! "

Soon a tall, portly gentleman entered the room, evidently in a state of great bewilderment. He did not recognise me.

" Whom have I the honour of addressing, and what, pray, may be the nature of your business ? It is very late. It must be something of unusual importance."

I have a very strong objection to pronouncing my name—it almost always throws people into a state of consternation; so I took out my card, and handed it to him.

He held it close to the candle, but could not read it. He then took out his spectacles, and made another attempt. This time he was more successful.

" God bless me ! what can have brought *you* here? The very person I wished of all others to see. Excuse me if I did not recognise you. But one candle, you see, and my sight is not so good as it once was."

" I am, I regret to say, the bearer of very painful

intelligence. The duty has quite unexpectedly devolved upon me, and I must discharge it. You have a daughter?"

"Do not keep me in suspense. What do you know of her? We are most anxious about her. I have just returned from seeking her, but cannot find a trace of her movements since she left this house at six o'clock, promising to be back in a quarter of an hour."

"I know where she is."

"Thank God! my mind is relieved. Where is she, then?"

"I left her at Charing Cross Hospital about an hour ago."

"What! has any accident happened to her?"

"There has—a fatal one, I fear."

He staggered to a chair that stood near, and sank into it in an agony of terror and alarm. He had no power to speak, so completely was he overcome.

It has often fallen to my lot to be the bearer of fatal tidings; yet I have not made up my mind as to the best mode of proceeding in communicating them—whether to tell the *whole* truth at once, or to gradually prepare the mind to receive it. It must come at last, and then the shock seems to me to be quite as great as when you seek to prepare the mind to receive it, which I think but prolongs the agony. Perhaps the mode of proceeding should be adapted to different dispositions and natures.

In the present case I acted as I have usually done. I

endeavoured to palliate the effects of what I knew would prove a dreadful shock to the father's feelings. I cannot congratulate myself upon my success.

"I must go to her immediately. Perhaps you will be so kind as to accompany me?"

"Certainly, sir; but I would suggest that you wait a little while until you recover yourself. Your daughter has been well cared for, and wants for nothing now."

He looked at me inquiringly, as if he would have asked for further explanation, but dared not hear it. I could not summon the resolution to tell him the whole truth at once.

In a few minutes he rose from his chair, and staggering to the sideboard, took out two decanters of wine. He made a sign to me to help myself. Pouring out a tumbler of port for himself, he swallowed it at a draught.

"I am ready to go with you now," he said.

Then ringing the bell, when the servant answered it, he requested her to inform her mistress that he was going out with the gentleman who had called, and that he would be back as soon as possible.

Upon reaching the street he took my arm, and we proceeded together slowly along.

"We have been in the greatest distress about my daughter. Her absence was wholly unaccountable. Perhaps you will favour me by telling what you know about her?"

I thought this a good opportunity to break the sad truth to him, so I minutely described all I had witnessed on that eventful evening ;—the scene in the park between his daughter and young Moneybags, her sudden illness, my conveying her to the hospital, the discovery that she had taken poison, my *rencontre* with young Moneybags, his accident, and admission into the same hospital as contained his victim.

"It seems like a dream," he said, and then made me repeat the whole story over again.

Still I could not summon up the courage to tell him his daughter was dead, although I gave him no hopes of seeing her again alive. But he clung to the idea of her possible recovery so tenaciously, that I could not be guilty of the cruelty of destroying his hopes.

But I did not want him to go to the hospital at that unseemly hour. I doubt even if he would have been admitted. I explained this to him, and so far prevailed as to induce him to defer his visit until the morning. He promised compliance, upon condition that I would make inquiries at the hospital as to the state his daughter was in. I knew such inquiry was useless, although I pretended to make it. When I returned to him I said his daughter was in a deep sleep, from which she could not be disturbed.

"And did you inquire how that villain Moneybags was?"

"I did not. I do not think his injuries very serious."

But they were more serious than I had imagined : in falling upon the broken glass he had divided an artery, and wellnigh bled to death.

" It is too late for you to go home to-night; go and take a bed at my house, and we will come again to the hospital the first thing in the morning."

I saw no objection to this, so I complied, and accepted his invitation.

The servants had all gone to bed when we returned; but he let himself in, and soon placed before me a good supper of cold sirloin and pickles.

By this time he had somewhat recovered his equanimity, and could converse calmly on general topics. He was very curious to learn if I knew anything about young Moneybags.

I did not consider it advisable to communicate *all* I knew of that gentleman's proceedings, so I contented myself with remarking that I thought he was giving himself up to dissipation.

" A rich man's son, sir, and, like all such, spoilt—irretrievably ruined. He has never known the pleasure and satisfaction of working for money, and considers only how he can spend it. He has talents. Had he been a poor man's son he would have made his way up to a good position in society; as it is, he is but a drone in the hive, no good to himself nor to others, abandoned to sensuality and indolence. I never approved of my daughter's attachment to him, although I did not wish to oppose her inclinations. I gave her my unbiassed opinion of the man of her choice, so that she made it with her eyes quite open."

Next morning, after an early breakfast, we proceeded

again to the hospital—he to recover his lost child, I to bring away her corpse!

I sought the head nurse to explain to her my dilemma, and to consult with her as to what should be done about the deceased young lady, provided her father persisted in seeing her.

The good woman smiled while I was speaking. When I had concluded she said,—

" Lor' bless you, sir, she's not dead."

" What do you say—not dead ? Do you know who I mean ? "

" Certainly I do. The young lady you brought in last night poisoned."

" Exactly. Why, I saw her dead myself last night."

" You *thought* you did; so did we all. She was very low, and we thought she was gone; but she only swooned, and this morning she is quite nicely and comfortable like."

" Well, you do surprise me. I am quite rejoiced, I assure you."

Leaving the father to the enjoyment of his interview with his daughter, I proceeded to ascertain the condition of young Moneybags.

He was in a much worse condition than his victim. Completely prostrated by loss of blood, together with his constitution shattered by dissipation, it would be a long time before he could leave his bed. He was safe for a few weeks at least.

I had yet a duty to perform to my client, old Moneybags, as I could now venture to give him an account of his son. I bent my steps during the morning down to Eastcheap. Upon arriving at the warehouse I was surprised to find it closed.

Knocking at the door at a venture, without any expectation of its being opened, it was answered by Mr. Barton.

"How is this, Mr. Barton? No business to-day?"

"No, sir. The old gentleman died this morning."

"Old Moneybags dead?"

"Dead, sir, and we cannot find his hopeful son anywhere."

"You can find him any day for the next month at Charing Cross Hospital."

Thus ended my mission with Moneybags and Son. I learned quite accidentally, some months afterwards, that the son, now become the principal in consequence of his father's death, had reformed, and was married to Henrietta. He may prove an exemplary husband. I hope he may for her sake.

THE GAMESTER.

I WAS called one evening to a certain gambling house at the West End, where some victim had quarrelled with his luck, and was revenging himself by breaking everything he could lay his hands upon. Chairs, mirrors, decanters, were shivered beneath the violence of his assaults, and the occupants of the room had much ado to avoid the missiles aimed at them. The place, at that moment, seemed to have justly earned its title of "hell."

I arrived just in time to see a heavy decanter sent flying against a large mirror over the chimney-piece, and smash it into a thousand pieces. The decanter rebounded, falling upon the bald pate of an elderly military-looking gentleman, who fell stunned by the blow.

Several of the company were vainly endeavouring to restrain the man's violence, but afraid to grapple with him. As I entered he caught my eye, and desisted in a moment. I went up to him, and laid my hand on his arm.

"What is all this about? Are you mad?"

"I think I am; so would you be if you had been robbed as I have been."

I could see he had been drinking, and was in a very excited state, as much like madness as anything you ever saw. My policy was to soothe him.

"What have you lost, pray, sir?"

"My money—everything in the world; and now, sir, I am a beggar. And that is not the worst of it."

"Do you expect to recover it by this violence?"

"I do not; but I have been cheated, swindled. The whole concern are a set of infernal thieves, and I must have my revenge."

At this juncture a person, who appeared in charge of the concern, addressed me.

"Remove this man. I shall give him in charge."

The culprit, who was evidently a gentleman by birth and education, looked at him contemptuously.

"Give me in charge, will you? It is I that should give *you* in charge, and all your gang. Black-legs! cheats! swindlers!"

"Better come away from this," I remarked. "I do not suppose this gentleman means to give you into custody."

"But I do, though. I am not going to submit to this fool's insults and injuries quietly, I assure you. If he could not afford to lose his money he had no business here. He would have made none of this fuss if he had won twice as much as he has lost."

"If I had lost it fairly I would not have cared; but I know that I have been cheated, tricked, swindled by a gang of thieves, and I'll not submit to it quietly."

"How much have you lost?" I inquired.

"Twenty-five hundred pounds in cash, and I O U's for as much more."

I endeavoured as much as possible to soothe him, and managing to draw him gently aside into the recess of the window, I whispered in his ear:—

"Come with me quietly, and I'll put you in a way of recovering your money."

He took the hint. I was obliged to convey him to the station; for the proprietor, or whatever he was, persisted in giving him in charge. While waiting for his bail he gave me the following particulars of his life:—

"I am of good family. My early days I may pass over, as they exhibited nothing eventful, but were an even round of joy and happiness. I fell in love, and, upon arriving at the age of twenty-one, I married a lady of my own rank, of great beauty and no inconsiderable fortune. My love for her was equalled only by her devotion to me. This mutual affection continued unabated for several years, during which two lovely children were born, proving a source of additional happiness to both of us. About that time my father's health began to fail, and his medical adviser recommended that he should try the efficacy of the waters at Baden-Baden, and it was settled that he should spend the ensuing summer there.

"He objected, however, to going there alone—indeed, he was unfit; and my mother being dead, it was proposed that I, my wife, and children should accompany him. We willingly assented, and thither we went.

" I was well aware of the temptations of the place; I had been there before, but had resisted them all.

" Baden is charmingly situated, and much of its society is choice and unexceptionable. This season was one of unusual brilliancy: several Russian nobles were there, and many aristocratic families from various continental states and from England. We entered into all the gaieties : three times a week to the *soirées* at the *Salle des Réunions;* on Saturdays to the ball at the *Grande Salle;* joined the picnics and the *fêtes champêtres* which were given almost daily at the *Jäger Haus* and *La Favorite.* We never failed to attend the promenade before the *Conversations Haus* at the fashionable hour, where on several occasions we were distinguished by an invitation to join in the dances, charades, and the *tableaux vivants* so frequently got up at the residence of the Russian Princess Lebanoff.

" My wife enjoyed this gaiety immensely, and perhaps the more so, amiable as she was, for the general admiration which her beauty and grace excited, and the adulation they gave rise to. I was content to witness her felicity ; and my father partook of the universal joy, since he had been chiefly instrumental in procuring us so much gratification and pleasure.

" Such happiness could not, in the course of things, last for ever. A cloud was slowly gathering in the unseen distance, which was destined soon to throw its darkness and gloom over our sunny path. One disengaged evening—they came but rarely—I strolled out to enjoy the softness of the evening air, and to take a moonlight view of the charming scenery of this enchanting place.

"As I stood gazing abstractedly on the starry heaven above me, lost in admiration at its spangled radiance, a friend, or rather a fiend, accosted me jocosely, saying,—

"'Are you an adept in astrology, that you gaze so intently on the stars? Can you tell me whether those twinklers which rule my destiny are in such a position that I may venture to stake a hundred louis to-night at the table?'

"I made no reply; but he quickly caught me by the arm, and added playfully,—

"'Come with me to the table, and see if your readings be correct;' and we went together towards the place he indicated.

"I made no effort to refuse. I saw no danger. I need not play. Following the circuitous guidance of my tempter, I passed between those doors over which might have been written the lines Dante inscribed over the gates of his Hell.

"A novel sight presented itself to my view. There were the piles of gold, and the excited victims who vainly coveted it, hazarding certain ruin in their mad attempts to gain it. But when within the charmed circle, what had appeared to me as madness in them, became an easy achievement for me. As I inhaled the intoxicating air of this infernal den, and saw the heaps of gold that fascinated the eyes of those who gazed upon it, I became intoxicated, and rushed to the table, and commenced a career that ended in misfortune, and laid the foundation of a vagrant life to me, and of misery and grief to every other member of my family.

"Irritated at my losses, mortified at my want of skill, maddened by the wine so liberally supplied to the victims of the table, and suffering under the bitterness of self-reproach, I returned home a demon.

"It was late, and my wife, alarmed at my unusual absence, had not retired to bed. For the first time since our marriage I concealed from her where I had been; and I even spoke to her in a tone and with a degree of harshness I had never used before. In this manner I repaid her anxiety and care, and although she did not even look at me reproachfully, I saw that her brilliant eyes were dimmed with tears.

"The fatal spell was upon me. Those innocent pleasures in which I had hitherto indulged, and which were so joyously shared by my wife, now became distasteful to me. Nothing but the excitement of the gaming-table would satisfy me. Both my father and my wife soon discovered my resort, and in the greatest alarm they implored me to resist the fearful temptation. But all in vain! I was fascinated beyond the power of reason—no thought or care for consequences; and although I was neither a cool nor a skilful player, and rarely left the table a winner, still I continued to win money, and to dissipate it as fast as won, for no other purpose than to appease an insatiable appetite.

"Night after night my wife and father sat awaiting my return in wretchedness at my apparently incorrigible conduct, for I had added drunkenness to my gambling propensities; so they determined to seek a remedy for my dreadful malady in quitting Baden. This determination was announced to me upon my return late one night from the gaming-table, where I had been a loser. The fury I exhibited was great; but my father was inexorable, and took the opportunity of expressing some severe remarks upon my general conduct. I rushed from the house to the gaming-table again, resolved to risk all I possessed, in the wild hope of recovering what I had already lost.

"While in this resolution I approached the gambling saloon. The door flew open as soon as I was observed (for even Satan is courteous in temptation), and I entered.

"The usual scene presented itself. The piles of gold were undiminished, though a frenzied group stood around gloating upon the destroyer. Some had fallen to the rear in this desperate encounter, and had made way for others better provided for the conflict, but not a particle better qualified for victory. The minds of these excited men, however, partook of all the feelings of the actors in the scene. As they could never become actors themselves again, they threw all their hopes, fears, and expectations into the fortunes of others.

Completely ruined themselves, they stood to watch and exult in the inevitable ruin of others.

"I was not daunted by these ordinary scenes in a place of that character. No whisper of prudence, no caution of experience, could alter my resolution. The spell was on me, and I absolutely hugged the hideous vice as the only friend that could offer me immunity for my losses.

"I commenced; I played with desperation; I staked small sums and large sums with the same result—uniform ill-fortune. I retired to the wine-table, played again, and again was loser; but receiving fresh vigour with my fresh potations, I summoned up every energy for a last bold trial. I cast my envious eyes upon the glittering heaps of wealth, to which I had added an incentive to my present effort. I thought not of wife, children, home, nor my kind, indulgent old father, but only of that gold to which the brilliant lights and dazzling mirrors of the *salon* gave such resplendent charms. I could pause no longer; the treacherous hour had come. I hurried on to meet my fate.

"The heartless banker, hardened to his profession, and accustomed to human sacrifices at his board, perceived my frantic resolution, but looked on callous and unmoved. I staked. Then I stood with uplifted, clenched hands, waiting the result of the hazard of the die.

"The game went on. My forehead was bedewed with a cold perspiration. I scarcely breathed, while I

trembled from head to foot. Had the torture of suspense continued but many minutes longer, I verily
believe my heart-strings would have burst.

"The game proceeded in deadly silence.

" 'ROUGE PAYE!'

"O horror! All my little remnant of wealth was
engulfed in those fatal words. All my hopes and
expectations were in a moment swept away.

" '*Rouge paye!*'

"I had staked on *rouge*, and lost!

"Now my thoughts, so long truant, wandered to my
home. I jumped up from the table, rushed about the
room tearing my hair, grinding my teeth, and swearing and blaspheming in my delirium. Then I drank
copiously of the wine, but could not drown my remorse.
As I disturbed the tranquillity of the demoniacal
temple, I was for a moment the object of attention to
the worshippers. But they had no time or sympathy
for penniless fools : they looked around for other dupes
upon whom they could fatten, and, unmindful of my
example, willing ones soon took my place at the
table.

"The heated room soon became intolerable to me. I
felt stifled, suffocating. I rushed out into the open air.
It was evening. I flew along, smiting the air with my
clenched fists, and gnashing my teeth, until I found
myself again on the same spot where, innocent and
happy, I had stood gazing on the starry heavens on the

evening when I was first tempted on the demoralising and destructive career of vice that so soon left me a ruined, wretched man.

"In the silence of the night I heard a footstep approaching. I wished to shun the contact of my fellow man, for I felt a fearful animosity against every human being, and prepared to move away, lest I might be tempted to add another crime to those I had already committed. But my steps were arrested by a voice saying,—

"'Again questioning the mysteries of the stars?'

"I would rather have heard the roaring of a hungry lion in the desert, or the howling of a famished wolf in the forest, than those accursed tones of my tempter. Had I possessed the power, I would have annihilated him on the spot. As I turned away he saw my face. It inspired him with horror: terrified, he turned and fled hastily away. 'Twas well he did so, or there would have been murder. Nothing would have satisfied my deadly hatred of that serpent in my path but to have torn him limb from limb.

"He had vanished in the darkness of the night. I followed in the path I supposed he had taken, and soon found myself in the wood at the back of the *Conversations Haus*, where many a ruined man had sought relief from his grief and shame in suicide.

"There I paced frantically to and fro, calling upon the spirits of those who had so untimely perished to aid me in my revenge. Then, in despair, I cast myself

upon the grass, and endeavoured, by beating my forehead upon the earth, to procure insensibility to my
tortured brain; but in vain. At length, weary with my
ineffectual attempts to obtain forgetfulness, I bent my
steps towards my blighted home.

" But how was I to face my fond and gentle wife, or
the frowns of an indignant father? I arrived before
the house, yet had not the courage to enter, but paced
up and down, watching the dim light that shone through
the window of the room where I pictured them sitting,
anxiously waiting the return of the wayward husband
and son.

" Summoning up all my resolution, I entered the
house and the room where my wife and father were
sitting.

" They were appalled at the figure I presented; they
seemed to doubt the evidence of their eyes. My wife
uttered a scream; but my father was silent with
astonishment.

" I faltered. Such a reception enraged me. Was I
branded with the mark of my guilt on my brow, that
they should so recoil from me? My rage was un-
bounded. I frowned with every expression of hatred
and contempt I could master upon those very beings
who would have sacrificed everything, or even life itself,
for my advantage.

" My wife fainted. I tried to move to her assistance,
but my feet seemed glued to the floor. I could not stir
a step; something seemed to whisper that I should pol-

lute that pure creature with my touch.   My father
assisted her, and she slowly recovered.

"As soon as she could speak she exclaimed,—

"'You are ill, you are ill!   What has happened to
you?'

This question was more irritating to my feelings than
the scream.   I managed, however, to restrain myself,
and thought to quiet all suspicion by saying:—

"'There's nothing the matter with me.'

"But a fond woman's eye penetrates deeply into a
husband's soul.   She could not be satisfied with an evasion.

"'Oh, tell me the truth!   Something serious, perhaps
ruinous, has happened to you, I am sure.   Never before
did I see you look as you do now.'

"This was but the language of affection; but the
suspicion her words conveyed to the ears of my father
maddened me.   I wished she had reproached me, spoke
harshly—anything but what she did say.   Could I have
made her angry with me I should have been appeased;
but now my anger became ungovernable.   I clenched
my fists, yet was ashamed to strike.   I gnashed my
teeth, and in the extremity of my rage I lifted the urn,
which had been kept hot for my return, in the event of
my wishing for coffee or tea, and hurled it violently
upon her.

"Never shall I forget her agonising scream—it rings
in my ears even now—as she fell to the ground.   I was
appalled at the atrocity of my own mad act.

"My father rushed to the assistance of his suffering

daughter, for he loved her much; while I, terrified at my own iniquity, attempted to escape. Accidentally I came in collision with my father as he crossed the room. The shock threw him down with great violence, and, from his inability to rise, it was evident that some bone was broken. This proved but too truly the case : a fractured thigh kept him in bed, a cripple, until his death.

" The little household had become alarmed at the disturbance I had created, and soon assembled in the room where these terrible scenes were being enacted. Seeing no one there but the members of the family, they could not comprehend the nature or the cause of the tumult, till my wild efforts to escape from the scene gave them a clue to the culprit. My children, attracted from their beds by the cries of their mother, came screaming in, and added, by their lamentations, to the disorder.

" Picture to yourself this scene, if you can. No, it is impossible ! What a beast is man when overcome by drink ! Everything that should be prized on earth is wantonly sacrificed to the demon of intemperance. Surely the temporary sensual gratification is but a poor exchange for the loss of health, honour, virtue, domestic peace, and love.

" You may imagine that the peaceful and happy home that I had converted into a den of misery could be no place for me, the cause of all the ruin and destruction brought upon it. I was fit only to herd with wolves and hyenas. My name I knew would be execrated by all Baden ; I should be pointed at with the finger of scorn ; nay, more—the criminal courts would demand of me the penalty of my crimes. I must flee, and quickly too.

" How I escaped from the house I hardly know. The efforts made to detain me, an infuriated madman, were futile. I only remember finding myself in a tavern, imbibing large draughts of brandy till I became unconscious, and then awakening from my stupor to find myself lying on the ground beneath a tree, a few paces from the roadside.

" I felt in my pockets—they were empty. Which way could I turn, penniless and degraded ? Bewildered with the recollection of the preceding night's events, I could not at first persuade myself but that I had had a horrid dream ; but gradually the terrible truth became evident to my mind. I arose and made my way as quickly as possible along the road that led from the town, and never stopped until exhausted. Seeing an apple tree, a branch of which hung within my reach, I plucked some of the fruit, and thus allayed both the hunger and thirst that devoured me. I then washed my face and hands in a little brook that flowed along in front of the garden fence, and, while doing so, recognised that I had a diamond ring on my finger. The sight of this roused my flagging energies. I could sell this jewel, and with the proceeds escape to England.

" I reached Hamburg, and from thence took passage to England, where I arrived, ignorant of any profession or calling by which I could expect to obtain an honest living.

"I had a few pounds left, the remainder of the money I had obtained for my ring. I resolved to stake this at the gaming-table, with the vague hope that fortune, always fickle, seldom kind, would take pity on one she had treated so harshly, and enable me to retrieve in some measure my error and crimes, and again become a good citizen.

"I was not long in discovering a place suitable for my operations. I determined to proceed cautiously; so the first night I did not play at all, but contented myself with merely looking on. Next night I staked a small sum, and in a few moments found myself in possession of forty pounds. Elated with my success, I staked again, and again I won.

"I kept on for nearly an hour, when my companions began to exchange significant glances with each other, which I thought boded no good to me. They could hardly suspect me of foul play; for they took every precaution to prevent that. But my continual winning was so singular that they could not conceal their astonishment and disgust.

"Several times the game was changed, but the result continued the same. I won every time. I who had been in Germany knew something of German *diablerie*, and I grew half suspicious that the tempter was at my elbow, luring me by success to inevitable destruction.

"Making an effort, I resolved to stop playing; but

when I announced my intention of doing so my companions protested against it. They wanted to win their money back again; so I was perforce obliged to continue playing.

" The cards were shuffled and cut, and cut and shuffled again, but without changing the result to me— nearly every game was mine.

" At last my companions all rose abruptly from the table, exclaiming that they were willing to play against any man, but not against the devil.

" I cannot tell you how rich I found myself that night, nor how many good resolutions I made for my future conduct. I husbanded the money, and endeavoured to find a means whereby I might establish myself in some honest calling.

" I never ventured to write to my wife or father, nor did I dare to crave their pardon or forgiveness, for I felt that my offence was most unpardonable. Once, during many months, I took up my pen; but no sooner had I done so than the enormity of my offences paralysed me, and the pen fell from my hand. The bottle has been my only resource when the agonies of remorse have been too keen for me to endure.

" Occasionally I have heard of my family. My father I know is dead, and I, perhaps, am his murderer. It is thought that I am dead, and my son inherits the family honours, of which his miserable father is so unworthy. I wander through the world with the curse of Cain on my brow.

" I did not succeed in my efforts to obtain employment ; for, in truth, I was quite unfitted for anything useful. My store of money gradually dwindled away, and again I saw no resource but to resort to the gaming-table.

" All my store of wealth amounted to twelve pounds, ten of which I resolved to venture, and then, if it were lost, to desist, and put an end to my existence.

" But Fortune (wanton jade!) wooed my favours, and showered her gifts upon me most profusely. I could not lose, play as carelessly as I might. That night I returned home with what was to me a little fortune.

" But my success was unfortunate for me. I fancied that I bore a charm or spell which would always insure my winning. I returned next night to the gaming-table, and *lost*.

" But not *all*. I kept a reserve, which I had the fortitude not to touch to hazard it. Upon this I drew for my moderate wants, until I grew weary with the monotony of my existence.

" One night I drew a sovereign from the hoard, with a secret resolution that if I lost it I would pinch myself of everything, except bread and water, until the time elapsed during which, in the ordinary course, I should have expended it.

" This coin I staked, and won. I staked and won again. Marvellous fortune ! I was again rich, comparatively.

" From that night I became a professional gambler ;

that is, I made it the business of my life.   I act
cautiously, and pay my losses with my gains.

"But I make no friends.   I am alone, cut off from
all human sympathy.   The men I associate with are
scarcely human in their passions, but what poets feign
demons to be.   Their friendship would sink me into
the bottomless pit.   No, I must live, even if it be in
penance and remorse, in obscurity and oblivion, to
expiate my crimes; and time may bring many unlooked-
for changes.

" You found me in a place where I had not been
before, where I was unknown.   Sharpers, they took me
for a novice, and practised tricks upon me.   I lost my
money, and I became irritated.   Drink infuriated me.
You know the rest."

ROBBING THE MAIL.

THERE were mail coaches in those days. We've seen the last of them, and, as for myself, I must say with some feeling of regret. There was something peculiarly English about them, and when they disappeared an interesting institution was sponged off the national slate.

It was known to me that the Yarmouth mail would, on a certain night, convey a certain passenger, the bearer of a large quantity of valuables, and I was requested to go down to Yarmouth and escort him up.

My instructions arrived rather late, so that I missed the coach by which I should have gone; therefore, when I arrived at Ipswich, I concluded that as the mail would be along in an hour or so, I would remain there and await its arrival.

I was sauntering up and down in front of the inn at which the mail stopped, when I was accosted by a warder of the jail in that town, who informed me that a notorious highway robber, one "Martlesham Jack," had broken from prison, and escaped clear off.

The time for the arrival of the mail approached, and you know mails were proverbial for punctuality; but this one I was expecting failed to make its appearance either at the time it was due or for twenty minutes afterwards.

A little crowd, which, when the mail is punctual, quickly arrives and as quickly disperses, had now gathered about the coach-office, discussing the delay of the mail, and speculating as to the cause.

When a full hour had elapsed, and no mail had made its appearance, the anxiety of the crowd became intense.

"Something serious must have happened—perhaps an upset. Suppose some of us go and see if we can find out what is the matter?"

This proposition was received with general approval. A gig and a saddle horse were procured. I took possession of the latter, and off we started. Shortly before we arrived at Rushmere Heath we saw the light of a lantern approaching, borne, as it proved, by the guard of the missing mail.

We challenged him, inquiring the cause of the delay, and of his appearance under such circumstances.

"The mail's been stopped and robbed. The coach-man is shot dead I'm afraid, and I am wounded, but not badly. The passengers have made off, and I am looking for assistance to bring the mail on."

"We thought something had happened, and we have come to assist you. How far off is the mail?"

"About a mile."

We took the guard up into the gig, and hastened to the scene of the disaster.

Arrived there, we made an examination. It appeared that the expedient resorted to for stopping the mail was to place three hurdles, brought from a neighbouring field, in the middle of the road, just in the horses' track. As the night was rather chilly, it is probable that the reeking and breathing of the horses prevented the coachman seeing the impediments; for the leaders, stumbling against them, fell down, and the wheelers, becoming alarmed, fell down also.

The sudden stoppage of the vehicle, as the guard informed us, threw him forward. At the same moment two shots were fired, one of which hit the coachman; the other hit the guard, passing through the fleshy part of his right arm; and immediately the guard felt himself seized behind, dragged down into the road, and thrown into a ditch, where a man stood over him with a pistol aimed at his head.

The coachman was dragged from the box down among the horses. Meanwhile, a couple of men proceeded to rob the passengers. There were but two—the bearer of the valuables I was to have escorted, and a young midshipman.

As soon as the coach stopped, the bearer of the valuables, acutely sensitive of danger, whipped out his knife and ripped a hole in the coach lining, and thrust his parcel into it. He happened to have made up a duplicate of the parcel, a dummy, which he carried in the breast pocket of his great coat for "ballast," as he described it.

When the robbers presented themselves at the doors of the coach, pistol in hand, they demanded "Money, or your life," according to custom in such cases. The middy wanted to show fight, but his fellow-traveller counselled submission, and quietly surrendered his purse, watch, and the dummy parcel, which he intimated contained bank notes.

The robbers appeared to be well satisfied with their spoil, and politely closed the doors of the coach, wishing the travellers "good night." They then proceeded to rob the mail-bags, contenting themselves chiefly with selecting small packages. The letters they scattered about the road in mere wantonness.

As soon as the robbers had gone the passengers got out and helped the guard to rise. The bearer of the valuables, having secured his treasure, proceeded to a neighbouring farm-house, with the owner of which he was acquainted, the middy accompanying him. The coachman was found tied to a tree, his head reclining upon his breast. He had been shot through the heart, and had two fearful stabs in the breast, either of which was sufficient to cause instant death.

The robbers had cut the traces, so we had to rig up with the harness in the best way we could. We put the body of the coachman inside the coach, and made the best of our way to Ipswich, first collecting all the scattered letters.

I remained at Ipswich till next day, antieipating the appearance of the bearer of the valuables. He came along in the course of the morning, and I accompanied him to London, where we safely arrived with the treasure.

Of course this mail robbery and murder caused some considerable excitement; and, as soon as the nature and extent of the robbery were ascertained, full particulars were scattered far and wide. Among the parcels taken from the mail-bag were two containing a quantity of bank notes, the numbers of which, of course, were known.

About a week after this occurrence I was walking along Whitechapel in company with a brother officer, when he gave me a signal to be on the alert.

"Yonder," said he, "at the door of that public-house, I see a fellow that answers to the description of 'Martlesham Jack.' Do you know him?"

"I do," I replied. "Had the care of him a few years ago on suspicion; but the case could not be proved against him. I'll go and speak to him, and do you follow on and quietly take him."

I approached "Martlesham Jack," and inquired how he was getting on. He appeared uncommonly nervous, and gave me very unintelligible replies. I gave the signal to my fellow-officer, and he came forward and took Jack into custody on the charge of escaping from prison. There was a suspicious-looking fellow lounging along in company with Jack. We took him into

custody also, at which he loudly protested, as there was
no charge against him.

We had no suspicion, at the time of making this
arrest, that Jack had been concerned in the mail
robbery. We merely knew that he had escaped from
jail, and that a reward of twenty-five pounds had been
offered for his re-capture.

Of course they were searched at the station. Jack
wore a curly wig, red hair. In the lining of this we
found a thousand-pound Bank-of-England note, one of
those lost from the mail. In a belt fastened round his
waist, worn under his shirt, we found a considerable
quantity of bank notes, all stolen ones. On Jack's
companion we found a banker's case containing
promissory notes, bills, and bank notes to a considerable amount, all stolen from the mail.

We congratulated ourselves upon our extraordinary
good luck; for there was a reward of five hundred
pounds offered for the apprehension of the robbers of
the mail, and a per centage on the value of the stolen
property that might be recovered.

We kept our own counsel upon making this discovery. It was important to find out where Jack
lodged. We found a key in his pocket, which we had
no doubt belonged to the room he occupied.

I remembered seeing a girl speak to Jack just before
he was arrested, and I had no doubt that if I could
find her I should be able to discover his lodging.

So I proceeded to the spot where we had taken Jack,

and visited the neighbouring public-houses, in the hope
of meeting with the girl. Some hours elapsed before I
fell in with her. As soon as she appeared I went up to
her, and told her that Jack had been looking for her,
and was inquiring for her just before she came in.

"Be Jases, and haven't I been looking for him all
this blissed day! Well, sure, and I think I know where
I 'll find him this time."

She started off at a rapid pace, and I followed at a
discreet distance. She looked into every public-house
that she passed, but of course did not meet with Jack
for obvious reasons; he was safely under lock and key
at the station.

After the girl had exhausted all probable public-
houses on her road, she suddenly dived into a narrow
court, and into the first open doorway she came to.

That was enough for me. Here was Jack's habita-
tion, as sure as last Sunday was a wet day. I retired
a little out of sight, awaiting the damsel's re-appearance.
She soon returned, and I heard her inquire of a man
she met, as she was coming out of the doorway,—

"Have you seen anything of my Jack?"

"What, don't you know? Why, he 's copped."

"O C——! you don't mane that? Where 's he
cribbed?"

"Close by. You had better go and take him some
'bacca."

The damsel shed a few natural tears, and started off.

I darted up the staircase she had just quitted.

As I ascended the stairs, the tenants of the various rooms I passed—a motley herd—came out to gaze at me, some eyeing me with curiosity, others with scowls. I kept on until I came to a closed door, which I knocked at, but received no answer. I then applied the key found in Jack's pocket, and it fitted exactly.

When I opened the door a scene presented itself that would have stirred up the bile of many a banker. Bank notes, bills, letters, mostly torn, were strewed about in all directions. In a broken red earthenware pitcher I found some fifteen hundred pounds in bank notes.

I carefully collected the scattered spoil, and folded it up in a newspaper, and was not a little amused to see pinned against the wall two handbills, one of which offered a reward for the capture of "Martlesham Jack," and the other for the apprehension of the mail robbers.

There were others concerned in the robbery, or at least one other, but we had no clue to them as yet. Many persons of doubtful character were arrested on suspicion, but discharged for want of evidence.

One evening a couple of young men went into the shop of a dealer in ready-made clothes. After making a purchase they tendered a five-pound bank note in payment. The shopkeeper, well informed of the mail-coach robbery, suspected that this might be one of the stolen notes; and as his shop was not far from a police-station, under pretence of getting the note changed, he sent his shopman to the station to ascertain whether this note was one of those stolen, and, if it were, to bring a policeman along with him.

He returned in a few minutes not with one policeman, but with two. They immediately arrested the two men. As they did so, one of the men was observed to drop something: it proved to be a parcel of the stolen notes.

Upon being searched at the station, other notes, all stolen, were found upon them, together with a key that opened a trunk at their lodgings, which was found to contain a large quantity of stolen property.

Of course no doubt existed that these men were a part of the gang who robbed the mail and murdered the coachman, although, upon their examination before the magistrate, they vehemently protested their innocence.

But from the quantity of the stolen property found in their possession, and the very improbable story they told as to how they became possessed of it, no doubt existed that they had participated in it. They were remanded for a further examination. They urged that they were respectable men, gave their names as Henry and William Kesgrave, that they had a brother living at Woodbridge, another at Lowestoft, and a sister in London, which statement proved correct.

Upon this arrest becoming known, I was desirous to ascertain which of the gang was the murderer of the coachman; so I called upon "Martlesham Jack," and informed him of the arrest of the brothers Kesgrave.

This intelligence threw Jack into a state of nervous

trepidation, so much so that he inadvertently admitted his connection, which he afterwards stoutly denied.

The prisoners were all indicted, and true bills found against them.   The ablest legal assistance was engaged for the defence, proving that the prisoners must be amply supplied with the means of feeing them.   Never was there a greater display of tact in the examination of witnesses and sifting of evidence than was exhibited on this occasion.

It was determined to try "Martlesham Jack" separately, for it was supposed that, being a hardened offender, it was he who murdered the coachman.   An offer was made to Jack's companion, who was arrested with him, that he should turn king's evidence.   At first he refused, but he subsequently accepted the offer.

This man testified that the robbery was planned by the brothers Kesgrave, and that he was invited to join in the plot; that after the thing was planned, and the night fixed upon for committing it, "Martlesham Jack" broke out of jail, and went to Kesgrave's house for shelter and concealment.   He was invited to join in the business, and did so.   Being a strong, powerful man, he took the lead in the affair, and he it was who bound the coachman to the tree.

The brothers Kesgrave were young men of good education, but of dissolute habits.   They had both lost situations and character, and were out of employment at the time they planned the robbery.   Their intention was to escape to America as soon as possible after the

affair; but, as most of the money they stole consisted
of bank notes, they had some difficulty in changing
them so as to procure the means of paying their passage
money. It was in making the attempt to change a
note that they were apprehended. The younger of
the brothers was but twenty years old; yet it was he
who had shot the coachman. The poor man was
much alarmed, and begged piteously for them not
to kill him, as he would make no resistance. But
"Martlesham Jack" insisted that he should be shot,
else they would surely be detected, he being the only
one who could recognise the robbers. There was some
difficulty in deciding who should commit the foul deed,
and the decision fell upon young Kesgrave. He hesitated for some time, till threatened by his companions.
He then stepped up to the helpless man, who still
implored them to spare his life for the sake of his poor
wife and little children, who depended upon him entirely for their support, and placing the pistol close to
his body, fired. Upon receiving the contents of the
pistol the unfortunate coachman gave a terrible scream,
and then all seemed to be over. The villains then
started from the place; but "Martlesham Jack," to make
sure of the man's death, returned and felt his pulse.
Finding some signs of life still remaining, he plunged a
knife twice into the man's body, and then left him.

They proceeded together some miles across the
country, till about daybreak, when they went into a
chalk pit, and there divided the plunder.

Upon this evidence, and upon that derived from their possession of the stolen property, the prisoners were convicted.

Upon being asked if they had anything to say why the sentence of the law should not be pronounced upon them, young Kesgrave rose up, and in a calm and graceful manner made the following eloquent and touching address :—

"I thank the honourable court for the privilege it thus allows me of saying a few words, which are probably the last I shall utter in public during my brief sojourn in this world. I improve the moment to declare to this honourable court and to the world that I have not a single objection to offer against the just sentence of the law being passed upon me. I am but too sensible of the enormity of the awful crime for which I must suffer an ignominious death. I fully acknowledge the justice and legality of my punishment. The only regret that I now feel—the bitterest pang that afflicts me at this moment—arises from its not being in my power to make restitution to her who has been made a widow by my crime, and to the innocent, helpless children whose honest father I have wickedly slain. I am preparing to die. I expect no mercy from earthly tribunals, nor do I deserve any. The only hope I dare to have is in the Redeemer's blood, and to him will I look and plead. I can only crave the honourable court to allow me as long a time as may be compatible with its sense of justice and propriety, to improve what time I may yet remain on earth in preparing to meet a just, but offended God."

During this brief address a solemn silence pervaded the crowded court, and all present were deeply affected by the unhappy fate of so promising a young man. The other prisoners were silent, but greatly moved, yet showed much fortitude, and seemed perfectly resigned to their fate.

Owing to the youth, and some mitigating circumstances in the younger Kesgrave's case, a powerful effort was made to obtain a commutation of his punishment to transportation, but in vain. The day fixed for the execution was the 15th of October, and on that day they were executed in the presence of a large concourse of people. The culprits seemed to be truly repentant.

Previous to being launched into eternity young Kesgrave made the following address to the multitude:—

"My dear friends, in taking my last farewell of you on this earth, I beg leave to say a few words, especially to the young men who are now witnessing my fatal doom. I was brought up by a kind, indulgent father with every care, and strict regard to my future well-being. I had his good advice and his moral instruction. I had been taught to avoid evil company, and shun that which was vicious ; but, little by little, I was led into error, and I indulged in what I thought harmless violations of duty, until all the good advice and moral precepts of my kind father were forgotten, and his aged heart was broken by the follies of a disobedient and ungrateful son. Ah! my dear young men, let me implore you to avoid the fatal rock upon which I have been wrecked. Be you obedient to your parents. I trace all my errors, all my follies, and even my crimes to the use of tobacco. I smoked tobacco contrary to the express injunctions of my father. Smoking led me to drinking and bad company. I became idle, dissipated, and lost my character. In this extremity I resorted to crime—the awful crime for which I am now about to suffer. Oh! had I but my life to go over again, and could I but restore the peace of mind to that aged father who tried so hard to save me from this ignominious end—could I but restore the life which I have taken, what earthly punishment would I not undergo! But it cannot be. My only hope is that God will be merciful to me, and repair the injuries which I have inflicted upon others."

A letter written by this unfortunate young man to his father, a few days before his execution, will speak for itself. It carries with it its own comment, and should be written upon the heart of every young man in the land, and stand as a beacon light to warn others of the sunken rocks which beset their paths.

"IPSWICH BOROUGH GAOL.

"MY DEAR SORROW-STRICKEN FATHER,

"I am daily and anxiously expecting a letter from you. On Wednesday last I received my awful sentence, which I acknowledged to the court then, as I have before to you, the strict justice of. I know that my hands are polluted with the blood of an innocent fellow being; and my conscience, O my conscience, is burdened with the dreadful crime of murder. Oh, my dear poor father, little did I ever expect, when I took my leave of you and my once happy home—little did I think, when I parted with my dear sisters and brother, that before we should again meet my hands would be imbrued in the blood of a fellow being, and I should now be immured in a gloomy dungeon, under sentence of death. Would to God I had rejected the wicked proposal when it was first made to me! I was not aware of the design to murder until the moment it was committed. Would to God I had been stricken dead upon that fatal night! But then I should have died as I had lived; yet now, though I have brought sorrow and disgrace on you, my dear father, yet my guilty soul may be saved through the merits of the Redeemer. Oh, dear father, believe me when I assure you that when the poor man begged his life I told him I would spare him, and I meant to do so—indeed, I pleaded for it earnestly; but my companion was inexorable, and assured me that if he was not killed we should surely be detected, and I was ordered peremptorily to shoot him, or be myself shot. In that dreadful moment my fears unmanned me; and oh, God forgive me! the terrible deed with a trembling hand was done. Oh, my dear father, I do not write this to excuse my guilt, but to console you by the assurance that there were yet left upon my wayward heart some tracings of your teachings, and the many fervent prayers which you had offered up for me in youth had not been entirely obliterated from my memory. I was not wholly without the smitings of a conscience. Oh, may God preserve my dear brother from the evil of bad company, and enable him to soothe a heart which my crimes have lacerated! The poor woman, too, from whom I have torn away the husband of her heart, and the children whom I have made helpless orphans, if I could but be spared to work for them all my days! But God will care for them in his infinite mercy. Oh, what pangs of conscience do I not suffer at the wrong I have done to these poor people! Oh, father, this is a time of shame and sorrow to me, your erring and very disobedient son. I pray God to help me to repent, and blot my sins from the record of his remembrance. I read my Bible most of my time, and other good books; but the Bible is now my constant companion. Now I can refer to the many passages which, when but a little boy, you used to point out to me. Now I find their worth. O that I then but properly appreciated them! 'Though your sins be as scarlet, they shall be made white as snow; though they be crimson, they shall become white as wool.' Oh, father, this is a consoling hope to me now in my time of trouble. How often have you, my dear father, told me these things; yet, oh, how perverse, how obdurate

was my heart, that did not hearken to you then! Oh, I
have resisted your good and oft-repeated advice. I
have preferred the paths of disobedience and guilt to
those of virtue and honour. I cannot plead ignorance.
I have sinned against light and knowledge, and am
doubly guilty. I have nothing to hope for but the
unmerited mercy of God. One thing more, my dear
father, and I have done. Mrs. Hill, the poor widow,
made so by my hand, is a poor and helpless woman,
with several small children. As a last wish, it would
smooth my pathway to the grave to know that you
had contributed to her aid. Let me have that consolation ere I die. She is a deserving woman, and will
not abuse your charity. Oh, help her to such an
extent as may be in your power, and God will reward
both you and yours. Now, my dear father, my dear
sister, my dear brother, farewell. To you, my dear
brother, hear the words of a lost brother. Be obedient
to your father, avoid evil company, resist temptation,
and seek an interest in Heaven for your guilty and
stricken brother,

"HENRY KESGRAVE."

This letter melted the public with pity for the unfortunate writer. Had his lot been better cast he
might have proved a good and useful citizen.

THE BURGLAR'S HAT.

" HELP ! murder ! Help ! "

If you were to hear those cries in the middle of the night, of course you 'd run, wouldn't you ? Well, so did I. As I approached the house from whence the voice proceeded, I saw a woman in her night-dress at the parlour window still screaming " Help ! "

" What 's the matter ? " I inquired.

" Oh ! make haste in ; I 'm sure there 's murder going on."

" Then you must let me in. Open the door, quick."

" Oh ! I cannot ; I should be murdered."

" What do you mean ? Who 's hurting you ? "

" Oh ! not me, but my mistress. Somebody I 'm sure is murdering her. I heard the blows, and I hear her groans now. Hark ! Oh ! don't *you* hear them ? "

It was no use to stand there parleying. The street door looked too heavy and strong to be easily forced in, so I mounted the railings, and, by the aid of the water-pipe, somehow or other, I can't tell you how, reached the window ; and, with a little assistance from the woman, who clutched me by the coat collar, I managed to get into the room.

"Now, young woman, what is it?"

"Hush! there's some one murdering missus upstairs."

"How do you know?"

"I heard them break into the back-parlour window and go upstairs. I was afraid to stir. Then I heard them go into mistress's room. I could hear them strike her, and then she screamed, and then her groans. O dear, we shall all be murdered!"

"Now you keep quiet. Which way is it?"

"I'll open the door softly. Can you find your way up?"

I crept cautiously up the stairs, and, by a dim light shining through a door standing ajar, I was guided to the scene of action. I heard a noise of keys and of rummaging as I approached the door, and taking out my staff, I prepared for an encounter.

As yet I had no knowledge of how many villains I should have to engage with; but as I gently pushed open the door with my left hand and looked in, I saw, by the light of a lantern held by one ruffian who was searching a bureau, that there were three of them. The other two were acting as sentinels—one over an old lady lying in the bed, the other with his back to the door by which I entered.

Of course my appearance was quite unexpected, and disturbed the operations of the villains. The fellow with the lantern was the first to see me, as he happened to turn the light full on my face just as I put my head in.

" A peeler, by G—d ! "

The fellow's head was bared for the blow, and I struck it. At the same moment the other two fellows sprang upon me, and with some heavy instrument—a *jemmy*, or life-preserver, or something of that sort—struck me two or three violent blows on the head, and I lost my consciousness.

When I recovered my senses I found myself on the floor of another room, with the young woman I had first seen bathing my temples with vinegar. Two other policemen stood looking on.

" Well, old fellow, feel all right ? "

" What 's all this ? " I inquired. " What does it mean ? "

" It means that you have had a good thump on the head, and have been to sleep over it."

" Well, I thought I 'd been dreaming : where 's those rascals ? "

" We were just going to ask *you*. Come, tell us what you did with them."

" I have some recollection that I gave one fellow a token of remembrance, and——"

" And — he returned the compliment ; so you 're quits."

" I feel very queer," I said, putting my hand to my head, and feeling a lump as big as an egg.

" No doubt you do. You 've had that which would make any man feel queer. Hardly expected to see you open your eyes again. Who gave it to you ? "

"I think I know; but I must consider. But what brought you here?"

"I brought 'em, sir," answered the maid-servant. "I listened after you went upstairs, and I heard a scuffle, and I thought perhaps the villains would murder you too; so I opened the street door, and let these gentlemen in."

"Yes, and when we came upstairs we found you lying stiff on the floor beside the bed where the old lady lay murdered. The staircase window was open. We looked out, but could see nothing; but, upon listening, could hear a noise like some one scrambling over a wall. I ran round into the court at the back of the house, but was too late; the fellows got clear off. How many of them were there?"

"I saw three."

"Did you recognise them?"

"I have seen one of the fellows' faces before, but my head's so confused I can't say where now."

"Take time to consider. The old lady's dead — you'll have to attend the inquest."

In searching the premises for traces of the murderers we found an old hat in the back yard, which had evidently been dropped in the flight. I took charge of this, hoping some day to find the owner.

The usual inquiries were made on the neighbouring beats as to the appearance of any suspicious characters, but nothing satisfactory was elicited.

I took particular care of that hat; there was nothing

very remarkable about it, but still I held on to it with a kind of apprehension that it would serve as a clue. It was the only one I could reckon upon, so I made the most of it.

At that time I kept a little spaniel, one of King Charles's breed, which I had found astray in the street one night. I used to lock him in my room while I was on duty. One day, upon returning home, I found he had been amusing himself with that hat, and in his sportiveness had torn the lining out. Of course I scolded him; but, from his frisking about, I think he fancied I was expressing approval of his conduct. However, I picked up the hat and restored the lining to the inside: in doing so I saw a little slip of paper, quite saturated with grease, adhering to the felt. Upon removing it I found it to be the fragment of a letter, evidently torn off to preserve the writer's address, which was, "Henry Miller, —— Street, Salford." The street was illegible.

I set myself to working out this clue. The owner of the hat was doubtless acquainted with this Henry Miller. I must see Miller. But how to find him? He might not be a resident at Salford, or, if he were, only a temporary one—perhaps a transient lodger.

However, I started immediately for Manchester, and instituted inquiries among the police authorities if any one of that name was known to them.

There was none.

I next proceeded to the post-office, and, although

every facility was afforded me, no Henry Miller was known to any of the carriers. After reiterating my inquiries, one old man said he thought he remembered that name, and directed me to the house where he had delivered letters for it. To this house I bent my steps, but no such person resided there, nor was the name known to the present tenant. I returned again to the post-office, and while relating my failure, a person accidentally present suggested that I should apply to a certain retired publican who was the oldest inhabitant of that neighbourhood, and who probably knew everybody that had lived in it for the previous thirty years. He had retired from business life to a comfortable little villa some three or four miles off. I made the best of my way thither, and was very courteously received.

He remembered the name of Miller. It belonged to a gentleman who had taken a newly-built mansion in —— Street, but from some cause or other connected with the state of the house, had quitted, after occupying it only three months. He did not know where he was gone; but the man who removed his furniture lived in the same neighbourhood, and could probably give me the information I required.

I found out this man without much difficulty. He informed me that Mr. Miller had gone to live at Atherstone. He described him as a gentleman in easy circumstances, without any trade or profession.

You must know that the old hat was my companion on the voyage of discovery, safely locked in a travelling hat-ease. I made the best of my way to Atherstone, and introduced myself to Mr. Henry Miller.

I frankly stated the matter to him, showed him the hat, and the slip of paper with his name upon it that I had discovered under the lining.

"I remember it well," he said. "That hat was mine, and that slip of paper I put where you found it one day when I was travelling by rail to London. I put it there to identify my hat among the many others it might happen to be mixed with at the various public places to which I was going."

"And did you lose the hat, sir, while in London?"

"No, it got knocked about a good deal, so before leaving town I gave it to my man-servant."

"Is he with you now?"

"No, the foolish fellow got married and remained in London."

"Do you know his address?"

"O yes! He keeps the coffee-shop at No. —, Holborn."

This concluded my negotiation with Mr. Miller. My next step was to return to London and see his *ci-devant* servant, and the desired interview was soon obtained.

Of course I introduced the subject of the hat.

"Your late master, Mr. Miller, has, for particular reasons, a desire to refer to a hat he gave you when you quitted his service; it happens to contain some memoranda of importance which he wishes to refer to. Have you that hat still by you?"

"No, I am sorry to say I have not. It did not fit me, so I disposed of it."

"Of course you remember to whom?"

"O yes! I exchanged it for some trifle with Hodson, the greengrocer."

"And where is Mr. Hodson to be found?"

"Well, he lives up by Golden Square. I know his shop; but I do not know what street it is in. However, you can easily find it, as it leads out of Little Pulteney Street."

"Thank you, that is sufficient."

Mr. Hodson fortunately was at home when I called. He acknowledged the transaction of the "hat," but *he* had not got it. He had sold it to—he did not know who.

"But you have some knowledge of the man, surely. Did you never see him before? have you never seen him since?"

"O yes! I used to see him pass my shop almost every day. I had that hat in my hand one morning, brushing it up a bit, and he came up and asked me if it was for sale. I had no particular fancy for it, so I said, 'Yes, for half-a-crown;' and he bought it at once."

"Of course it fitted him? Have you seen him with it on?"

"Yes, but not lately. I think it must be a fortnight since I saw him."

"And you don't know where to find him?"

"I do not; but there's a neighbour there who I think does," pointing to a public-house nearly opposite.

"But who am I to ask about?"

"Ah! I did not think of that. Well, I don't know his name, but I think I can describe him."

We crossed over together to the public-house, and called for some ale. The greengrocer put certain leading questions to the publican, which caused the latter to recognise the worthy of whom we were in search.

"Yes, I know. He had not been here for a week or so, but came last night. Said he had been laid up. Wanted to sell me a gold ring. I did not buy it; but he left it with me to try and sell for him. There it is."

"This," said I, "is a lady's ring. I know a young lady I think it will suit. I will bring her to look at it. Do you know the owner's name?"

"His companions call him Bob Lester. I don't know where he lives, but I dare say he will be here this evening."

"Will you send him over to me?" said the greengrocer.

"Certainly. Perhaps you may do a little business together."

"Not unlikely. Send him over."

I was not sure that I might venture to take the greengrocer into my confidence; so I thought I might work the oracle by means of the ring. I wanted the servant of the murdered old lady to see this ring. Perhaps she might recognise it.

I brought her up immediately to the public-house. When the ring was shown to her she at once identified it as having belonged to her late mistress.

It now seemed highly probable that Bob Lester was one of the gang who had robbed and murdered the old lady.

The price the publican was instructed to ask for the ring was two pounds. I wanted to negotiate with the owner, if possible; so I made an offer of one pound twelve, and was to call in the evening for an answer.

I arranged with the greengrocer to negotiate for the ring, for I did not deem it advisable to show myself in the matter at present. I would remain in his shop while he made the bargain, and brought the owner over to me to conclude it.

According to appointment, I was at the greengrocer's at seven o'clock. He went over to the public-house while I waited in his shop.

An hour passed away and he did not return, and I began to grow fidgety, when my attention was attracted by a crowd in the street following a drunken man in charge of two policemen.

At the same moment the greengrocer came in laughing.

"There he goes. That's our man who has the ring to dispose of. He came into the public-house quite drunk, and made such a disturbance that he is going to be locked up."

I quickly followed him to the station. Arrived there,

x

I made such a communication to the inspector in charge as induced him to have the man searched.

In his pocket we found a small canvas bag containing a few trinkets, a key to a Bramah's lock, and a quantity of duplicates. A key of a room door was also found in another pocket.

I had no doubt these articles were the proceeds of the robbery at which I had figured, but I could not identify this man as one of the three I had encountered. In fact, from the momentary glance I had of two of them, there was scarcely time to recognise their features. Of the other I saw enough to enable me to identify him in the event of meeting with him.

At the station I left instructions that if any one called to see the drunken man he should be detained.

I then proceeded to the residence of the murdered lady. Her servant was able to identify all the articles found in the drunkard's pocket, and the Bramah key was found to fit a writing desk among the lady's property.

Late in the evening I made a visit to the station. There I found a man who, coming to look after his friend, the drunkard that was locked up, had, agreeably to my instructions, been detained.

Upon seeing him I had little doubt that he was the man whose face I had seen on the occasion of my encounter with the murderers and thieves.

Next morning, on being taken before the magistrate, they were both charged with the robbery and murder, and remanded for a week. I had not previously been able to ascertain where these men lived ; but they were recognised in court by several parties, and their whereabouts easily discovered.

Upon searching the lodgings of the man first arrested, a complete set of housebreaking implements was found, besides many articles the evident produce of burglaries.

There was yet another of the gang to be found, and the way I fell in with him was rather singular.

I was standing one Sunday evening at the bar of a certain public-house in Albany Street, Regent's Park, taking a quiet glass of ale, and "looking on," when a buxom little maid-servant came in for her supper beer, with a jug in one hand and a door-key in the other.

She told the barmaid how miserable she felt, all alone in the big house, as the family had 'gone out for the day, and they would not return until very late.

There were two men drinking gin and water at the bar at the same time, who overheard what the tattling girl had said ; and as she left the public-house they quickly followed and spoke to her.

Not liking their appearance, and thinking they meant no good, I asked the barmaid if she knew what house the girl had come from. She told me it was No. — in the same street. I finished my ale, and went out to see what was going on.

As I approached the house, but on the opposite side, I saw the girl in conversation with the men, and after a time they all went into the house together. I remained in front of the house, watching.

After the lapse of about half an hour I saw the front door opened, and shut again; *but no one came out.* Shortly after this I saw a light in the second floor, and the shadow of a man moving about the room.

I at once understood what was going on; and I immediately returned to the public-house, and requested that a messenger should be sent (quietly) to the station for assistance.

It speedily arrived. In the course of half an hour the street door, at which we were stationed, was cautiously opened, and a man, with a large parcel in his haud, was about to pass out, when he suddenly found himself pounced upon and walked off to the station. We left an officer at the door of the house.

Upon searching our prisoner we found enough of jewellery, plate, and other valuables in his pocket to stock a small shop. Among other articles was a purse made of a woman's hair; and as it was the only one of the kind I had ever seen, I particularly remarked it. It only contained a bent seveu-shilling piece, a gold coin which probably you never saw, as none have been in circulation for the last forty years.

Having locked up our prisoner, we returned to the house. All appeared quiet there. After waiting some time, it occurred to me that the other fellow might be murdering the girl, or worse; so I gave a loud double knock and ring.

After a longer delay than appeared to me necessary, the door was opened by the girl. I inquired if her master was at home.

She replied that he was not—that there was nobody in the house but herself.

"Where," I asked, "are the men you let in with you when you fetched your beer?"

"I let no men in," she replied, greatly confused; "they are gone."

"One is gone, but there's one inside now, and he's after no good."

"How can you say so? I'm sure——"

"I'm sure the house has been robbed. We are policemen, and must search the house."

"What do you mean? I don't understand you."

"We'll soon explain everything."

We entered the house, and proceeded to the kitchen in search of the other rascal, but he was nowhere to be seen. We had a long search for him, and at last found him in the water-butt, up to his knees in water.

We quickly conveyed him to the station. When searched, nothing was found upon him but a silver spoon.

I did not at all associate these men with the murder of the old lady; but I happened to mention the story of the capture to her servant, and when I spoke of the hair purse and the seven-shilling piece she exclaimed,—

"Why, that must be poor missuses. She had such a purse, and has shown it to me many a time. I could swear to it if I could see it."

" You shall see it."

When, on the Monday morning, I visited the fellows I had arrested on the Sunday night, I fancied the face of the one upon whom the purse was found looked familiar to me. Come to furbish up my memory, I at length arrived at the conclusion that he was the one upon whom I fetched so unlucky a blow. I asked the divisional surgeon to examine his head, to see if there were any marks of a recent wound.

The result of his examination was quite conclusive and satisfactory. I had no doubt of my man, and certain evidence produced at the trial confirmed it.

The three villains, upon very good circumstantial evidence, were all found guilty, and suffered the extreme penalty of the law. I doubt if they would have ever been detected had it not been for the BURGLAR's HAT.

APPENDIX.

ON THE MEANS OF DETECTING SPOTS OF BLOOD.

IT is of the utmost consequence to the ends of justice that a sure means should be established of recognising spots of blood upon clothes, iron, steel, &c. Many methods are already known to the chemist; but the task of analysis is sometimes so delicate and difficult, that we think we shall be rendering some service to the cause of justice if we describe the surest method of detection now known.

In most cases the spots of blood have not been exposed to a high temperature; consequently there is no coagulation of the globules of the serum. Berzelius advised the operations of the investigation to be conducted in the following manner:—Place the stained tissue or iron in a footed glass half filled with cold water. The hematine and albumen gradually dissolve, and form red streaks, which fall to the bottom of the glass, while the fibrin remains insoluble in the state of a soft and elastic substance easily detached by mechanical means. The red liquor is divided into several portions, and submitted to the following tests :—

Upon adding chlorine the liquid becomes first green, then colourless, lastly opalescent, and leaves a white flocculent deposit. On the addition of ammonia the colour does not change; but red pigments used in dyeing—such as cochineal, Brazil wood, &c.—assume a blue tint. Nitric acid produces a greyish-white precipitate,

Tannin precipitates the colouring matter without altering the hue. Lastly, a fifth portion, submitted to ebullition, coagulates, or, if the liquor be very dilute, it becomes at least opalescent.

M. Persoz recommends the use of weak hyperchlorous acid, holding a little chloride of mercury in solution. Upon moistening the suspected spots, if they are blood they assume a very peculiar green-grey hue, while they become quite colourless if they are of any ordinary colouring material.

According to the chemist Rose, the most striking characteristic of blood is the di-chroism of its solution in potash or in caustic soda, which is red when viewed by reflected light, and green by transmitted light.

But the tests given by the above and other chemists, although on the whole very satisfactory, are still far inferior in precision, clearness, and facility of execution, to that indicated by Dr. Brücke, of Vienna, and which is based on the formation of the crystals of *hemine* of Teichmann, of Göttingen.

Teichmann discovered, in 1853, that red blood, under the influence of acetic acid, gives rise to red or reddish-brown crystals of hematoïdine in the shape of rhomboidal plates; and he gave to them the name of *crystals of hemine,* in order to distinguish them from the red crystals of *hematoïdine* which are sometimes met with in stagnant blood. The crystals of hemine are formed with so much facility and so surely, and are at the same time so characteristic and so easy to distinguish under the microscope, that Dr. Brücke, considers them as the most exact means of recognising the presence of hematoglobuline.

The method he recommends for dealing with the spots of blood is as follows :—

Begin by washing the spots with cold distilled water, as already indicated by Berzelius. The red liquid, to which a few drops of a solution of common salt are added, is evaporated to dryness in a watch-glass, with some sulphuric acid, under an exhausted receiver. The dry residue is examined under the microscope to make sure that it contains nothing that may be confounded with the crystals of Teichmann. A little glacial acetic acid is then put on the above residue, which is evaporated to dryness on a *bain-marie*. The residue is again moistened with a few drops of distilled water, and examined anew under the microscope. It will then be discovered whether the spots are really blood or not, as its presence is exhibited by the appearance of thousands of crystals of hemine.

The chemists Scriba, Simon, and Buchner have repeated the directions given by Dr. Brücke, and have found them completely confirmed by experiment. The extract of even a very small spot of blood upon a cotton or linen substance, or upon wood or metal, presents, by inspection under the microscope, thousands of crystals of hemine. According to these experimentalists, the addition of common salt is necessary only in certain cases. The evaporation *in vacuo* and with the *bain-marie* may also be dispensed with; still, to obtain well-defined crystals, it is always useful to evaporate slowly and cautiously at a temperature of 100° F. to 140° F. When the spots of blood are still fresh, or merely dried without having been washed, we can operate more rapidly by boiling the woollen or cotton cloth with the spots, or the wood upon which they may be found, or still better, the matter detached from the metal, with a little monohydrated acetic acid in a small matrass; afterwards evaporate a few drops of the solution to dryness upon a watch-glass placed in a sand bath heated to a temperature of 140° F., and examine the residue under a microscope. The crystals may also be obtained with ordinary acetic acid, but it is safer to employ monohydrated acetic acid.

When the spots of blood are old, or partially washed with water, which may remove the salts contained in the blood, the addition of a little common salt, before evaporating to dryness, is indispensable; and for this reason it is best to employ it at the first in medico-legal researches, when there is but a small quantity of the material at disposal. In cases where too much salt has been added, it can be removed under the microscope by rapidly washing the dried matter with a little cold distilled water, which will dissolve the marine salt first. Of all red-coloured substances the only one that gives crystals resembling those of hemine is *murexide*; but it is easy to distinguish them from crystals of hemine, because they are formed without the addition of acetic acid, and also by the murexide becoming blue under the action of caustic potash, while the crystals of hemine give a di-chroic solution with this reagent.

There are also means of distinguishing human blood from that of other animals.

There are three crystalline substances derived from the colouring matter of the blood.

1°. The crystals of *hemine*, described above.

2°. *Hematocrystalline*, or blood crystals, observed by Funké, and studied by Lehmann, which are obtained by treating an aqueous solution of clotted blood, freed from serum, first by a current of oxygen, and then by a current of carbonic acid gas. These crystals obtained from the blood of different animals possess neither the same form nor the same solubility in water. The crystals of the blood of the horse, dog, hedgehog, fishes, &c., are prismatic, and the most soluble; those of the blood of the marmot constitute rhombohedrons or hexagonal plates, a little less soluble than the preceding; those of the blood of the squirrel present large hexagonal plates, or hexagonal prisms grouped as rosettes, still less soluble; those of the blood of the guinea-pig, rat, and mouse, constitute tetrahedrons, or other forms of a regular system, and are the least soluble of all, requiring for their solution 600 times their weight of water. All these crystals are more or less deep-red in colour, and decompos every quickly, especially upon contact with air.

Their aqueous solution coagulates at 145° F. Nitric acid gives a white precipitate, but there is no precipitate with sulphuric, hydrochloric, and acetic acids. Caustic potash does not dissolve the crystals, but changes their colour to a dirty yellow. Ammonia readily dissolves them, giving them a peach colour.

It is not improbable that these crystals of hematocrystalline are carbonates of the same compound of which the crystals of hemine are the acetates.

3°. *Hematoïdine,* under the form of microscopic needles, or of small oblique rhomboidal prisms (angle of the rhomb = 118°), hard, brittle, bright orange-red in colour, heavier than water, insoluble in alcohol, water, ether, and acetic acid. Ammonia rapidly dissolves them, with an amaranthine hue, which quickly disappears; incinerated, they leave scarcely a trace of ashes. It is very probable that a relation exists between these three crystalline substances, and that hematoïdine may really be a species of base, of which hemine and hematocrystalline are combinations with acids and salts.

Hematoïdine is the name given by Virchon to crystals observed for the first time by Sir Everard Home in some effused blood, in the substance of the tissues of a living animal.

THE END.

WINCHESTER: PRINTED BY HUGH BARCLAY.

www.ingramcontent.com/pod-product-compliance
Lightning Source LLC
Chambersburg PA
CBHW020809060726
47498CB00017B/1155